The deep dark of Svartleheim, realm of the Black Elves. The Ivald monks called it a shortcut.

They lied.

For once you enter their tunnels, the Black Elves never let you leave.

In this ninth volume of Glenn G. Thater's Harbinger of Doom saga, Theta arrives at Jutenheim, hot on the heels of Korrgonn and the League of Shadows. Their fateful confrontation fast approaching, if only they pass the Black Elf king and the ancient evils that lurk in his subterranean domain. But do the Black Elves serve the dark powers or the light?

BOOKS BY GLENN G. THATER

THE HARBINGER OF DOOM SAGA
GATEWAY TO NIFLEHEIM
THE FALLEN ANGLE
KNIGHT ETERNAL
DWELLERS OF THE DEEP
BLOOD, FIRE, AND THORN
GODS OF THE SWORD
THE SHAMBLING DEAD
MASTER OF THE DEAD
SHADOW OF DOOM
WIZARD'S TOLL
VOLUME 11+ (FORTHCOMING)

HARBINGER OF DOOM
(COMBINES *GATEWAY TO NIFLEHEIM* AND *THE FALLEN ANGLE* INTO A SINGLE VOLUME)

THE HERO AND THE FIEND
(A NOVELETTE SET IN THE HARBINGER OF DOOM UNIVERSE)

THE GATEWAY
(A NOVELLA LENGTH VERSION OF *GATEWAY TO NIFLEHEIM*)

THE DEMON KING OF BERGHER
(A SHORT STORY SET IN THE HARBINGER OF DOOM UNIVERSE)

To be notified about my new book releases and any special offers or discounts regarding my books, please join my mailing list here: http://eepurl.com/vwubH

GLENN G. THATER

SHADOW

OF

DOOM

*A TALE FROM THE
HARBINGER OF DOOM SAGA*

This book is a work of fiction. Names, characters, places, and incidents herein are either the product of the author's imagination or are used fictitiously. Any resemblance to actual persons, living or dead, events, or locales is entirely coincidental.

Copyright © 2015 by Glenn G. Thater.

All rights reserved.

SHADOW OF DOOM © 2015 by Glenn G. Thater

ISBN-13: 978-0692616222
ISBN-10: 0692616225

Visit Glenn G. Thater's website at
http://www.glenngthater.com

January 2016 Amazon Print Edition
Published by Lomion Press

PROLOGUE

PRESBYTERIAN HOSPITAL NEW YORK CITY

Present Day

"He's never been sick before," said the woman as she stood beside the hospital bed. Her husband lay there, his eyes closed, his breathing labored, mumbling something under his breath. "The first time in ten years that I've known him. He's never even had a cold, but now this."

"Everyone gets sick," said the doctor as he scribbled something on his chart, his handwriting illegible. "Even a man with muscles like his. It's just part of being human. It's a bad fever, I admit. Something exotic is behind it, I imagine. You mentioned that he travels a lot. To tropical countries? Jungles?"

"He goes everywhere," she said. "For work."

"Well, this time he brought back something nasty," said the doctor as his eyes surreptitiously scanned her, a woman of uncommon curves. "But I've a feeling that he's tougher than it is. Some heavy duty antibiotics, acetaminophen, and a lot of rest and fluids. That and time is all it will take."

"But why is he saying such strange things?" said the woman. "You heard him when you came in. He's been mumbling weird things all day. It doesn't make sense. Is he dreaming? Has the fever affected his mind?"

"The human mind is a strange thing," said the doctor. "I've seen people do all sorts of odd things with a high fever. We'll know more when we get the bloods back, but I wouldn't worry about it. Once we get the fever down, he'll be back to his old self again in no time."

When the doctor left, the woman reached out her hand to grasp her husband's, but then she jerked it back. The last time she'd reached out to him, he squeezed her so hard that she thought her hand would break. It was still stiff and bruised. It wasn't his fault. He wasn't even conscious; not really. But it hurt all the same.

She pulled the sheet over his feet, which dangled over the edge of the bed, though the top of his head was but an inch from the headboard. His eyes opened for a moment, and then his eyelids fluttered for several seconds before closing again. "The black el-ves took it," said the man, his voice weak, barely above a whisper. "They took the orb. Not what you think. They thought to keep it secret. To keep it safe. They carried it down Thoonbarrow way. Dropped it into the Well of Eternity. They thought no one would ever find it; that no one would ever know or think to look there for it. They were wrong."

"Oh dear God, what are you saying?" said the woman. "Please, be quiet. Be still. You have to rest."

"The Old One – the gnome – he is relentless," said the man. "Scoured all Midgaard for it. Delved deep. Deep. Found the orb, he did, by what evil craft I know not. But he found it, to the bane of us all."

The man's eyes opened again. He tried to sit up.

"No. Don't." She put her hand to his shoulder. "You have to rest. You have to lie still."

The man's eyes were bloodshot; his eyelids fluttered; face pale; sweat on his brow. His eyes moved up and down the woman and then from one side of the room to the other, slowly, taking in every bit of it. "This be not Lomion. This be not Midgaard. Who are you? Tell me true and speak quick."

"It's me. Your wife." She looked like she wanted to run from the room. As if she were with a stranger that she had no business being alone with.

His eyes studied her, but they were unfocused. "I know your face," he said. "I remember." He inhaled deeply, as if searching for a familiar scent. "The Woman on the Wind."

"What?" she said. "It's me."

"I have to go back," he said. "Is it within your power? I have to go back. This time, I will not let them pass. Where be my armor? My shield? My weapons?"

"I don't know what you're saying," said the woman.

"No matter," he said. "I will make my stand, alone if I must, naked if I must, but I will hold fast the gates to Abaddon this time. For if I don't, the Duergar and the demons will rise and all Midgaard will fall. I will hold them at the gateway. I must. I will not fail again. I must go back. Please send me back. I will not fail again. I swear it."

1

EVERMERE BAY
ISLE OF EVERMERE
THE AZURE SEA

Year 1267, 4th Age
37th Year of King Tenzivel's Rule

OB

Ob couldn't believe his eyes. He'd seen *The Black Falcon* go down. He'd watched in horror as it happened. A giant sea beast — something what looked like a snapping turtle, but one that was as big as a castle, lifted the entire ship clear out of the water and smashed it down to the inky surface of Evermere Bay as if it were naught but a child's bath toy. The impact shattered the ship, blasted it to bits, and sent whatever men aboard not killed instantly, into the bay's frigid waters, struggling to stay afloat while weighed down by armor and gear.

That sea creature was bigger by far than anything Ob had seen or heard tell of. Far bigger than the largest holyphant. Bigger than any whale. Much bigger. The size of a small mountain, it was. Who ever heard of such a monster?

Nobody whose head was set on straight.

Nobody who wasn't dead drunk or befuddled with age. Only in fairy stories did such monsters exist. Only in children's tales about the *Age of Myth and Legend*. All bunk and bother. Nothing but humbug.

But Ob saw it. And it was real — a living beast. It was true. Or else, he'd lost his mind, which, of course, was quite possible. Maybe he'd been hit in the head one too many times. Maybe a lot too many times.

That giant turtle thing wasn't done even after it destroyed the ship. Not by half.

Then it went after the men.

With teeth and claws, it plucked them from the water — them few what had fought their way to the surface, stunned and half dead. They never had a chance. Brave, strong fighting men were they — them what Ob and company had brought aboard. And Slaayde's reavers — they were tough men too. Tough as nails. But it didn't matter. They never had a chance. No man had a chance against such a monster. Might as well fight a mountain or duel a storm.

It ate them, that thing did.

It ate the men.

Its jaws so massive it bit men in two in an instant, except when it chose to swallow them whole, which was no trouble for it at all; its maw bigger than the double doors of Dor Eotrus's great hall.

Ob saw the glinting light off the men's armor as it snatched them up, one after another, out of the water from on-high. Its great head, pecking down like a bird of prey, over and over, its long neck stretching. Ob saw men struggling within its grasp. Like gnats caught in a man's hand. They had no chance, no hope.

Not a goodly way for a man to die. Not that there were many goodly ways, but Ob could think of several that were better than getting eaten alive. For himself, he still held out for extreme old age.

When the turtle's feast was done, no survivors of *The Falcon* remained.

Not one.

Not one was able to swim away, not from that thing, not in that frigid water. Not one man clung to floating debris. The beast was thorough. Little or no wreckage floated about the bay's surface, as if even the flotsam feared to show itself to the great beast.

Ob watched that all transpire during the prior hour. One of the hardest things he'd ever seen in a hard life

So then, what in Odin's name was *The Black Falcon* now doing cruising through the waves and shooting flaming pitch at the Evermerians? Wasn't it broken on the bottom of the bay? Yet there it was before his eyes once again. Still afloat. Still intact. And fighting. It was a mad notion. It made no sense unless . . .

A ghost ship.

That's what it had to be. A specter of what once was.

Unless Ob was losing it. Imagining the whole thing. But he didn't think so. His head still felt on straight. Or thereabouts.

It was a ship of the dead.

The dead come back to Midgaard to fight

blood-sucking cannibals on the Eotrus's behalf.
 It made no sense. Not much did anymore. Not since old Mister Fancy Pants showed up, all high-and-mighty, spit-and-polish, boasting and bragging. Everything went to shit after he showed up. That stinking bastard. That no-good harbinger of doom.
 Ob saw Claradon Eotrus on that ghost ship. He saw him. The boy stood at *The Falcon*'s prow. He was pointing. Shouting orders. Men were scrambling all about the deck. The catapults were firing like mad. The ballistae. All of them. The Malvegillian archers were there — nearly a full squadron of them. All dead now. All ghosts. Phantoms. Just like Claradon. They were lined up along the deck rail. Taking aim. Firing. Again and again at the giant beast. Sir Kelbor was there. Ob saw him at Claradon's side, reliable even in death. The Bull too. And young Sir Paldor. Other men were on deck, but Ob couldn't make them out quick enough.
 Apparitions. Spirits, one and all.
 The ship was coming on fast. Almost close enough for Ob to reach out and touch it as it passed. Maybe the cold water was getting to him. Muddling his brains.
 Or else, mayhap Odin sent the ship and her crew back. Back down to Midgaard. Its mission. Its purpose. Not yet done. Maybe he still had plans for The Falcon, Odin did.
 And then the truth hit him.
 It wasn't the All-father what brought *The Falcon* back. It was Old Pointy Hat that saved her. Pipkorn and some strange thingamajig he'd gifted

Claradon before they left Lomion City. A Ghost Ship box he called it. Ob had long since forgotten about that bauble, as honest folk were wont to forget things arcane. The knowledge slipped away from normal folk, like memories of dreams. But as Ob focused his thoughts on it, he remembered. Pipkorn claimed that the box had the power to create a duplicate ship — a twin to *The Falcon*, crew and all. And Claradon had used it to trick the giant turtle — that was the only answer that made sense. And that meant that the *Falcon* that went down was not the real one, but an illusion created by Pipkorn's magic. So Claradon and the others weren't dead men. They weren't ghosts. They were alive!

Ob's legs had gone numb, treading water in the icy bay. His hands too. Part of his arms. Everything was getting numb. His head throbbed. He couldn't stop shivering. Now don't forget, gnomes weather the cold far better than Volsungs. Hardier folk, you know. But even still, that water was too cold for any man to bear. Much too cold. And Ob had been in it too long already. He was tired. Dead tired. And he was feeling weak. Lethargic. A voice in his head told him it was time to let go. To be done with this life. To be done with Midgaard. To let Old Death come and claim him at long last. Give up his sorry life and join Aradon, Gabriel, Talbon, and the rest, in the realm of spirits.

Ob looked up, blinking through the spray that hit his face, his eyes searching. He didn't see the Valkyries, the shield maidens of Odin. They were not circling the bay on their winged horses. They were not waiting for him to die. They were not going to scoop him up and carry him up Valhalla way, to drink and dine with the gods and the honored dead in Odin's great hall.

And in that moment Ob felt sorrow; he felt despair. He thought they'd be there at the end. For him. After all he'd done. He thought that he deserved the honor. He hoped that he did. Had he failed to measure up in the eyes of the gods? Had old Odin judged him unworthy of Valhalla? Or did it just mean that it wasn't yet his time?

Well, if the first be true, then, to Helheim with Odin. And to all the gods with him, the stinking Aesir. Ob wasn't done with Midgaard yet. Not yet.

2

EVERMERE BAY
ISLE OF EVERMERE
THE AZURE SEA

SLAAYDE

Captain Dylan Slaayde had been in more brawls, skirmishes, and all-out battles than he could remember. He and his crew had seen action up and down every major river on the continent, from their northern headwaters, all the way south to the Azure Sea. And they'd sailed it, the great sea: the Azure. Not just on that quest with the Eotrus, but many times.

Slaayde had braved the sand and stone of many islands not shown on any charts except those he'd had drawn up. On those travels, he'd seen wonders most folk wouldn't believe. Good things. Beautiful things. Impossible things. And horrors to make a man's blood run cold.

It was a big world out there. A lot bigger than almost anyone realized. Most of it wild. Unexplored. Dangerous. Exciting. And ancient. More than anything else, it was ancient. Civilizations had risen and fallen throughout Midgaard over ages uncountable. Some of those past civilizations had produced wonders —

wonders beyond that of Slaayde's modern, enlightened world. He knew that. He'd seen the ruins. He'd held the artifacts: the books, the tablets, the strange devices. There was a lot more to Midgaard than most folk ever dreamed.

Even those cosmopolitan folk of Lomion City, who had thrived on trade from near and far for centuries, had no idea of what was out there.

But Slaayde knew.

Or he thought he knew before he set out on that voyage with the Eotrus. Even Slaayde had never experienced anything like what had happened on that trip: monsters and mayhem, magic and mischief, traitors and triumph.

And it was all about to end in a battered longboat, adrift in a bay off an uncharted island halfway between nowhere and never was. An evil place that was home to a legion of depraved cannibals. Blood-sucking superhuman flesh eaters that were nigh impossible to kill.

To call them human was too generous to them, and an insult to the rest of us. During the day, the Evermerians hid behind a facade of normality and polite society, carrying on as if they were regular folk, all civilized and such. But that was naught but an illusion. A snare set by cunning predators. Foul ghouls were they. For all Slaayde knew, they sprang up straight from Helheim. Nightmares come alive.

When midnight approached, their beauty slipped away and they revealed their true faces. Black eyes they had. All black. No whites at all. Claws as long as knives. Teeth, sharp as razors. Skin, a sickly pale gray. Strength of two or three men. And resilience beyond belief. Arrows didn't phase them. Stabbing neither. Take an arm off. Take a leg. They kept coming.

They weren't remotely human. They couldn't be. Wild wanton killers were they. Depraved beasts. Such was their nature.

When the bloodlust took them in the black of the night, they fell into a frenzy. A mania of violence and ravenous hunger. A hunger that couldn't be sated. A thirst that couldn't be quenched.

If he hadn't seen it himself, Slaayde wouldn't have believed it. Any of it. The very idea was madness.

But perhaps it wasn't any crazier than much of what he'd experienced on that voyage. That voyage of the damned. Everything had turned upside down the day that Theta had first set foot aboard *The Black* .

Theta.

If that even was his name. If he even was a man, and not some thing himself. Some creature out of Helheim. Slaayde had his suspicions. Not that it mattered.

Where Theta went, death followed. So too did madness. And black sorcery, otherworldly beings, bounty hunters, and vengeful gods. They flocked to him, moths to a flame.

Darg Tran, Slaayde's traitorous navigator, called Theta a harbinger of doom. As far as Slaayde was concerned, that's what he was. Truly. A harbinger of doom.

Ever since Theta showed up, *The Falcon* had been attacked over and over again. And every time, it was by creatures. Monsters. Things. Impossible things. Unthinkable things. Things that shouldn't exist. In all Slaayde's travels, he'd never seen their like. Never heard tell of them, except in fairy tales and fables. But where Theta walked, fairy tales came to life. Myth merged with Midgaard.

And everyone around him died.

One by one.

Bertha, Slaayde's beloved.

She was dying. She might already be dead.

He hadn't been able to check on her for many minutes. Last he knew, the bleeding had stopped, and she was still breathing.

Slaayde glanced down at her several times between the Evermerian attack waves, but he couldn't tell if she still lived. Still breathed. She'd lost so much blood. Too much. She was so pale. So still.

She'd always been so full of life. Strong. A commanding presence. A good match to Slaayde. Kept him on his toes. Kept him sharp and focused and grounded. And she was the best darned quartermaster he'd ever known. Now he was about to lose her.

He couldn't protect her. He couldn't save her.

He tried. But he couldn't. He failed her. He couldn't even protect himself. Not against the Evermerians.

But it wasn't his fault. He hadn't made any mistakes. Except for one, for which he would ever regret: taking Duke Harringgold's money to ferry the Eotrus boy and his retinue after *The White Rose.* A fool's errand from the start. The Rose was too fast, even for *The Falcon*.

The entire mess was Theta's fault. That stinking bastard. He'd brought them to that accursed island: Evermere. Led them there on a madman's quest.

The Falcon should never have been there. It should be sailing the Hudsar, moving cargo, fair or foul, up and back. Up and back. A dangerous life, but that was Slaayde's trade. That's where he and Bertha belonged.

A very dangerous trade if truth be told. A lot of the folk that he dealt with were criminals. Some were cutthroats. Some were straight up killers. But most were business folk just looking to buy or sell whatever it was they had or wanted. They came to Slaayde when the government or some such, didn't approve of the sale or wanted to take a cut when it wasn't their due. That's what the government did. Tried to control things. Take the freedom from the people. Make money off every transaction. Every sale. Every bit of labor. And then take that money and redistribute it as they saw fit. Or else waste it entirely. Lots of folk had no stomach for that..So them what was in the know went to Slaayde to procure what they needed.

Be they fair or foul, he could deal with those kinds of folk. He could manage them. He was an expert at it. And when things went bad, well, he was an expert at dealing with that too. His crew was the toughest on the water. Man for man, they could take on anybody. Fancy spit-and-polish knights included.

But what went on in that bay, during that

battle, was different. It wasn't a fight so much as a feeding frenzy. The Evermerians swarmed around them like ants flocking to a picnic feast.

Ravel was dead at their hands. Torn apart. The best darned trader that Slaayde had ever served with. He could fetch a king's ransom from a group of beggars for a pile of fresh dung, and leave them happy for it. You didn't find that kind of skill every day. The man was irreplaceable. And he was a decent healer too. The only one *The Falcon* had.

And Guj was dead. Good old Guj. Dumb as rocks, but just as solid. Loyal. Trustworthy. Tough as steel. He'd fought by Slaayde's side countless times. Been with him since he was a boy. And now he was dead. All thanks to Theta. Mister Fancy Pants. Mister Bigshot. He's the one that should be dead after all the trouble he'd caused. All the killing he'd brought about.

But Bertha. The only woman that Slaayde had ever loved. There had been other women. Before her. But she was the only one that mattered. She was — the one.

He couldn't even hold her hand. Couldn't comfort her in her last minutes. Couldn't look into her eyes. Couldn't tell her how he felt. All he could do was stand over her. And try to keep them off her, the bloodthirsty evil things.

And he would. He wouldn't let them have her. Wouldn't let them touch her. Not again. Not while he yet lived. Not while there was a single breath left in him.

Some men, not many, but some, could hold their own in a fight. Even a big fight: a true battle to the death between men what knew what they were doing.

But not Slaayde. He didn't hold his own in those kinds of fights.

He dominated.

He took control of the fight. Went right at his opponents. Usually, killed them dead before they knew the fight had started. Most of the time, he took them down with a single blow. Skewered many a man straight through the heart with his saber. He wasn't ashamed of it, the killing. He told himself that they were all bad. That they all had it coming. And he believed it too. Maybe he was even right about that. He tried not to think on it too much. What good could come of that? Better to go through life with few regrets and even less guilt. Happier that way. And that's what life is about, isn't it? A grand quest to be happy?

His saber skills didn't work with the Evermerians.

It didn't kill them.

It didn't even seem to hurt them. If anything, it just made them mad.

What was that about? Cut through their hearts and they kept coming. How could that be? How could a man, a beast, or whatever they were, live without a beating heart? It made no sense.

Or maybe, they weren't alive at all. Maybe they were dead.

Dead things that walked.

Slaayde had heard tell of old stories about such creatures. Duergar they were called by some. Draugar by others. Ghouls, blood lords, and shamblers were other names he'd heard. The undead.

Maybe that's what they were. Slaayde didn't know. And there, trapped in that longboat, he didn't much care. It didn't much matter. All that mattered were that there were far too many of them. Alive or dead, there were too many of them.
Slaayde knew that he was about to die, and so were all the people in the longboat with him, Bertha included. Even Theta. They were all going to die.
In the fight of his life, and his saber sat useless in its sheath. How ironic. Instead, he held an oar. An oar! A lousy piece of wood. No edge to it. No point. Not even much weight. Just a clumsy club. Swung it with one hand at times; two at others. He beat them back.
Swing after swing. He broke one oar over an Evermerian's head, but found another. Broke that one in two, but kept fighting with what was left. Over and over he swung that wood. Most of it from a kneeling position. Every time he stood he risked a hammer blow to chest or back from friendly fire. Artol was swinging left and right with that big mallet of his. Little Tug went wild with Old Fogey. Theta had a hammer too. He went at them from the prow. Those three giants smashed the Evermerians to pulp every time one tried to set foot aboard the longboat. But the ghouls kept coming. Wave after wave. Nothing could stop them. Not the hammers. Not Glimador's magic. And certainly no lousy wooden oar. Nothing.

3

CITY OF STARKBARROW SVARTLEHEIM

THROONBILG BILN MAC-MURTH

Ramluk the Diresvart, High Magus to Throonbilg biln Mac-Murth the King of all Starkbarrow and Grand Lord of the Jutenheim Deeps stood before his king wearing the traditional dark blue robes of his station, and gripped a seven foot long bone staff in his right hand. Ramluk was the tallest Svart in all Starkbarrow, standing a full head above his fellows, and all the taller still for the blue conical hat that sat ever upon his bald pate.

King Throonbilg was half his height, though more robust of chest and limb, and far darker in complexion — a scion of an ancient, unpolluted bloodline that harkened back unto the Dawn Age. The king's face was sullen and lined, his eyes sunken. He leaned forward, perched on the edge of his throne, chin on his palm.

"A Portalis Nifleleir must not reach Anglotor," said Throonbilg in Svartlespeak. "Not now. Not ever."

"My king, we do not know for certain that the intruders have a Nifleheir. We have not seen it. In fact, none has been seen in Jutenheim since the Second Age."

"Karakta niln Bertel has seen much through

her stone since we last spoke," said Throonbilg. The king gestured toward Karakta, the only other person in the throne room, giving her leave to speak.

Karakta was a Svart seer. She sat atop a carved stone stool of tall, spindly, single leg, higher by far even than the king's throne. Her limbs and torso were as spindly as the leg of her chair; her head, bald as that of the king, though her complexion was two shades the fairer. Her seer stone was set before her, atop a small round table that matched her stool.

Karakta turned her head toward the Diresvart, her torso remained directly facing her seer stone, her neck turned unnaturally far to face him — far enough to snap the neck of a Volsung, yet it caused her no harm or distress. "They have a golem born of elven craft," said Karakta. "It carries an object of great power in a box blanketed in sorcery that is ancient and alien to me. The Nifleheir lies within. They call it the Orb, which describes it well enough, I suppose."

"If they have a golem, then there is a wizard of great power amongst them," said the High Magus.

"Not one," said Karakta, "but five or six. Perhaps more."

"A master and his apprentices," said Ramluk.

"Masters all," said Karakta. "Wizards of power one and all, each to match your Diresvarts and more."

Ramluk's mouth dropped open. "Now we know why the monks let them pass. They could not hope to stop them."

"There is more," said Karakta. "With them travels a Red Demon of Fozramgar."

Ramluk shook his head. "This I cannot believe. Your stone must be faulty; your reading, confused. Those things are but nightmares best forgotten. Long, long dead."

"I have braved the stone's vapors to see it myself," said Throonbilg. "Karakta speaks true, as always and ever."

"The demon is not the worst," said Karakta. "With them travels another thing not born of Midgaard. A creature of Nifleheim. A great lord of that place. A being of power beyond imagining. Ancient as the mountains. Old as the wind."

"Show me," said Ramluk.

"There is little to see," said Throonbilg. "The Nifhleheim Lord wears the face and form of a man, though he is much more."

Ramluk made a gesture with his hand and he rose up into the air until he reached the height of the seer's table. He placed his hands against the table's rim but did not dare to touch the Starkbarrow Stone. "Show me," he said.

Karakta ran her hands over the stone and said her words. Soon appeared an image of the Leaguers, trudging through the tunnels. The image flitted about, as if seen through the eyes of a flying insect that buzzed about the space. At last, the image settled on Korrgonn.

Ramluk leaned close and gazed deeply, his face growing pale as nausea crept over him — it was always the same when he drew close to the stone. Then, as if sensing the stone's spying, Korrgonn's gaze turned toward the stone and his eyes narrowed. Karakta immediately broke contact and the stone went dark.

Ramluk dropped to the floor only partially slowed by his magic and puked up his lunch.

"Forgive me, my king," said Ramluk.

"For doubting me? Or for ruining my floor?" His tone harsh. Then he waved his hand as if to dismiss the whole notion. "It is of no matter any longer."

"It senses us watching," said Karakta. "The first time that I studied the Nifleheimer, it reached into my mind and tried to possess me, to take me over, mind and body. I barely broke contact in time. Never before have I seen such power.

"This creature is beyond my knowledge, my king," said Ramluk.

"It is beyond us all," said Throonbilg.

"How many have invaded our caverns?" said Ramluk.

"Hundreds," said the king. "An army fitted for war. We must stop them at all costs. I have sent word to every duke and chieftain, and have called up all our warriors. Every last Svart that can hold a weapon: male, female, and child. Even now they pour from every cavern and warren in Starkbarrow, and all our demesne beyond."

"If their power is as great as we fear," said Ramluk, "this battle may be the end of us. The end of our race."

"If they reach Anglotor with the Portalis Nifleleir," said the king, "it may mean the end of all Midgaard. This is why we are here, why we've always been here, down through the ages. To keep safe Anglotor. To never allow one of the spheres of power to be brought close."

"If they pass us, Lord Uriel will stop them," said Ramluk.

"Perhaps," said the king. "But we cannot count on that. It is we that are here to protect him, to lessen his burdens, not he, ours. We must safeguard all Midgaard from this evil. A portal to Nifleheim must never be opened again."

"I will gather my Diresvarts, my king," said Ramluk. "We will pool our powers and together, we will rouse the Rock Elementals from their slumbers. All our sorcery will be brought to bear to stop these villains. We will send them all down to Helheim where they belong."

"You must kill them all," said Throonbilg, his voice solemn. "The fate of all Midgaard hangs in the balance. This deed must be done. No matter the cost to our lives, to our honor, or to our souls. Do you understand me, wizard?"

"It will be done," said Ramluk. The Diresvart turned and took his leave to begin his preparations.

"What will you do, my lord?" said Karakta.

"I will visit the chamber of our ancestors. I will gaze into the Well of Fate and my tears will pollute its ancient waters, for today I know that I be the last king of Starkbarrow, the last Lord of the Jutenheim Deeps. For whether this day brings victory in battle or defeat, it marks the end of the Svarts of Starkbarrow. Today we meet our doom.

4

EVERMERE BAY
ISLE OF EVERMERE
THE AZURE SEA

THETA

The Duchess lay at Theta's feet. She was dead at long last. Her head severed. Her body broken. Theta saw the shock on her minions' faces when she *fell to his sword. What were they – those Evermerians?*
Ghouls?
Demons?
He had hoped that killing her, and making a spectacle of it, would put them to flight. But it did not. The Evermerians remained undeterred. The volleys of arrows that they launched at the longboat while he still held her head aloft was proof of that. Her demise gave them but a few moment's pause.
And then on they came.
Roaring, howling, mad with bloodlust the like of which Theta had rarely seen, even amongst those taken by the berserker rage. Some of the Evermerians wielded swords, some swung clubs, but most came at them with only tooth and nail, albeit, teeth akin to sharpened spikes and nails as long and deadly as daggers. Formidable foes were

they despite their lack of battle skills. The rage, the frenzy, and their preternatural resilience made them terrible opponents.

Theta swung his hammer – that ancient mallet that he had carried since time immemorial. Despite its effectiveness it had never been his favored weapon. He preferred a blade — wide and heavy; steel to slice, cut, and crush as his needs demanded, without fear of breaking. But against the Evermerians, he found that the hammer was a wiser choice, for his sword only stopped them if he severed their heads. Even for Theta, in the frenzy of battle, that was no easy feat. But the hammer – it could crush their defenses, splinter their arms, stave in their chests. All blows that slowed them or stopped them. And then a followup strike to the head to shatter their skulls to bits of bone, brain, and pulp. And then repeat as the next one came in.

And so he swung the hammer, over and again. Gripped it in his left hand, his shield in his right. And did what he did best.

He fought.

He killed.

And killed again.

He saw the endless tide of Evermerian boats all about them, brimming with bloodthirsty ghouls. There seemed no end to them. Several thousand at least yet remained, including the swimmers that came at them from the beach. A glance to his right showed him that his fellow warriors fought on. They held the fiends at bay. The line was solid. It was sound. Artol swung his hammer with uncanny skill. Little Tug the same.

Glimador threw magic worthy of a skilled battle mage — blue fire and arcs of electricity rained down amongst the Evermerians, springing from the young warrior's sword. The boy was far more skilled than even Theta had expected; his mother had trained him well.

Theta couldn't tell how the others fared – there was no time to look.

He was proud to serve with the men in that longboat. Warriors worthy of the *Age of Heroes*.

But despite all their skill and grit, he wondered how long it would be before only he remained. Before all the others were dead or pulled down. And then he'd be fighting alone. And then what would he do? Even for him there were too many. Far too many. There could be no victory there. No victory.

They might take him down. Perhaps even end his long existence. He would not allow that possibility. If it came to it, into the water he would go. He'd swim for it. Make for the other side of the island and develop a plan.

There was little other choice. If it came to that.

But he didn't think it would. Though hope was never a strategy that Theta employed, he held out hope that his deductions were correct. That *The Black Falcon* had not been destroyed. He suspected it as soon as the longboat reached the mouth of the bay. There should have been debris; a great field of it — from when the ship splintered and crumbled under the blows of the sea turtle. But there was no debris field. None at all. Unless, somehow they were at the wrong spot and the debris was hidden from their sight by darkness.

But he didn't believe that. It should have been there. It had to be there. And since it wasn't, that meant *The Falcon* hadn't been destroyed. That meant it was still out there. Its destruction but an illusion. An illusion whipped up by the magic of old Rascatlan, whom the Lomerians called Pipkorn — his hand at work even out there, so far from the land he called home.

And then Theta heard the whine that the great ball of pitch made as it flew through the air and arced toward their position. It was a sound that he knew well and identified at once. A fiery ball launched from a ship's catapult. From *The Falcon's* catapult.

And as Theta swung his great hammer he smiled. Deliverance was at hand. The great quest would continue.

5

ABOARD THE BLACK FALCON
EVERMERE BAY
ISLE OF EVERMERE
THE AZURE SEA

CLARADON

The Falcon's catapults were working at full capacity, launching two hundred pound balls of flaming pitch, lead, and iron shot doused in oil, hundreds of yards through the air. The projectiles roared and sparked as they arced across the morning sky, the sun threatening to peek over the horizon. The missiles shattered on impact spreading murderous shards and hungry flame for many yards in all directions.

On Claradon's orders, the crew held nothing back. They worked the ship's weapons as fast as they could. And by the gods, they were fast. Even the master bombardiers of the Dor could not match them in speed, precision, or general expertise.

The sailors at the ballistae were no less skilled. Shot after shot did they fire. Their massive harpoons blasted through boat after boat, sending many Evermerian crews into the water, the surface of which was aflame, far and wide. More than a few Evermerians were pierced through head or torso by the great shafts and were thrown in the water, broken and bloody.

The Evermerian boats were afire. Their swimmers were burning. The screaming of the fiends was a terrible sound to hear; a cacophony of the dying and the damned, as they were devoured by flames that the bay's water could not quench. But it was a wailing that meant victory. Victory for the Eotrus. They would live to see another day. Their great quest would continue.

"We've done it," said Claradon as he stood on the foredeck, his face, pale and drained, Kayla stood beside him on his right, Sirs Kelbor and Paldor on his left. "Their ships are scattering. They're running."

Sir Trelman dashed up to Claradon's side. "The swimmers," he said. "They're turning back — what ones aren't aflame. They're turning back!"

"It's over," said Kayla. "Please, let's head back to your cabin. You must rest. You're not ready to be up and about yet," she said as her eyes focused on the heavy bandages still strung about Claradon's chest. As yet, no blood seeped through.

"It's not over until our people are all back aboard," said Claradon.

"Kelbor can stand in for you," said Kayla. "The battle is over. There's nothing more that you need do here now."

"It's my place," said Claradon.

"The wound will open. You'll bleed. I can't go through that again. You can't. We almost lost you."

Claradon paused, considering her words for a few moments before he turned toward Paldor and Trelman. "What have you seen?" he said to them.

"The longboat looks full," said Trelman.

"I see Theta, Artol, Tug, and Slaayde," said Paldor, a spyglass held to his eye. "Several more are aboard. I think they're all there. Maybe they all made it."

"That would be a miracle indeed," said Claradon. "Let's get them out of the water, as fast as we can."

"What of the islanders?" said Kelbor. "Let them flee? Or have at them?"

"We should kill as many of them as we can," said Trelman. "Those things are not men; they're monsters. Did you see the teeth? The claws?"

"No doubt, they are fiends called up from the Nether Realms by The Shadow League," said Claradon. "And left here to greet us. Just as they sent those others against us before as we passed the Dead Fens. Such creatures as them deserve no mercy. They warrant no compassion."

"So we continue the assault?" said Kelbor.

"I want you to blast them," said Claradon. "Blast them all back to Helheim. Destroy as many of them as you can."

"Even those that flee?" said Paldor.

"Aye," said Claradon. "The gloves are off. Let's be done with them."

6

ABOARD THE BLACK FALCON
EVERMERE BAY
ISLE OF EVERMERE
THE AZURE SEA

CLARADON

Claradon leaned over the rail as the longboat pulled beside *The Falcon*, and the men tied her off. They strung the lines to the gantry system and began to raise the longboat as the dawn sun shown into it. What it revealed was a frightful sight. Artol and Glimador were dumping bodies and body parts – what was left of who knows how many Evermerians – into the water. Every man on the longboat, and the boat's every surface, was red with blood. They were covered in it. Head to toe. Bow to stern.

Claradon's eyes scanned the boat, searching out each man. Each friend. Tanch was there, but he was down. He couldn't tell whether the wizard was alive or dead and that set his heart to pounding for Tanch was like a brother to him. As was his cousin, Glimador, who looked unscathed. So did Artol. But where was Ob? Where was the old gnome? Slaayde was there. But Claradon didn't see any of Slaayde's men except for Tug. There were two seamen at least in that boat that Claradon didn't know. Men that weren't part of Slaayde's crew. Who were they? Why were they aboard?

Where was Ob? Claradon didn't see him anywhere. Not in the boat; not in the water. Mayhap he was hidden behind one of the others. Or maybe he was gone. Lost. Dead. Dead gods, he prayed that that was not so. Let the gnome be alive. Of all his comrades, each one valued, even loved, Ob was the one he needed the most. The rock that he leaned on; that he depended on more than any other.

Claradon made to move toward the ropes, to get a better look into the boat, but he stumbled. For a moment he couldn't tell which way was up or down, his balance far off normal. He turned to Kayla, gripped her arm for support, and then he felt himself falling. And everything went black.

7

TUNNELS OF SVARTLEHEIM, BENEATH THE ISLE OF JUTENHEIM

FREM SORLONS

Wave after wave of bloodthirsty Svarts (commonly called, "black elves") rushed Captain Frem Sorlon's line, howling and snarling, no mercy planned, no quarter given. Skirling sounds of metal clashing against metal came from farther up the tunnel where the rest of the expedition was fully engaged. The Svarts had flooded out of the small (oftentimes, tiny) side tunnels to either side of the main and simultaneously assaulted a large swath of the League of Light's expedition. Frem and a few dozen stalwart men, mostly knights and soldiers of Frem's Sithian Mercenary Company, were at the very rear of the expedition, cut off from the main force by the elfin attack.

Frem's men stood shoulder to shoulder across the width of the narrow tunnel deep below the Monastery of Ivald on the Island of Jutenheim.

The Ivald monks had convinced them that the tunnels were a shortcut under the deadly swamp that dominated much of Jutenheim's interior, and that taking the subterranean route would shave off at least a few days from their journey — a trip to an ancient temple of power where Korrgonn and the wizards of the League of Light sought to open a portal to the heavenly realm of Nifleheim, and in doing so, enable their patron Lord, Azathoth, to return to Midgaard and restore his kingdom.

They need only avoid the black elves and stick to the path marked on the map the monks gifted them to place them days closer to their destination. That underground path proved easy to follow. Avoiding the black elves proved impossible. The elves attacked them en masse only hours after they'd entered the tunnels. No call for parley, no warnings or threats, no fanfare announcing their approach. They just sprang from ambush. Running from out of the darkness, howling for blood, illumed only by the sparse light given off by the Sithians' torches.

The expedition's goal was no longer to get through the tunnels faster than they could have passed the swamp.

It was to get through the tunnels alive.

Frem's knights formed an impenetrable line of steel: sword, hammer, and mace; shields locked together in the front row, dented and bent, spears and pikes behind, red enameled plate armor gleaming in the flickering torchlight. The spearmen struck overtop of their fellows, skewering the onrushing Svarts and stopping those many that sought to leap over the Sithians' line in their frenzy. Despite all their skill, each of Frem's men was struck untold times by the Svarts' wavy black blades; only their heavy armor saved them from fatal wounds, though the Svartish weapons did their damage — the Sithians' armor was gouged, mangled, and criss-crossed with scars that glowed from the strange residue left behind by those hellish blades.

Frem stood the third row, looming over the tall knights in front, his friend and squadron wizard, Par Sevare Zendrack, ever-present at his side.

"How many elves are left?" said Sevare, distracted by the dark blood that leaked past the Sithian line and pooled beneath his feet. The smell of that blood was heavy in the air, along with an odd, lemony scent that came off the Svarts — they exuded it like sweat."Can you see any end to them?"

"I see an end to us if they don't give up soon," said Frem. "There are hundreds. All crawling over each other to get at us."

"Bloodthirsty little buggers," said Sevare. "After all of them that we've killed, to still come at us in such a frenzy. . ."

"Squad, back two steps," shouted Frem. A moment later, as one, the two rows of soldiers in front of Frem shifted back exactly two steps — a maneuver Frem had been forced to use time and again since the skirmish began, for the Svart blood made for poor footing; Frem wanted the Svarts hampered, not his own. And too, did the Svarts use the piled bodies of their own as step stools, negating much of the Lomerians' height advantage.

"Good thing that only a few can come at us at once," said Sevare as his red and blistered fingers began to weave another incantation, the hair on his arms standing straight up due to the influence of the magic. His hands shook, his digits only marginally responsive — perhaps from pain, or else from the effects of channeling too much sorcery from the Grand Weave of Magic.

"Squad, back two more," shouted Frem.

"Even better that there are no side tunnels hereabouts," Frem said to Sevare. "That's what's done in Thorn's Stowron. The elves are still puking from half a hundred holes all around them. They never had a chance."

"How many Stowron are still up?" said Sevare as he tried to see over the men in front. The wizard was tall, several inches taller than most men, but that wasn't enough to see much from where he stood. Frem towered over everyone and had a better view than anyone else.

"Rounding that last bend a while back put all but a few out of sight," said Frem. "Only a single squad managed to follow us. They're pinned down. How they're still alive at all, I can't fathom. They fight till their last breath — every one of them. Tough men, them Stowron, despite their odd looks."

"You figure that Ezerhauten and Korrgonn can hold on at the center?" said Sevare.

"There are no side tunnels up where they are, best as I can remember," said Frem. "So I expect they're set up much the same as us, except they've got two fronts to fight on, instead of one."

"But a lot more men to defend with," said Sevare.

"Ezer will see them through this," said Frem,

"so long as Ginalli doesn't muck things up and Thorn doesn't kill him."

"No," said Sevare. "It'll be Lord Korrgonn's powers that will save us today, if we're to be saved at all. I'm certain of it."

"Keep your faith all you want," said Frem, "but I prefer to rely on my weapons, my squadron, and myself. Are you ready?"

Before Sevare could answer, a Svart landed two steps from him. Somehow it had vaulted over the Sithian line.

Before the black elf got its bearings, the wizard's staff arced down.

Square atop its head did it hit.

Its skull cracked like a melon.

"On three," said Sevare loud enough for Frem to hear.

"Squad, down on three," shouted Frem.

"One.

"Two.

"Three."

As one, all eight men in the front two rows dropped low. They braced their shields before them. Pikes overtop. Sevare and Frem stood tall behind them, Sevare's hands outstretched toward the Svart horde; a blast of yellow fire exploded from his fingertips. The mystical fire roared over the Sithians, sped toward the elves.

Hungry, ravenous fire was it, pulled down from the Grand Weave by the strength of Sevare's sorcery. That spell vaporized the elves at the van, but did not dissipate in the doing.

Black ashes were all that remained of the elves' front line.

The next row of elves fell to the same fire.
As did the next row.
And the next.
And the next.
And on and on.

Sevare's sorcery rocketed down the tunnel, and incinerated nearly everything in its path; fiery death its only offering. Only a sharp curve in the tunnel ended the spell's advance; the fire fizzled out.

A score of crispy Svart corpses marred the magic's wake. The ashes of dozens more clung to the tunnel like soot in a chimney.

A clutch of three battered Stowron huddled at a spot along the tunnel wall, spared by the sorcerous fire, their weapons and cloaks soaked of blood, some, their own. They took but a moment to get their bearings. Then they ran headlong for Frem's line. The Sithians made a hole to let them through.

Meanwhile, Sevare cursed and spat as he frantically shook his hands before him, smoke rising from his flesh. A trooper doused the wizard's hands and arms with the contents of a canteen of water. The first drops sizzled and steamed on contact with the wizard's bare skin.

"Troop, switch out the line by rows," Frem bellowed. "Move your tails, boys, they'll be on us again in a moment."

Eight fresher men took over for those from the front two rows, who retired to the rear to rest. Of the eight new ones, only three were Sithian Knights, two were Lugron, and three were Stowron, but all wore Sithian armor, borrowed from the dead or wounded. Without the heavy armor, the line couldn't hold — not against the Svarts.

The line had barely reformed when a horde of Svarts rounded the far bend and raced toward them, howling and screeching in the darkness.

"Archers," shouted Frem as he ducked down on one knee, his hand upraised.

When he pulled his arm down, a volley of arrows soared over him and the Sithian skirmishers and crashed into the Svart line. Half a dozen black elves dropped, arrows to head, neck, chest, and groin.

"Again," shouted Frem.

Another volley of arrows sprang forward. Six more black elves fell.

But still, their fellows charged forward, undeterred. They knocked their wounded comrades aside, or ran straight over them and their dead — no compassion, no empathy, not even for their own. Worse, they had no fear. No fear of the Lomerians at all. Not even of Sevare's terrible magic.

The melee men stood up. They readied their shield wall; braced for the impact of the charging elves.

"Troop, reserve pikemen to the line," shouted Frem. Eight more men with pikes and spears came up behind their fellows and braced against their backs, pole arms upraised at the ready.

"Squad, hold steady," shouted Frem as the Svarts barreled forward.

The black elves crashed against the Sithian line.

Some ran headlong onto the pikes.

Others barreled shoulder first into the shield wall. Some few tried to leap over the line, but the spears and pikes caught them all.

With the impact, the Sithian line staggered but held. The black elves, for all their fervor, had neither the mass nor the strength to break through the Sithian's wall of steel.

And so, the wild melee went on.

No respite.

No reprieve.

No end in sight.

"Frem," said Sevare through gritted teeth as a trooper wrapped bandages about his hands and forearms. "Can we hold them here? Is there a chance?"

"So long as they don't throw any wizards at us, we'll last a good while yet," said Frem as he looked back toward their rear. He'd done the same several times during the battle.

"You're expecting an attack from that end too?" said Sevare.

"That's what I'd do if I were them," said Frem. "Back two steps," he shouted. "Hopefully, they've no way to get back there; at least not anytime soon. How many more times can you throw that spell or one like it?"

Sevare looked at his hands. His arms shook. "Two times more. Maybe three, but don't count on that."

Putnam's whistle sounded from the rear.

"And there it is," said Frem. "Four pips. A major attack. Troop, squads one through three stay here. Hold the line no matter what. I'm going to reconnoiter the rear."

Frem barreled down the line, pushed past the others, and pulled Sevare along with him, though the wizard was in a daze. When Frem got to the rear, he saw a dozen dead elves lying in the tunnel. Sergeant Putnam, Clard Lugron, Sir Carroll, and Sir Royce stood amidst them, weapons bloodied, breathing heavily, but otherwise unharmed. Men were passing pikes to them. Frem moved to Putnam's side.

"We're in the deep stuff now, Captain," said Putnam hefting a pike; he aligned it with those of the knights on either side. "Real deep stuff."

"What is it? What did you see?" said Frem. "Do they have a wizard?"

"The monks," said Putnam as a battle cry rang out before them. From around the bend, just entering the edge of the lantern light, charged every last monk and guardsman from the Monastery of Ivald. All in full battle garb. Howling for blood. Several Svart charged along with them, thick as thieves. Brother Abraxon, the monks' head man, at the van

"Oh, shit," said Frem.

8

ABOARD THE BLACK FALCON, THE AZURE SEA

CLARADON

Even before he opened his eyes, Claradon knew he was back in his stateroom on *The Falcon*. He had spent so much time in that bed in recent weeks, he knew its every lump and divot.

Kayla was at his bedside, just as she had been over the prior weeks. She tended to him nearly every moment of his recovery, as he lay there, struggling to survive the terrible chest wound that he received at the hands of one Milton DeBoors — the infamous bounty hunter of song and story. A man hired by House Alder to kill him.

In truth, Kayla was a woman that he barely knew. Yet she doted on him as much or more than a good wife, a loyal sister, or a loving mother. Why she had such depth of feelings for him, given their brief acquaintance, he didn't know. But he was thankful for it. Thankful for it every day.

To think, it wasn't many weeks before, that they had first met. In Tragoss Mor, the city of the Thothian monks. Claradon and the others had rescued her. Plucked her from the auction block in the central slave market. Saved her from a life of bondage and abuse. A life likely not worth living. Grateful, she was, of course. Who wouldn't be? But it was more than that, Claradon was certain. Much more. She had true feelings for him. And he was developing the same for her.

And what more could any man want than the likes of her? A quick wit. Caring. Loving. Loyal. The face and curves of a goddess. And a warrior herself. Brave and strong. Capable. And of elven blood. Noble elven blood, if her tales be true — and he didn't doubt them. A woman he would be proud to present to his father and mother in the grand hall of Dor Eotrus. A woman worthy to marry a Dor Lord.

But his parents would never meet her.

His mother gone these past few years. His father, lately joined her in Valhalla. He needed no one's permission now. No one's approval. He was the patriarch of the House. The Lord of Dor Eotrus. Though he felt that the honor was put upon him long before his time. Long before he was ready to bear it.

Strange that he should think of such things, so far from home. Would he or Kayla even live to see this quest through? He knew not. But he had to admit, the odds were against them. Against them both. But a man could hope. A man could dream. He had had a lot of time for both of those over the prior few weeks. He still needed to regain his full strength, and retake his rightful position as leader of the quest.

A few more days. That's all he needed. And he'd be on his feet again. He'd be himself again.

"How do you feel?" said Kayla.

"Like a darned fool for not listening to you," said Claradon. "I should have headed below deck when you advised. I'm lucky I didn't end up headfirst over the rail."

"I would never have let you fall, my lord," said Kayla.

"I know," said Claradon, his eyes locked on hers, a hint of a smile on his face.

Her gaze lingered on him. Then she leaned over the bed. She kissed him gently on the lips. Sweetly. Tenderness in her touch.

He pulled her close, and kissed her harder, once and then again, and lingered in the embrace.

"Are you strong enough, my lord?" she said, her eyes alight, a grin on her face. "I can wait, if you are not," she said, her voice now breathless.

Claradon smiled. "Let's find out."

9

SVARTLEHEIM

JUDE EOTRUS

"**B**e ready, Brother," whispered Jude Eotrus to Brother Donnelin as the sounds of battle reached them from far up the tunnel and from far back. "This may be our chance."

"Our chance for what?" said Donnelin. "To get lost in these tunnels on our lonesomes? No light, no supplies, and hunted by Shadow League nutcases and black elves too? No thank you, Master Jude. We're quite better off where we are — for now. Our time will yet come, but we must be patient."

"I've been a Tyrian Knight for five years, Brother Donnelin," said Jude.

Donnelin looked confused for a moment, and then realized what Jude meant. "When you've bounced a child on your knee enough times, and wiped the snot from his nose, it's hard to see him as a man, even when he's full grown. You'll pardon me, I trust, Sir Jude."

"And if I don't?" said Jude, his voice serious, his face stiff.

"Well then," said Donnelin, his voice just as stern, "I can always kick your behind and remind you to respect your elders."

They stared at each other for a moment, and

then both smiled.

"My hands are almost free," said Jude.

"Good, get them free, but hide it," said Donnelin. "Do nothing more. Like I said, we have to bide our time."

"If we stay here much longer, we may never leave," said Jude. "From the sound of it, the Leaguers are losing. Ezerhauten is the only one of them that knows tactics, and the priest and the wizards won't listen to him. They're fighting him on everything."

"You don't know that," said Donnelin. "We've only caught snippets of what they've said."

"I heard enough," said Jude."

"Then you should know that it's not Ginalli that's in charge," said Donnelin. "And not Korrgonn. It's Thorn. The others are all afraid of him, Ginalli included."

"If Korrgonn is the son of Azathoth as they say, how is it that he's not in charge?" said Jude.

"A fish out of water is he," said Donnelin. "He knows little of Midgaard or of men. He watches. He listens. He doesn't say much. So long as the Leaguers follow his purpose he lets them decide things. Where he thinks they go off course, he gets them in line."

"How could you possibly know that?" said Jude.

"The olden magic runs strong in me, dear boy," said Donnelin. "Prisoner or no, I have powers."

"If the fighting reaches us," said Jude, "we need to make a break for it. I need you with me on this."

"I've served the Eotrus since before you were

born," said Donnelin. "I'll not abandon you now, no matter how thick your head. But we have to use our brains. We can't survive in here without light and supplies, if even then."

"All we need to do is head straight back the way we came," said Jude. "As long as we pick up a torch, we'll make it. We got here in two hours, we can get back in less than half of that if we move with speed."

"The monks will turn us over to the Leaguers straight away," said Donnelin.

"Not if they don't catch us," said Jude. "We'll slip into the monastery's basement, then make our way up and out before they know we're there."

"And if the basement door is locked?"

"We'll knock it down. You've got more than enough olden magic to do that, am I right?"

"Every monk in the place will hear the door coming down. There will be no sneaking by them. And too many to fight."

"It's our best chance," said Jude.

"It's a lousy one."

"What's the alternative? Give them the slip somewhere in the interior of Jutenheim? Out in the jungle that they were talking about? Or the swamp? Then where do we go, and what do we do?"

Donnelin shook his head. "Make for the coast. Look for a boat. I don't know."

"I don't know isn't a good plan," said Jude. "We need to go back the way we came and get down to Jutenheim town. Then by hook or by crook we hop a boat and sail home straightaway. That's our best chance. It may be our only chance to see Dor

Eotrus again."

Donnelin nodded and stayed quiet for some moments, thinking. "Maybe I've gone scared in my old age. Scared of getting trapped here in the dark. Scared of dying. Scared of losing you, same as I lost your father and the others."

"What happened in the Vermion that night?" said Jude. "The truth this time."

"Too long a story for now, but I'll tell you when we've the time. Just know that your father died a hero's death. He's looking down on us even now from Valhalla; proud of you, I'm certain. And you're right about the tunnel. Heading back is our best chance. Even if it's a lousy one. But we need weapons and torches to make it work. Without torches we're dead for certain."

"We'll get them," said Jude.

Teek Lugron moved close to the two prisoners.

He shoved Donnelin and smacked Jude across the back of the head. Made a show of it too, grunting like he'd thrown everything he had into the strike, but the blow had no power behind it.

It was a fake.

Jude fell to the ground, feigning injury. It just seemed like the thing to do.

"Stop your jabbering, you scum," said Teek, loud enough for those Leaguers nearest to him to hear.

"Get up, you no good slacker," said Teek. "Sniveling weakling; I barely touched you." The Lugron helped Jude to his feet, but took his time about it. He slipped something into Jude's back pocket when he leaned in close and whispered. "You played me square enough back on the ship, and old Teek don't forget, Judy boy. Wait to make your move until you can't wait no more, and then hightail it; Big Red is watching you close even when it seems he's not."

"You'll come with us?" said Jude.

"Maybe, Judy boy," said Teek. "Depends on them darned elves."

10

ABOARD THE BLACK FALCON, THE AZURE SEA

CLARADON

Someone was screaming. Claradon didn't know who, but it was loud, yet muffled; at a distance. A woman's voice. He listened closely, and then he realized that that voice was familiar. He couldn't be certain, but – was it his mother? Was it her? Calling for him? Screaming for help? Dead gods!

Claradon's eyes opened even as he jolted upright and bounded from the bed, his chest stiff and sore. "Kayla," he shouted as consciousness returned. He took two steps towards the door, his legs not fully sound, his head groggy, his eyelids felt glued down, hard to see. And then he realized all he wore was his nightshirt. He spun; eyes searched for his weapons. For anything of use. He didn't see them. He couldn't think. His head was spinning.

He heard sounds from the hallway. A violent scuffle.

To hell with the weapons. He ran for the door, opened it. No one was there. There should have been a guard.

He stepped out into the hallway and looked

one way and then the other. A trooper, face down in a pool of blood. His guard. Stationed there to protect him. Either Frost or Parnel, had to be. Good men both. Farther down the hall, toward the end, two figures struggled on the floor.

"Help," spat Kayla, though the words were strained and muffled. He barely heard her.

He ran down the corridor, uncertain whether he was awake or in the throes of a nightmare. He'd had plenty of those in recent weeks. But he ran. Kayla needed him. And then the person atop her turned toward him.

It was seaman Gurt, the bastard!

But yet it wasn't.

His eyes were black – entirely black, no whites to them at all, or so it seemed in the poor light of that corridor. His face was pale almost to gray. And fanged. He had fangs for Odin's sake! They protruded from his mouth. Fangs like a viper. Like daggers.

Kayla's hand was at Gurt's throat, straining to hold his head back away from her. Her other hand gripped one of Gurt's.

Claradon sprang to action. In a blink of an eye, he was on them. He kicked Gurt in the face with all his strength. The blow was jarring because his foot was bare. Gurt shook his head from side to side like a wet dog and then stared back at him, the blow of no effect. Claradon kicked him again, this time aiming the blow, putting all his power into it.

His heel slammed into Gurt's jaw. But it was Claradon that was thrown back. He stumbled against the wall even as Gurt stood up. The kick again had no effect.

Claradon didn't understand. He hit him with everything he had. Was he so weak now? Was he so feeble?

And what happened to Gurt? He had come in on that longboat with Theta and the others. What happened to him in Evermere? It made no sense. He looked more monster than man. Another creature of Nifleheim? Had he been in disguise all along? A hidden monster in their midst?

He didn't know Gurt well. But he knew he was the best knife fighter on the crew. Gurt's hands held no knives but each was now a dagger unto itself — with claws several inches long.

Claradon backed up, still groggy from sleep, his vision blurred. Still dizzy from his injuries. He fell into a fighting stance. The way Sir Gabriel had schooled him. He clenched his jaw and his fists and waited until Gurt lunged in.

Sir Gabriel had taught him many ways in which to fight an armed opponent when he himself was unarmed. A dangerous battle it would be every time. But Claradon knew the maneuvers. He'd learned them all. Practiced them endlessly with Ob and others.

When Gurt's claws swiped at him, he stepped back and to the side. He brought his hands together and struck at Gurt's wrist. He bent it, twisted it, and turned it over in his grip. He pushed down on Gurt's wrist and hand with all his might, dropped to his knee as he did so — as fast and as hard as he could.

He heard the bones splinter: wrist, hand, and forearm. Even so, Claradon barely got his arm up in time to catch Gurt's other forearm as the seaman brought his other claws to bear.

Claradon lunged forward, tackled Gurt; a knee dropped hard on his chest. One hand held Gurt's arm back; the other at his throat — to choke him out. He had to.

But then Claradon flew through the air. Somehow, Gurt pushed him off and flung him. Tossed him as if he weighed next to nothing.

Claradon hit the floor six feet from where he had been. He rolled, spun, and was up in an instant. Even that wasn't too soon. Gurt charged him. One step away when Claradon dodged aside. Claradon's chest wound threatened to tear open. The pain, terrible. He pushed it down; ignored it.

And then they were locked together again. Claradon tried to hold Gurt's clawed arm at bay; the seaman's other arm limp at his side, broken in multiple places. But Claradon's two arms were not strong enough to hold back even one of Gurt's.

Elbows flew. Knees crashed. Claradon headbutted Gurt, but that strike did him more harm than the seaman.

Gurt tried to bite him over and again. He lunged at his throat at every opportunity. It was all Claradon could do to hold him back. The seaman was half his size, but had at least twice his strength. It made no sense. Claradon's left hand was at Gurt's throat, held his head back, kept those fangs at bay even as his right hand fended off Gurt's claws. Claradon couldn't win. Gurt was too strong. Too resilient. His best chance was to attempt a throw. Get Gurt off him, grab

Kayla, and slip into a state room; bar the door. Hold out until help came. And it would come. Claradon's men would put Gurt down.

Just as Claradon was about to attempt the throw, Gurt stiffened, and a blade sliced through his chest — through his heart. Kayla had stabbed him through the back.

Gurt spun, spitting blood. He went after Kayla. Claradon grabbed Gurt by the hair with one hand. Pulled the dagger out of the seaman's back with the other. Gurt stumbled. Claradon tackled him. They both went face down to the deck.

Before the seaman could throw him off, Claradon drew the dagger across Gurt's throat — once and then again. "Stomp on his arm," shouted Claradon. "Hold it down."

Kayla was there. Battered but battling. She threw herself atop Gurt's arm; held it down though it bucked and writhed.

Claradon sawed at the seaman's neck. Cut him deep. Severed the jugular. Impossible though it was, that wasn't enough. Gurt kept fighting. Struggling. His strength, limitless.

Claradon kept cutting. He had to. He couldn't stop. He didn't. Not until Gurt's head separated from his neck. Only then did Gurt go limp.

Claradon was covered in blood. He couldn't believe what he had just done. What he had had to do. Disgusted by it. The blood was everywhere. The walls, the ceiling. Sprayed with it. Kayla's face awash with it.

A moment to catch their breaths and then they embraced.

"You saved me," said Kayla, tears in her eyes.

"You saved me again."

"You did half the saving," said Claradon, breathing heavily, his chest throbbing. "The bastard was strong. How did Gurt become one of those monsters is what I want to know."

"What a fool I am," said Kayla. "I thought I could beat him alone. I thought to make you proud."

"I am proud," said Claradon. "Few folk could hold their own against such as that. Thank Odin that your screams roused me in time to help."

Kayla's brow furrowed. "Screams?"

"It woke me up. I was dead to the world," said Claradon.

Kayla shook her head slowly. "My lord, I did not scream."

11
SVARTLEHEIM

FREM

Brother Abraxon and his vanguard ran headlong toward the Sithian mercenaries, as if they had no fear of death. Illumed only by bobbing torches, their shadows cast frightful figures on the tunnel walls and ceiling that made them look as giants. Their war cries, amplified by the narrow confines, sounded like tens of thousands of wild men. But for all Frem knew, with the black elves included, mayhap there were that many of them. So far, he could see no end to them.

Frem stood behind the pikemen, hammer and dirk at the ready, itching to get into the fight. But he knew he had to hang back. He had to direct the others. Not that they needed much directing — the Sithians were experts — but his tactics, honed over long years, made them all the better.

Sevare was at his shoulder. The wizard rarely needed direction from Frem as to what sorcery to throw or when to throw it. He just knew.

He stood there, Sevare did, his hand upraised toward the ceiling, mouthing his words of power — guttural words, harsh and discordant, more animal sounds than human speech. Each syllable Sevare spoke sent a sharp pain through Frem's head, beginning at each ear. The other soldiers felt it too; Frem saw them wince at the sounds, but they held their positions; they didn't let the magic distract them. Luckily, most had served with Sevare long enough to know what was happening.

Pain or no, Frem was certain that the troops welcomed those mystical words, as he did, for they heralded the Sithians' most devastating attacks. Sevare was a war wizard without peer in the Sithian ranks — at least since the passing of Cotter the Dandy some time back. What Sevare's esoteric words meant, if they meant anything at all beyond the sounds themselves, Frem could not hope to know, and never bothered to ask. Some things were better left alone. Usually, a word or two was all it took to launch Sevare's sorcery — that quickness was one of the things that made him great — but this time, he droned on and on until the monks and black elves were but a few strides away.

Only then did the sorcery spring forth from his fingertips. Swift as an arrow it sped, but wide as the tunnel. A dark cloud it was, a shadow that moved of its own accord.

In the darkness of the tunnel, and in their own frenzy, the monks likely never saw it coming. But they knew, however briefly, when that shadow touched them. When it did, for the briefest of moments their bodies lit up, as if bathed in bright light.

Then their flesh disintegrated.

Midstride, they vaporized into wisps of smoke. Only gray bones and acrid odors left behind. And those bones — it was as if they knew not that their bodies had been destroyed. They came on still — a step of two, bones alone, before they collapsed, crashed to the tunnel floor, and scattered. A spray of bones blasted into the front row of pikemen, though it did them no harm save to their nerves.

The first several rows of monks were destroyed like this, from that single sorcery. Fifteen or twenty men all told.

But not Brother Abraxon.

When the black shadow of death went for him, something repulsed it — some ward he carried, some token of protection. In his mad fervor, he didn't even notice his fellows dying at his sides. Or else he didn't care.

Brother Abraxon's sword knocked aside Clard's pike with surprising skill and stepped within its reach. Before the Lugron could pull his sword, the monk bashed him on the head. Frem lunged forward and stabbed the monk in the shoulder with his dagger. Even that didn't slow Abraxon. The monk turned toward Frem with the wild eyes of a zealot, teeth bared,

12

ABOARD THE BLACK FALCON, THE AZURE SEA

SLAAYDE

Captain Dylan Slaayde sat at Bertha's bedside, both his hands cupped around one of hers. Slaayde's eyes were red, his cheeks wet, his jaw tightly clenched. A rare display of emotion that was for the good captain. But they were alone in the captain's cabin; no one to see her dying; no one to see him grieve. No one to think less of Slaayde for it.

Not that Slaayde cared. Not anymore. Not after staring helpless at Bertha's face as life drained away from her. Seeing the love of his life like that, changed something inside Slaayde. It put an end to some part of him. Some important part, though he couldn't name it. Something from deep down at his core. What that meant for him, how that would affect him, he didn't yet know. But he knew he felt different.

Empty.

Devoid of any notion of happiness, contentment, or joy. As if he'd never be happy again. Or whole again.

He was no child; no starry-eyed lover; no fool. He'd suffered loss before. He knew grief. He knew that time would dull its edge. He just wasn't certain that he cared anymore. Without Bertha, what really mattered?

Her face was white like the bed sheets on laundry day. Her skin, cold. The life, the warmth, the love, the support — it wasn't there anymore. Cold and dry in his hands.

Cold like a corpse.

And that's what she should be, and he knew it – after all the blood she'd lost. The wound at her neck never stopped bleeding — pressure, bindings, and compresses all did no good.

The red seeped through.

And kept seeping. No end to it. How she still breathed, how her heart still beat, after losing that much blood, he didn't understand. He'd never seen the like, though he'd seen a lot of wounds. Half as much blood lost should have killed her.

But yet she hung on. Clung desperately to life, somehow. A fighter was she. A tough woman. He was proud of that. Of her. He should have told her that more often — if even he told her at all. But now it was too late. His life was weighed down with would haves and should haves. They followed him like a pack of hungry hounds nipping at his heels, never letting him be. Never letting him forget.

There was no leren aboard *The Falcon* to patch Bertha up properly, if that were even possible. There wasn't even a second-rate healer or crotchety old herbalist like The Fourth Hammer had. Hell, with Ravel gone, Bertha had the most medical knowledge of anyone on the ship. That left no one to see to her in her time of need — at least, no one that knew what they were doing past binding a wound or setting a bone.

That meant that Bertha didn't have a chance. And that made Slaayde angry. Angry at the world. At the gods. At the Eotrus. At Theta. But most of all, it made him angry at himself. Himself! And when Slaayde was angry, he was dangerous. Deadly.

Slaayde was the captain. He selected and hired the crew; nobody else. He could have hired a skilled leren for the ship at any time, but he didn't. He should have done it years ago. The need was there. There was no excuse for it — with all the action that *The Falcon* saw. Instead, he relied on Ravel's half-baked and field-honed skills. That was darned poor judgment. And that mistake was all on him. A top leren — somebody with real knowledge of herbs, medicines, and such, somebody with a bit of magic to back that knowledge up — could have given Bertha a fighting chance.

Maybe.

A chance to live through that wound. To heal up and recover. To be herself again. To have a life with Slaayde — the two of them, together.

Maybe.

But thanks to Slaayde's foolishness, there wasn't anyone like that aboard, so no chance did she have. No chance at all. Except maybe for Theta and his bag of tricks.

13

SVARTLEHEIM

FREM

Sevare was down.

The men poured water over him. When it touched his flesh, much of it bubbled, boiled, and turned to steam. How such a thing was possible, Frem could not say. How did magic heat him up like that? How could his flesh withstand it? Frem had no answers. Like many things to do with sorcery, it was something odd that one just had to accept. And so Frem did.

Sevare cried out from the pain. His eyes rolled back in his head. Not a pretty sight. But Frem knew he'd recover. He always did. But Frem figured Sevare had only one more sorcery left in him that day. And if he used it too soon, it might kill him. He had to save it for the right time. Frem and the others had to give him that time.

With the destruction of their vanguard, the monks' charge broke, but only for a moment. Then they started up their howling again. The black elves amongst them took the lead. The whole mob charged forward anew. Back and back into the tunnels their line stretched, far beyond the limits of the meager torchlight.

"No end to them," mumbled Frem.

They broke upon the Sithians' pikes and kept

coming. They pushed forward, howling and slavering. The big knights in front of Frem got pushed back — one step and then another. Frem sent more men to the line to bolster the shield wall. The fighting was close and intense. Weapons darted through the narrowest of gaps between shields. The Sithians planted their shields to the ground and kept a foot on the lip that stuck out, anchoring the shield wall to the tunnel floor, as they fought above it with thrusting weapons.

Frem called out the orders using the Sithian battle code. The men thrust and withdrew in step, as a unit. First the front line struck, then the pikemen overtop, supported by a few archers. Over and over they thrust and withdrew one step, then again, and again. Even as the elves died in droves, they pushed the Sithians back. Every step squeezed them closer to the fight at the other end of their line. They had little more ground to give.

The black elves had surprising skill. They were fast and strong. They fought as individuals, each man for himself, oblivious of what their fellows did and how they faired. But what made them terrible opponents, was that they had no fear of death. Their eyes were wild. Their attacks single-minded. They plowed forward, and attacked, and kept attacking until they were cut down.

The Sithians held their line — a line of steel and skill that neither the monks nor the black elves of Thoonbarrow could hope to breach.

Instead of giving up, the elves tried another tactic. They began to leap forward en masse, vaulting from the shoulders of their fellows, to land on or beyond Frem's front line. And they knew their ground well. They picked just the right time for their new attack. Just when Frem had his back to a large chamber that the tunnel opened into. Once backed into that space, the elves could come at them from all sides.

And they did.

Frem's orderly line was infiltrated, first by a handful of elves, and soon by a score. Elves were behind him. Around him. Everywhere.

Order and discipline broke down.

Now, for the Sithians, it was every man for himself.

The battle turned to chaos.

There was no room to swing a sword. Little space to maneuver. Frem stood back to back with Royce and Putnam. He thrust with his dagger and swung overhand with his short battle hammer. Frem stabbed a monk through the mouth, then an elf through the neck, another through an eye. Frem wasn't certain how many he'd put down with his hammer: perhaps five, perhaps eight. Beyond all limits of fatigue, he fought on instinct, training, muscle memory, adrenaline. Soon it was just the elves that came at them. Had the monks all fallen? Or had they retreated? Frem couldn't say. His view of the battlefield had shrunk to the immediate area around him; no time to look around and size up anything. No time to give orders to the troops. He didn't even know what troops he had left, except that there were some, for he heard the larger battle about him, and caught glimpses of it as he fought.

14

ABOARD THE BLACK FALCON, THE AZURE SEA

THETA

Theta stood alone at *The Black Falcon's* prow, his hands on the rail, the breeze setting his cape aflutter. Dolan walked over to him, his face bandaged, swollen, and bruised.

"It be spring, yet every day it grows colder," said Dolan.

"You didn't stagger up the ladder to speak to me about the weather," said Theta. "Rest while you can. Once we get to Jutenheim, there may be little opportunity for it."

"You'll have us go back there, won't you?" said Dolan. "To that island. Evermere."

Theta answered, "If even one of them got off that island, got to a population center, there might be no stopping the spread of their disease. Midgaard could be eaten alive."

"There are thousands of them left," said Dolan.

"I'll find a way to bring them down," said Theta. "I always do."

"But not alone," said Dolan. "Not just us, right? You'll raise a proper force this time, won't you?"

"If such opportunity presents," said Theta.

"And if not?" said Dolan.

Theta smiled. "Then I'll do it alone, or with whoever will follow me."

Dolan was at a loss for words.

"Don't worry, we'll develop a fool-proof plan," said Theta. "They'll never know what hit them."

Dolan shook his head and couldn't help but smirk. They stood there for a time, enjoying the cool breeze, the warm sun, and the solitude of the empty sea.

15

ABOARD THE BLACK FALCON, THE AZURE SEA

SLAAYDE

Slaayde walked across *The Falcon's* main deck and approached the Captain's Den, hat in hand. As usual, the Eotrus had men stationed at the door. Slaayde understood the need for security. But he was the Captain. Those were his chambers. He owned the stinking ship.

Slaayde had come up on deck alone. His clothes were disheveled. Somehow he put on his old boots — the ones with the hole in the right big toe. He felt like he was in a daze; only half conscious.

He wondered if they were going to stop him at the door. Try and tell him that Theta was too busy to see him. Turn him away.

Let them try; he'd give them what for.

That was not a day to mess with Slaayde. Not a day to test his anger or his resolve.

Then Slaayde realized that Little Tug was trailing him. Tug would move them, if they needed moving. He'd get in. He'd get what he needed from Theta. He had to.

"Open the door," said Slaayde.

The man did so; one of the Eotrus sergeants. A veteran. He knew who was who. He knew his place. Slaayde respected that.

"Captain Slaayde is here," said the sergeant into the open door.

Theta sat at the big table in the middle of the room. Slaayde's table. Some of the others were there too. Who knows what they were up to, bastards every one. Stinking no good Northmen.

Theta eyed him as he walked up to the table. Slaayde couldn't interpret his expression. Was it concern? Pity? Or was it nothing at all? Pure indifference?

"Bertha needs a swallow or two of that witch's brew of yours," said Slaayde, though he barely got the words out, despite going over them a dozen times in his head before he left his cabin and more on the walk up from below deck. He just spouted the words out; he didn't even know what he was saying. He trusted that they were the right words, the ones he had practiced, but at the time, he wasn't certain. As he spoke them, Slaayde's eyes searched for the steel sphere that housed Theta's potion. Theta guarded that thing like it was the queen's jewels. But Slaayde couldn't see it. Theta was seated, and that big belt of his, which held more stuff than any fighting man should carry, was hidden behind the table, if he wore it at all.

"It won't work on her," said Theta. "Not on that wound."

Slaayde felt his cheeks flush. He expected Theta to give him a hard time, but he had hoped that he'd be reasonable. "She's bad off," said

Slaayde. "I wouldn't ask otherwise, but she needs it, so I'm asking. Without a healthy dose of that stuff, she's not going to make it."

"It won't work on that wound," said Theta.

Slaayde's eyes narrowed. "Name your price, you bastard."

Theta's words were slow and clear. "The elixer won't work on that wound. Wanting it to, won't change that."

"You want *The Falcon*?" said Slaayde. "Is that it? You want my ship? One sip. That's all I ask. One sip, for Odin's sake, and the ship is yours."

"I cannot help her," said Theta.

Slaayde's cheeks went from red to fiery crimson. "We're trying it," said Slaayde, his voice going deadly cold. "Where is it?" Slaayde's hand and arm began to twitch; his fingers, subtly searched for his sword belt. But it wasn't there. It lay on the table back in his cabin. He'd forgotten it. "Turn it over!" he shouted. Had his sword been where it should have been, he would've pulled it then and there, quick as lightning. He'd have lunged at Theta. He would've put the tip of that blade straight through his heart.

"What kind of heartless bastard are you, Theta?" said Slaayde. "You're talking as if that stinking potion is more valuable than Bertha's life. Is that what you think? Is it?"

"You're not listening to me," said Theta. "What ails Bertha is not within the elixir's power to cure. If I gave it to her, it would do her no good. No good at all. If I had something that could help her, I would. But I don't."

"I've seen what that stuff can do," said

Slaayde. "It's just a bite wound."

"It's more than just a bite," said Theta. "I think you know that. What happened to Gurt—"

"You no-good foreigner," spat Slaayde, trembling. "You just don't give a damn — about Bertha; about *The Falcon*, its crew; about anyone but yourself and your mad quest. Your stinking quest is going to get us all killed. Every one of us."

Theta started to say something more, but Slaayde turned and marched from the room, not hearing another word.

Deep down, Slaayde believed Theta. He knew that Bertha's wound was no common bite. Bandages and stitches — that's not what she needed. Something dark afflicted her, same as Seaman Gurt. Something evil was hidden inside that bite. Some kind of poison or venom, or else a disease or mayhap even a curse. A plague that transferred from the bloodsuckers to their victims through the bite. And when it did, it changed the victims. It destroyed them from within. It turned them from whatever kind of folk they were into whatever those bloodsuckers are. Into monsters. Bloodthirsty, flesh eating, crazed, maniacal monsters.

And now that was going to happen to Bertha. That's what was eating Slaayde up – even more than the thought of losing her. Of all people, to have that happen to her. It wasn't fair. It wasn't right.

He should have never brought her to the island with the shore party. He knew it was going to be dangerous, but he gave in; let her get her way, just as he usually did. And that got her hurt. If he'd just used his own good judgment, the same judgment every captain is required to have, she'd have been safe and sound on *The Falcon* the whole time. What happened to her was his fault for taking her. He failed her.

One more failure in a long line of them.

Bertha was a gentle soul, loud as she was when she got going. A kind heart she had. A good woman. The best Slaayde had ever known. And now, soon, she'd be a monster. She'd be one of them. A thing. And there was nothing in all the world that Slaayde could do about it. No way for him to stop it. Maybe no way for anyone to stop it.

16
SVARTLEHEIM

JUDE

For a long time, the battle seemed far away to Jude. The clash of arms was loud enough, the shouts and yowls were louder, but the action remained distant. It seemed to Jude that the fighting was closer in the rear, but it was hard to tell. Sound traveled strangely in the tunnels.

Jude watched messages passed to the expedition's officers from both fronts. He heard very little of what they said, but it was clear enough that the headmen argued incessantly. Ginalli acted like he was in charge, despite what Donnelin said about Thorn, but Ezerhauten butted heads with him on everything. Their arguments grew heated more than once. Jude saw Ezerhauten's hand fidget atop the hilt of his sword, where he rested it, more than once. Jude was certain that he would have pulled it and cut Ginalli down were it not for Korrgonn's presence. Mayhap the mercenary had a fiery temper that he had trouble controlling. Or else, mayhap he just hated the priest. Jude figured it was the former. Mercenaries were a violent and untrustworthy lot by nature.

The Nifleheim Lord lurked about, listening to everything, but rarely saying a word. He looked pale, even sickly. How a godlike being could get sick, Jude had no idea. Maybe Sir Gabriel was still in there somewhere, trying to kick Korrgonn out. Giving him what for every time he took a rest. That would be just like Sir Gabriel. But Jude knew that that wasn't the case. Only wishful thinking. Sir Gabriel was dead. All that was left was to avenge him. And Jude would. He'd avenge his father. Sir Gabriel. Par Talbon. Ranger Stern. Balfin. Marzdan. Dalken. And all the other good Eotrus men that the League killed. That they murdered. He'd avenge them all. Even if he died in the trying.

Eventually, a few wounded Sithian mercenaries staggered up from the rear of the troop. Ezerhauten set to interrogating them, but Ginalli scurried over and got in the way. No doubt, the priest asked after the weather back there, or inquired about the cut of the elves' trousers.

Soon, other battered mercs trudged down from the troop's front. Ezerhauten wanted to deploy Mort Zag and the remaining League wizards, but Ginalli would hear none of it. Kept his heavy hitters close, he did. To protect himself? Or Korrgonn?

All the while, Jude studied the scene. Donnelin did the same. The problem was, the Leaguers were all around them. And no matter whether Jude went forward or back, he'd be walking into a battle. He'd have to get past not only the Leaguers, but the black elves too. So he waited — and fingered the small dagger that Teek had slipped him. The first time Big Red stopped staring at them, Jude used the dagger to cut Donnelin's bonds.

Then of a sudden, the battle was on them.

Ezerhauten rushed forward with a few of his knights to see what was what, while men shouted in the tunnel just a short ways ahead. But before the mercenary could do anything, black elves charged into view. The little buggers were able to run past the soldiers, the narrowness of the tunnel notwithstanding.

In barely a moment, the elves were everywhere, wavy black daggers and swords swinging.

Jude had heard tell of their kind before. All Lomerians had. But he'd never seen one before. He'd thought them long died out, like the Mistkelstrans or the Zorns. But there they were. Short, gray, spindly, bug eyed, and agile as monkeys.

Mort Zag moved close to Jude and Donnelin even as the Sithians massed together to block the elves' advance.

"Stay behind me, and don't try anything," said Mort Zag, "or I'll let the elves have you."

All hell broke loose.

The mercenaries were fully engaged. They formed their battle lines; tight wedges of men that the elves could not hack through, but of which some were able to jump over and cause chaos from behind the lines. Jude lost track of Ezerhauten. Maybe they'd killed him, pulled him down by force of numbers, or else he was just too far up front.

When the elves got close, the League wizards let fly their magics: both protective and aggressive.

Green and red force shields went up here and there. They hovered about the wizards that birthed them. Cloaked them in mystical mantles of protection that kept the elfin blades at bay.

The Leaguers conjured up spectral knights from the ether; some stood protectively about their masters; their translucent blades held before them, sparking and crackling. Others charged the elves. Weapons swinging. No fear or hesitation. Their eyes, cold and stony. Devoid of life or emotion, soulless things that they were; they lived only to serve their masters.

Bolts of silver, red, and yellow energy blasted into the elves. Some sprang from the wizards' hands. Others erupted from the tips of their staves. The bolts cut the elves to pieces. Heads fell. Limbs lopped off. Torsos sliced in two.

Yellow fire poured down from the ceiling. Incinerated whole squads of elves. Burnt them to ash. The men that fought in their midst, untouched.

Holes opened in the tunnel floor. Swallowed up elves by the dozen. Closed a moment later. As if they'd never been there. The elves' cries cut off in mid-scream.

Despite the power and horror of that mystical assault, still the elves came on. In their thousands. Undeterred. Howling. Screeching. No fear of death did they have.

They even ran fearless at Big Red. Mort Zag scooped them up. One after another. Pulled them apart with bare hands. Popped their heads right off, without even straining. Dropped their corpses in a gruesome heap before him. He grinned all the while. Enjoyed it.

Until a tall elf with a long bone staff faced him.

That elf spoke his mystic words. They dripped from his lips with smoothness and confidence, as if they were old friends, comfortable and familiar. A moment later, a bolt of shimmering white light shot at Mort Zag's chest. It lifted the massive red demon from the ground. Threw him into the tunnel wall.

Mort Zag cursed, but was up in an instant. He grabbed the nearest elf. Threw him some fifteen feet to crash into the Diresvart. That sent the wizard sprawling. A dozen elves rushed Mort Zag. They stabbed him with their swords. Slashed him with daggers. Grabbed him about the legs. Tried to pull him down. Jumped on his back. Tried to gouge out his eyes. It did no good. His flesh was like iron. They couldn't cut him. They couldn't move him. They could do him no harm at all. He kicked one. Stomped on another. Smashed his fist atop another's head. And then another. With each strike, he killed one. Against him, the elves had no chance.

And then Jude saw Mason fighting. The man of stone was as formidable as Big Red, though he was hampered by the large box that he gripped in one hand — the box that held the Orb of Wisdom. Each of Mason's punches sent an elf flying through the air. Their weapons, equally ineffective against him.

Par Keld stood on a large rock in the middle of the tunnel. Even atop it, his head wasn't much higher than those of most of the Leaguers. His arms punched this way and that, almost in slow motion, his fingers crooked, his head bent low but his eyes up. With each punch elves far from him went flying as if clobbered by a giant maul. "Look at them," he shouted to anyone in earshot. "They're nothing to me. Nothing."

Despite their champions, the Leaguers were outnumbered at least ten to one. The elves were everywhere. No one was safe — no matter where in the tunnels they stood.

Finally, they came at Jude. No more pretending he was still tied up. He had to fight. Twenty elves rushed his position. Teek Lugron was there. So were some of Ezerhauten's knights. They interposed themselves between the elves and the prisoners. Showed their courage and their quality.

Some few elves made it past them.

Jude kicked one in the face. Disarmed a second one and took up his blade. Donnelin did the same. Slash and slice, stab and whirl, they did the dance of death with the elves. Jude was shocked at their skills. The elves were masters of the blade. One better than the last. And their speed was uncanny. Their resilience impressive, especially considering their diminutive size. They were amongst the most skilled opponents he had ever dueled, and Jude had sparred with some of the best knights in all Lomion.

And with that recognition, Jude marveled at the skill of the Sithians and the League wizards. For the elves, all their skills and grit notwithstanding, could only face the mercenaries and the Leaguers with great numbers, and even then, they suffered terrible losses. Jude realized in that battle, that the Sithians were each worth at least five Lomerian soldiers, some more than that. And the League wizards were likely as skilled as the best Archmages of the Tower of the Arcane. Perhaps even as powerful as the Grandmasters. What a shock that was. Jude had thought the Sithians were random mercenaries that the League had hired. And he had thought that the League wizards weren't much more than hedges. Now he knew better. And that did not bode well for his escape.

Ginalli fled toward the rear and urged Korrgonn along. They forced Jude and Donnelin to go with them, Teek and several soldiers as their guards. The Sithian knights and the League wizards formed an impenetrable line behind them.

Then orange fire blasted apart the Sithian lines. Men went flying. Others were on fire, screaming. Jude saw Mort Zag lit up like a torch, howling in pain.

The elves had magic too.

17

ABOARD THE BLACK FALCON, THE AZURE SEA

OB

Ob marched past the door guards into Tanch's stateroom. Upon his first breath, the gnome wrinkled his nose, for a strange burnt odor hung about the room. The wizard lay askew on the bed, his eyes closed, his face bright red – as if burned by overexposure to the sun. The bed clothes were disheveled; pillows fallen to the floor; the balance of the room a wreck. If Ob had been unfamiliar with Tanch's ways, he might have thought that someone had ransacked the place.

Ob cleared his throat, softly at first, then louder, but Tanch did not stir. "Magic Boy," he said to no response. "They said you were awake, you lazy bugger. They said you were asking for me."

Still, the wizard did not respond.

"Is anybody home?" said Ob loudly as he swiped at Tanch's feet. "Or are you back loafing about in La La Land?"

"I'm awake," said Tanch, squirming, his voice raspy and weak, and so different from its normal sound that Ob didn't recognize it. "Just trying to rest my eyes and gain back a bit of strength."

"You look like hell," said Ob. "Your skin is fried crispy. Like some Lugron half cooked you over a spit."

Tanch nodded. "Too much magic in too short a time. The body can't take it. Everything heats up. Heats up and burns out. I'm lucky I'm not dead. When a wizard goes too far, like I did out there – there's usually nothing left of him but a pile of smoking ash."

"You've tossed your share of spells before," said Ob. "I've seen it, but you've never gone all crispy."

"I've never thrown near so much sorcery before — never dreamed that I could. And never would have tried, but for the need we had. There were so many bloodsuckers on the docks. I figured I'd fry as many as I could. Give the rest of you a chance to get away. Gave them all that I had. Still, I don't know how I did it. How I killed so many of them. I should be dead after throwing all that magic. I should be dead."

"Mayhap the All-father was smiling down on you," said Ob. "They say he protects children, madmen, and fools. That covers you at least twice."

Tanch groaned and squirmed some more. "Don't make me laugh; it hurts too much already. I think maybe it's the ring," he said as he held out his hand and displayed the Ring of Talidousen for Ob's perusal.

Ob had seen the ring before. Big and gaudy. Something some frumpy old Baroness would wear to convince the blue bloods that the family fortune hadn't run out a hundred years ago. It didn't impress him much. Ob had no use for magic talismans and such. But this time, despite Tanch's intent, Ob didn't see the ring at all. All he could focus on were the ugly blisters that covered Tanch's hand; his skin a mottled mix of red and brown, wrinkled, like old leather. It made Ob cringe.

"The ring has got more power than I thought," said Tanch, "though perhaps not more than I should have expected, Talidousen being who he was. I wonder if Master Pipkorn knew just how much power the thing held when he gave it to me. He must have. In a way, it was Pipkorn who saved us. Without this ring – whatever it did – I could never have called down the magic that I did."

"Maybe it was the ring that added to your powers," said Ob. "Or maybe not. Maybe there is more to you than even you know."

"I just can't shake the thought that I should be dead," said Tanch.

Ob nodded and sat down in a chair toward the side of the room. "With all the craziness that's happened," said the gnome, "maybe you are dead. Maybe me too. Maybe we all are. Claradon included. Maybe that would explain all the impossibles that we've seen of late. I almost wish that it was as simple as that. But in my heart I know it's not."

Tanch's eyelids fluttered. He looked as if he was struggling to stay conscious. "The end is coming," said Tanch. "Death is creeping up on us even now. It's close."

"What say you?" said Ob.

"These are the end times, gnome," said Tanch.

"The end of Midgaard is at hand. It won't be long now. I've felt it coming for a goodly while. Long before this quest. But now I know it's true. It's no delusion, no fantasy. We don't have much time left."

"That's crazy talk," said Ob. "Why are you saying these things?"

"Because we have to be ready," said Tanch. "We have to prepare. There is much to do, and too little time to do it in."

18

ABOARD THE BLACK FALCON, THE AZURE SEA

SLAAYDE

"**A**nything?" said Slaayde as he approached his cabin's door.

"She hasn't stirred, Captain," said one of the seamen on duty.

"I don't want to be disturbed," said Slaayde as he turned toward Little Tug, who had been following two steps behind him. "I've no interest in visitors, well-wishers, gawkers, or vultures. Send them all packing."

Tug nodded and closed the door, leaving the Captain alone with Bertha.

Slaayde wanted to spend what time Bertha had left, alone with her in the cabin that they shared those last years. When she took her last breath he wanted to be at her side. And he wanted her to be at home. And the captain's cabin was her home. *The Falcon* was her home. And Slaayde was her family, and she was his — just as much as if they were married.

He thought about the plans that they had; about the promises that he'd made her. About how they'd retire in luxury someday. About how the

High Cleric himself would marry them in Lomion City's Odinhome on the eve of the summer solstice. And they'd live in a grand villa in Lomion City's High Quarter — a place on a hill with an expansive view, where they could look down upon the common folk from their pretty perch. They'd live out their days rubbing elbows with the nobles and drinking with high society folk. She'd wear pretty dresses and sparkly jewels that he'd gathered for her from around the globe. He'd amuse the snobs and the blue bloods with his talk of exotic travels and high adventure.

None of it was true — the plans or the promises. Sophisticated tastes aside, Slaayde wasn't meant for high society, or for soft living. He would die as he lived — on *The Falcon*, sailing the rivers or the seas. He'd never retire. Never give up his boots, his hat, or his sword. And certainly never his ship. He'd never give up the wandering life. She knew that, Bertha did. But still, she liked to hear the stories; she liked to help make the plans.

***

His orders aside, Slaayde wasn't surprised when he heard talking at the door, though it didn't make him any less angry about it. Tug was out there still, guarding and such. One or two of the boys were with him. Guj would've been there too, but he was dead. Loyal old Guj. Killed by one of the same things that had bit Bertha.

Slaayde had been expecting Theta to show up for some time. He always had to get in the last word. Had to make certain that his will got carried out — as if he were the All-father himself. Slaayde was surprised that he'd waited as long as he had to show up.

Tug opened the cabin's door after a brief knock, not even spouting a "by your leave." That surprised Slaayde. He expected some sort of scuffle in the corridor. He expected Tug to try to shove Theta off and that that would lead to a fight. But that didn't happen. Tug ushered Mister Spit and Polish right in, as if he'd been invited.

Slaayde supposed that Theta had earned Tug's respect. There was no denying that the foreigner was a warrior with few peers. Other soldiers naturally looked up to fighters like that. Slaayde couldn't blame Tug. He couldn't blame any of them. In another time, in another place, Slaayde might even have called Theta a friend.

But not now.

Not after all that happened. Too much blood spilled. And Slaayde knew that more was coming.

But if even Slaayde's best men started following Theta's orders over his, that meant he was losing the men's respect or their loyalty, or both. And if that happened, then he'd lose his command; he'd lose his ship. And that was all he'd soon have left. All that meant anything to him, except for Bertha.

Slaayde glanced toward the door for long enough to confirm that indeed it was Theta that had stepped into the room.

Theta didn't say anything at first. He just stood

there by the door, lurking like a grand blue gargoyle waiting to pounce. The bastard.

Some look or whispered word passed between Theta and Tug; Tug stepped back and closed the door, leaving Theta inside.

Slaayde ignored him. Let the bastard lurk. Let him wait. He knew what Theta was going to say and he didn't want to hear those words. Slaayde fixed his gaze on Bertha and tried to forget about the rest of the world.

Her breath was shallow. Barely detectable even with his hand upon her sternum. Her pulse was slow. But still the blood seeped from the wound, the red stains on the bandages, spreading, widening. The bedsheets were red. There was no stopping it, that bleeding. And Theta still lurked by the door, silently, looming over the room, sucking the air from it, distracting Slaayde, keeping his thoughts from what was really important.

Slaayde's heart beat faster and his blood began to boil. Just let me say goodbye in my own terms. In my own time.

Gods be damned, *The Falcon* was his ship. Who was Theta to barge into his cabin without leave?

"Get out," said Slaayde, though he didn't bother to turn his head toward Theta.

"You know what needs to be done?" said Theta.

19
SVARTLEHEIM

FREM

Frem watched as the black elves retreated. Back down the tunnel they scurried, their numbers thinned but still plentiful. Not in a panic did they run. Not in a rout. They simply turned, and ran back whence they came, climbing and vaulting over the heaped bodies as they went. Then Frem understood why. To an eerie whistle they responded — a strange cross between a hum and a flute it was. Their signal to withdraw. It repeated over and again until all the elves were out of sight, and carried on for a time thereafter.

Gore dripped from the head of Frem's hammer and off the face and edge of his shield as his arms fell limp at his sides, though a firm grip on his equipment remained. His heart pounded in his chest, his breathing so labored he couldn't control it. Sweat poured off his brow and chin, his clothes soaked through. He spat, coughed up a wad of phlegm, and spat again. He would've fallen to the ground, but there was no ground — just bodies, blood, and guts.

The dead were piled high all about the tunnel that he and his men had retreated down during the melee. In some spots one had to step atop heaps of corpses piled six or eight high.

A brutal ugly sight.

The smell of blood and entrails was nauseating. Above it all, the cloying lemony scent of the black elves.

That killing ground was one of the worst that Frem had ever seen. And he'd seen many.

Frem's armor was dented and gouged. He bled from at least two places on his legs where some black elfin blade had found purchase. Thank Odin they didn't use poison. His nose bled freely and he felt a cut across his cheek — how he received the last he didn't know, but it stung all the same.

Putnam and Royce were still beside him, tough bastards that they were. Battered, winded, and spent, but no worse were they than he. Carroll stood alone, farthest up the tunnel. He staggered over the bodies piled around him and fell to his knees more than once before rejoining the others. He looked half dead, a third of his armor torn off and hanging in tatters, one of his arms limp at his side.

Sevare emerged from under a heap of dead elves. From the looks of it, he'd been playing possum after the line got overrun. Smart that was. Kept him alive.

Clard Lugron was gone, buried somewhere amongst the heaped dead. A good soldier he was — loyal, brave, and tough. He'd be missed. One Stowron still stood, face and arms cut up and bruised but still some fight left in him. Ma-Grak was his name; one of their headmen. He didn't talk much — none of the Stowron did.

Several knights from 4th Squadron stood together a dozen yards back down the tunnel.

They'd managed to keep their formation and that had kept them alive. A shield wall was a powerful defense, especially against smaller opponents. Other men were farther back still. A good sized group, and that gave Frem some hope.

Then Frem realized that the ones back there, past 4th squad, were those that he'd left at the other front. Their lines had been compressed together. His rear guard almost wiped out.

Putnam and Royce set to killing the Svart wounded. How they had the energy or the stomach for it, Frem couldn't fathom. His gut told him to stop them. That it was wrong. He opened his mouth to give the order, but he stopped himself.

It had to be done. They couldn't have the black elves popping up and stabbing their legs or worse. There might even be some laying low, playing possum like Sevare, just waiting for them to lower their guard before they struck. Battle was an ugly business.

"Close ranks," said Frem. "See to our wounded. Look for any more survivors."

"Is it over, Captain?" said one soldier.

All eyes turned to Frem.

"No," said Frem. "Just a pause, I think, to regroup. So let's do the same."

For Frem, walking through that battlefield was a nightmare. With every step he felt the squishy flesh of corpses beneath him. And he heard and felt the crunch of bones. He worried that he'd crush one of his own wounded that lay there unnoticed, or that an elfin dagger would strike from the shadows in some last ditch effort to take him with them to the afterlife. Frem trudged over the bodies to the Sithian front line.

Sergeant Grainer was in charge there. Blood trickled down his forehead. His nose was broken and bleeding. He glanced over at Frem. "Two hundred at least still up around that bend, Captain. We don't have the men to push through. Or to hold against another wave."

"Our main force?" said Frem.

"The fighting up there went quiet as soon as they stopped coming at us here," said Grainer. "Best as I can tell, the Stowron rear guard are wiped out. Most of the Lugron too. The center of the troop, where are brothers are, may still be intact. Unless the elves withdraw, there's no way for us to rejoin them. If they're even still alive."

"If they weren't," said Frem, "the elves would still be on us. Ezer might be pinned down, but he's still up there. You can count on that."

"What do we do?" said Grainer.

"We're pulling out," said Frem. "There's fewer elves behind us than there are in front, so we're going to push through, back to the monastery. Right now, that's our best chance."

Frem pulled his men back as quietly as he could and formed them into a tight wedge. Sixteen battered men. Three too wounded to be of much use, two of which needed to be helped along. He wished he'd brought all the Pointmen with him to the rear instead of just one squad. Maybe then they'd have been able to hold the line.

They inched down the tunnel, one step at a time.

They had no choice but to hold torches in the front line, giving away their position and movement to all and any up ahead. Without the torches, they couldn't see at all, but Frem suspected that the black elves could. Soon they came to the chamber where the elves had tried to encircle them. Bodies were heaped everywhere. From the look of it, this was where most of Frem's men had fallen.

They were halfway across the chamber when they heard the strange humming of the black elves. Then they skulked from the shadows, massed in the mouth of the far tunnel. No end to them in sight. Frem heard the rhythmic chanting in tune to the humming. He felt his hair stand on end, static electricity in the air. He knew sorcery when he felt it, however alien its origin. One of their Diresvarts had arrived and was conjuring something nasty to throw at them.

Frem didn't need to say a word to Sevare. The wizard's hands were working despite the burns that afflicted them. His lips mouthed words. A blue sphere appeared around Frem's entire group — a mystical shield that Sevare often put to good use. It wasn't impenetrable, but held most magics at bay. It had saved their skins more than once in the past.

Then the chamber walls came alive.

Stone men, ten or twelve feet tall, stepped out of the walls, rock crumbling and falling around them, as if they'd been embedded for long years in the walls. They moved slowly at first, lumbering forward, awkward and stiff of limb. Then faster. In league with the elves, they were. Their purpose, clear enough to Frem. To kill him and his men.

And on they came. Creatures of rock they were. Not natural beings by Frem's reckoning. But things of dark magic. Conjured up by the Diresvart from who knows where.

"Back whence we came," shouted Sevare. "It's our only chance."

Frem didn't disagree.

The black elves began to pour from the far tunnel.

The Sithians wouldn't give them their backs, so they backpedaled as fast as they could.

The elves charged, howling and gibbering, but they were slowed by the dead. Frem, Putnam, Royce, and Carroll hacked at the elves as they backed toward the tunnel mouth, every step a risk, for the heaped bodies threatened to trip them up. They made the tunnel mouth when the nearest of the stone men was but ten strides away. The black elves were at them though, in full force. Frem stood the mouth of the tunnel, his hammer working, his dagger too. As fast as he was, elves slipped by him, under his weapons. He had to rely on Putnam and Royce to keep the black blades off his back.

"Frem, back up," shouted Sevare at the top of his lungs. "Ten paces back, double time."

Frem knew what that meant.

Sevare was about to throw some last sorcery.

Something terrible.

Frem turned and ran. Let the little buggers have his back for a moment. He feared the sorcery more.

The black elves didn't waste the opportunity. The tip of one blade and then another slammed into the back of Frem's armor.

It held.

The elves sliced him thrice to the back of his legs, high and low. But the plate and chain held there too. Good Lomerian steel. Worth every silver star he paid for it.

Frem made it four steps when a beam of yellow-orange light passed over his head from down Sevare's way. A terrible heat came off it. Frem thought his helmet would melt to his head. Mayhap his head would melt too, or else catch fire and explode.

But Sevare's beam was off course. It blasted against the tunnel ceiling instead of at the elves or the stone men.

A moment later, rock began to fall from the tunnel ceiling.

Now Frem understood.

The mouth of the tunnel exploded and collapsed.

Stone fell all around.

First Frem got pounded.

Then he got buried.

20

ABOARD THE BLACK FALCON, THE AZURE SEA

SLAAYDE

Theta's words repeated in Slaadye's head, over and again. "You know what needs to be done," Theta had said.

Slaayde's eyes clamped close, and his face scrunched up. "I know," he said through clenched teeth. "I know full well what happened to Gurt. I don't need you to tell me that. To tell me anything."

"Can you do it?" said Theta.

Slaayde's head turned toward Theta. His eyes were icy cold. "No one but me will touch her."

"Don't wait," said Theta. "Don't let her become one of them. She wouldn't want that."

"Don't tell me what she would want," said Slaayde, his voice rising. "You don't know what she would want. You don't know anything about her." Slaayde stood up and turned toward Theta. His whole body shook, quivering, barely containing a rage that threatened to explode about him.

"This is all your fault," said Slaayde.

"Everything that's happened – all the evils that have plagued my ship. All the deaths that have befallen my crew. Every one. Every one is your fault. You brought this down on us. This curse. You did. Not the Eotrus boy. Not your gnome, your wizard, or anyone else."

"It was you, Theta. It was you. You are the stinking no good harbinger of doom. Before this is over, before I'm off to drink in Odin's hall – I will see you dead," said Slaayde.

"Not today," said Theta. "I won't allow this sickness to spread. You do what needs be done and you do it quick. And if you don't do it, I will. And if it comes to that, and you try to stop me, I'll cut your stinking head off and pilot the ship myself. Do you hear me, Slaayde?"

"Go to Helheim," said Slaayde.

"I'll stand here until it's done," said Theta.

"You'll stand outside or anywhere the hell you want. But not in here. Not in my room. Not with her. Get the hell out, or I'll stick my sword through your stinking chest."

Theta held his ground for a few moments; long enough to show he had no fear of Slaayde or his threats. Then he stepped back toward the cabin door, and opened it. "She was a good woman," said Theta. "I saw enough to know that. She didn't deserve this fate. But I didn't bring it upon her." He stepped outside and closed the door; Tug peering in as the door closed shut.

Slaayde didn't hear any footsteps or conversation from the hallway.

He was waiting out there. Stinking Theta. Waiting out there for Slaayde to kill the love of his life. On his own ship, with his own woman, at the end of her life, he couldn't even have that bit of privacy, that bit of freedom, to do what he knew he needed to do. He had to have that stinking menace looming over him, standing outside the door, perched in wait like a vulture. He should just kill him. Kill him and be done with it. Drop his stinking body over *The Falcon's* side and let the sharks have their fun with him.

Maybe, just maybe, if he did that, the curse on the ship would be lifted. Maybe. But the bastard was right about one thing. He couldn't let Bertha turn into one of those things. Not Bertha. Never.

He had to end it while she was still Bertha. Still a human being. Still the woman he loved. But he wanted to give her every moment, every second of life that she had. She deserved that, didn't she? Every moment? Don't we all? He wouldn't deny her that.

He'd been thinking as he sat there all morning how he was going to do it. Trouble was, he wasn't even sure what would work and what wouldn't.

A dagger to the heart probably wouldn't be enough.

Decapitation would be, but he could never do that to someone he loved; it was too slow, too messy, too grotesque.

A dagger through the temple. That's what he'd settled on. He'd use the one he bought off that Southron trader some years back. Sixteen inches of wide blade, it was. Some strange alloy that Slaayde had not seen before or since; it was just as strong as Dyvers steel but held a keener edge. It would do the job. It had too.

She wasn't breathing any longer; not such that he could tell, anyways. He couldn't feel her pulse.

She was gone.

Bertha was gone.

Tears welled in his eyes. He could wait no longer. They were out of time.

He reached out and placed his hands on her head. Gently.

His heart raced. It was hard to breathe.

He turned her head to the side. Fearful that at any moment those eyes would open black. That Bertha would be gone; a monster in her place.

He had to be quick.

He picked up the dagger.

Tears poured down his cheeks. He blinked through the flood, barely able to see.

Then he plunged the blade through his beloved's skull.

She made no sound. No reaction. But a long groan of anguish slipped passed Slaayde's lips. Then he gasped for breath, the bile rising in his throat, his head spinning. He wanted to puke. He wanted spew out whatever vile stuff was lodged in his guts. To cleanse himself of the terrible deed he'd just committed.

He forced himself to keep his eyes open. Forced himself to focus on Bertha, to remain alert, in case she turned despite the dagger's blow, or in case she somehow opened her eyes for one last fleeting look at the world.

But neither happened.

Her eyes never opened.

Never turned black, thank the gods. The fangs

never grew. The claws never sprouted. The bloodlust never took control. She never became a monster. And for that, Slaayde was ever grateful. For his love died as Bertha Smallbutt, Quartermaster of *The Black Falcon*, and the one true love of Dylan Slaayde's life.

His hand still wrapped around the dagger's hilt, Slaayde heard the cabin door open. He took a deep breath and then another, and wiped his eyes quick as he could. When he'd half composed himself, however long that took, he turned, and saw Theta and Tug standing just inside the doorway. Theta's gaze met Slaayde's for but a moment, all the knight's attention focused on the dagger lodged in Bertha's head.

Apparently satisfied that the murder had met his expectations, Theta turned and left.

Slaayde felt numb. Detached from his body. As if he floated in a void filled of nothing but empty ether. Through that nothingness, he somehow heard Theta's steps as the knight walked down the corridor, as he ascended the stair. Strangely, each step was louder than the last, though each took him farther away. Each step boomed in Slaayde's head. They shook the ship and thumped like thunder — so loud that Slaayde wanted to press his hands to his ears to drown them out.

It did not escape Slaayde that Tug did not react to those sounds at all; he didn't seem to hear them. But Slaayde heard them. The steps of doom. He shuddered and felt a cold breeze from who knows where tickle his spine, base to nape.

Dylan Slaayde was afraid. Afraid of that man, Theta. That thing. Whatever he was. But it didn't matter. Nothing mattered anymore. He didn't know how or when, but one way or another, he'd see that bastard dead.

21

SVARTLEHEIM

JUDE

In a mad rush, the elves swept through the broken Sithian line. Howling and slavering. They threw themselves atop the men. Cut their legs and ankles. Pulled them down with their superior numbers.

Jude and Donnelin were swept along in the withdrawal to the rear. And that was fine with Jude. There was no way to escape toward the front — the elves were thick as flies and killing every man in sight.

Jude heard a loud rumbling. He looked over his shoulder and saw them. Several huge rock-like creatures lumbered through the tunnel toward what was left of the Sithian defenses. What they were, Jude had no idea. But for certain, he had no interest in squaring off with any of them. He ran toward the rear with the rest. Donnelin too.

A hundred yards down the tunnel, they came to the end of the line. Men were massed ahead of them, fighting more elves at the rear of the column. Jude realized that they were nowhere near what should have been the expedition's rear guard. The whole line must have collapsed.

Then he saw why.

The black elves attacked from side tunnels all

about. Poured from them, like ants from their hill. They'd torn the League's line to pieces. Jude and those with him were boxed in; nowhere to go.

Ginalli and Thorn were shouting. The priest tried to hold Korrgonn back, but Korrgonn pushed him aside. It was so strange for Jude to look at him — Korrgonn. He was Sir Gabriel — by face, by body. Exactly Sir Gabriel. And yet, in every other way: sound of his voice, manner of speaking, posture, disposition, the way he moved and walked — all were nothing like Sir Gabriel. Jude knew that appearances aside, Korrgonn and Sir Gabriel were as different from each other as any two people could be. That is, if Korrgonn could even rightly be called a person. How could a person inhabit someone else's body — take them over completely, their own body gone? Behind it, black magic. Evil sorcery the like of which was otherwise unknown to Jude. Unknown to Lomion. What else could explain it?

It didn't take long for Jude to see that person as Korrgonn, not as Sir Gabriel, despite his familiar face. An enemy with the face of a dear friend is an enemy still.

Korrgonn marched back the way they'd come, sword in hand. He strode toward the advancing black elves, their rock creatures, their wizards, and whatever else they'd put to the field.

Korrgonn swung his sword this way and that. He had speed and power that Jude had only seen one man possess before.

Sir Gabriel.

But the style was different. The maneuvers unfamiliar. The technique odd. Korrgonn had not learned to wield a blade in any fencing school or Chapterhouse in Lomion, of that, there was no doubt. His style was alien.

For a long time, Jude didn't believe that Korrgonn was a creature of Nifleheim. A son of Azathoth. He didn't believe the stories that Claradon and Ob had told him about that fateful night in the Vermion Forest. He thought they'd fed him and all the rest only half truths. A fable to cover up what really went on. But why? How could they do such a thing? And stick to their stories no matter the strength of his questioning? Didn't he have a right to know the truth about his own father's death?

He had no answers. Only doubts. Suspicions. He disbelieved. His only consolation was the certainty that he'd get the truth out of Donnelin, just as soon as they had the time to speak freely. Up until recently, Jude thought Korrgonn was naught but a wizard of skill, but yet, an impostor to greatness. A man that pretended to be a god to stroke his own ego and gather unto himself followers and power. Nothing other than that made sense. And even that was so far fetched because of the possession of Sir Gabriel's body. Jude's brain couldn't wrap itself around that, no matter how much he thought on it.

But the more he watched Korrgonn, the more he became convinced that Claradon had told him the truth from the start. Korrgonn was no man of Midgaard. He was from somewhere else. He was some thing else.

When he engaged the black elves, Korrgonn's blade glowed as if burning hot. Straight from a forge's fire. When it touched them, it cut through the elves with no resistance. Set them afire. Their bodies alighting as if doused by flaming oil.

They died screaming in agony.

When a dozen of them had dropped in as many seconds, their courage broke. They held back. Massed in the shadows. Awaited their stone creatures to emerge from the tunnels.

Nearly twice Korrgonn's height, dozens of times his weight, the stone creatures plodded forward. One. Two. Three. Four emerged from the shadows. The black elves pressed against the sides of the tunnel. They even stood atop one another, to clear as wide a path as possible for the stone things to pass. Even so, the creatures crushed many elves against the tunnel walls as they came on.

Korrgonn stood his ground. Swung his sword in a curious pattern as they approached. Around and around it spun. First, it moved down from his left shoulder toward his right hip. Then from right shoulder to left hip. And around again. Over and over. Faster and faster. So fast. A blur of motion. A loud humming coming from it.

And then when the first stone creature reached the front ranks of the elves, Korrgonn's sword abruptly stopped. Its point leveled at the creature. From its tip emerged a black bolt of arcane power. A shadow of energy. Its nature unknown.

Jude felt malevolence pour from that sword. A cold dark evil that crept from its tip. A shiver shot down his spine. The hair on his nape stood up. A tingling throughout his scalp. Brimstone filled his nostrils and stung his eyes. Made his mouth taste of iron.

That evil beam struck the stone creature in the center of its chest. A massive thump. A spray of shattered stone. It bore through it like an auger rotating at high speed. It cored through the thing. Only a moment it took. Then its torso exploded. Shards of stone flew in all directions at high speed. The nearest elves pelted with deadly shrapnel. A dozen or more went down, bleeding, screaming.

But the black beam was not yet done. It continued on. It blasted into the next stone creature. Stone shards flying. And then it exploded, just as the first. What little was left of it collapsed into a heap. The third creature and the fourth met the same fate. Only then did the spectre of death that shot from that blade become sated. The black beam vanished. Returning whence it came.

A great cheer went up through the expedition's ranks. The black elves, still in their hundreds, writhed and screamed from their wounds. Those that could, of which there were many, sought to close ranks. They started forward again. They would not give up. They would not retreat. They would fight to the bitter end. To the death.

22

JUTENHEIM

OB

"A civilized port," said Ob as *The Black Falcon* glided toward a long pier in Jutenheim's busy harbor. "A sight for sore eyes," he said as Claradon stood stoically beside him. Stone and thatch buildings filled the lands beyond the docks, narrow and twisty alleys connecting them, stone steps aplenty as the town was built up against the rock face of the great basalt cliffs that encircled the island. Many buildings were down by the water, many on the rocky slopes, and some few sat high up on the stone, precarious stone or wooden steps providing access for the fearless.

"Jutenheim is not Lomion City, or even the outer provinces," said Slaayde, looking gaunt and tired as he stepped up beside them at the ship's rail. It was the first they'd seen of the captain in a ten day, since Bertha's passing. "Their idea of civilized and yours may be a bit different," he said, his face devoid of emotion, his voice devoid of life.

"So long as they don't try to kill us and eat us," said Ob, "we'll get on well enough with them, I expect — assuming they serve up decent ale and fresh food."

"Food and drink they've always had aplenty, owing to trade and fishing," said Slaayde. "So no worries on that account, though if we're not mindful of our manners, they may take offense."

"So?" said Ob. "Why should I care?"

"If they take offense," said Slaayde, "they'll kill us — or try to. They're a bit prickly, the Jutens, especially with strangers, and they're a superstitious lot too. A bit backward they are, by Lomerian standards."

"I'm a wee bit prickly too, if you haven't noticed," said Ob, "so I'll forgive them for that. Captain," said the gnome, turning to face Slaayde, "on behalf of the Eotrus, I just wanted to say that — well — she was a fine lass, Bertha was. I'm sorry for what happened to her — we all are."

Claradon nodded, though it didn't appear that Slaayde noticed.

Slaayde stared toward Jutenheim, making no eye contact with the men. A single nod of acknowledgment was his only response to the gnome's words.

"Captain," said Claradon, "can you tell which me one of those ships in port is The White Rose?"

"None of them," said Slaayde.

"What?"

"I've been searching for The Rose from the moment we sighted the port," said Slaayde. "But I don't see her. I don't think she's here."

"Could she be somewhere else along the coast?" said Claradon, concern and confusion on his face. "Another harbor or some hidden cove?"

"The island is a rock," said Slaayde, "just like most in the southern Azure; tall cliffs of stone all the way around. And what stands before us is the only town."

"You're saying that this is the only harbor in the whole place?" said Ob. "How can that be? This is a big island. Very big, I've heard."

"It's the only place to land a big ship," said Slaayde. "You could come in a dinghy or a longboat elsewhere and scale the cliffs, but why bother? Beyond this town, there's nothing to see, a lot of rock, a bit of swampy jungle, or so I've heard tell."

"Could we have outpaced her?" said Ob. "Might The Rose still be out to sea? A day or two behind us?"

"Who knows," said Slaayde. "What with that storm that battered us and all the troubles we had – if The Rose faced similar trials, and how could she not have, she may well be at the bottom of the Azure. Or she may have been here, all fine and dandy, and left already. We won't know anything until we get over there and start asking questions."

"All this time," said Claradon, "I was so focused on us getting to Jutenheim. As if that were the goal – get here and it's done. Over. We get Jude back and we stop Korrgonn, all in one quick stroke. One final epic battle and then it's the homeward road for us. But now we're here and The Rose isn't. I wasn't expecting that. I don't have a plan for that. What do we do now?"

"I've been paid to track down The White Rose," said Slaayde. "And track her down I will. Don't you worry, I will find her, even if it's the last thing that I do."

"What ho," said Ob, pointing toward the nearest pier. "They've already assembled a welcoming party for us — though it's a sorry lot that they've sent: an old crone, unkempt and bedraggled. Attending her, a tall boy and his dog. No — a wolf it be. The boy has a pet wolf. Isn't that lovely?"

"The local seer," said Slaayde. "The Angel of Death they call her."

"A seer, you say?" said Ob, squinting. "You're right, captain. She wears the bones. This don't bode well. I doubt that fossil comes a calling on every ship that happens by."

"I've heard tell of her," said Slaayde. "Two hundred years old they mark her. Respected, but feared by the folk, she is."

"A bit young for you, Ob," said Claradon, "but still, she might fancy your beard."

Ob looked aghast. "No crone will be sidling up to me, boy, especially not one as tall as a tree. Fifty-nine years and five feet even are my limits, and both stretch well past my preferences. Any woman outside of that can look elsewhere. Being a gnome in my prime, as I am, I can afford to be particular."

23

SVARTLEHEIM

FREM

As Frem ran down the tunnel, he put his arms up to cover his face and neck. Thank the gods for his helmet, as stone after stone fell upon it and his shoulders and drove him to the tunnel floor only two steps from safety. The rocks fell all about, clanging against his armor, pressing him to the tunnel floor. He expected the crushing pressure of a ton of stone to break his back, but it didn't come. He was spared of that. He couldn't see, with the dust so thick, and the darkness of the tunnel. All he knew for certain was that he was alive. He could breathe, albeit with difficultly, hampered by clogging dust and at least a couple of hundred pounds of stones lying on his back. Otherwise, his limbs were responsive, though mostly pinned, rocks piled atop his legs and much of his torso. He seemed to be in one piece.

"Is he alive?" shouted Sevare as he dropped to his knees, wincing in pain, smoke rising from his hands and arms.

"Help me get him out," said Putnam.

Several minutes of careful digging and hauling of rocks later, and Frem was free. To the men's amazement, he stood right up.

"Odin was watching over you today, Captain,"

said Putnam. "Two big stones bridged over you, like an arch. That kept the heavy stuff off you. Kept you from getting dead."

Frem's armor was dented, top to bottom. His helmet was a shambles, his breastplate battered but serviceable, his greaves dented and gouged. But he had not a single broken bone and not one deep laceration.

"A lucky day, Captain," said Putnam.

"The day is not over, yet," said Frem. "How many are we?"

"Sixteen still," said Putnam. "But only fourteen what can fight. Orders?"

Then the rubble behind them exploded. Frem was pelted with stones and thrown from his feet.

Boulders shifted and flew. A grinding sound of stone on stone filled the air. Men were yelling.

Frem rolled over and bounced to his feet. Self-preservation had gifted him another blast of energy. There before him, rising out of the rubble, was one of the elves' stone creatures. It had been trapped under the rubble just as he was, and somehow found the strength to blast its way free. The rest of the tunnel was still blocked.

Men were down all around, moaning, groaning, bleeding. All hit by stone fragments.

Putnam thrust a pike into the stone creature's maw, but the thing swatted the weapon away as a man would swat a pesky bee. Two other Sithians came up with pikes in hand to support Putnam.

Frem still had his hammer; how, he didn't know. Without any plan, he ran straight at the thing. He slammed his hammer into the side of the creature's face as it bent low to go after the pikemen. That hammer connected with every ounce of strength that Frem could put behind it. When it hit, shards of stone broke off the creature's face, much of one eye was destroyed, and its nose was gone. The blow sent the thing reeling and it stumbled and fell on its rump. Green ichor poured from its wounds. A natural creature, after all?

Frem leaped atop it, yelling. "Hit it with hammers! Hit it with stones. Forget blades."

He pounded the creature about the face over and again as it lay stunned. The others attacked its arms, occupying them so that they couldn't go after Frem. The thing tried to roll over and get up, but Frem kept hitting it.

Ten times.

Twenty.

More.

Each hammer blow knocked off shards from its head. Narrow cracks and fissures formed about its head and neck. Finally, a swipe of its arm sent Frem flying through the air. He crashed into the tunnel wall. His armor took the brunt of the impact, but he was winded for a moment. That's when he saw the creature's open palm come down atop Craybin's head. It blasted him to his knees. The creature smashed its palm down again. There was a great snapping sound, perhaps Craybin's spine. The creature kept pressing down and squashed Craybin to pulp.

Frem charged in just as Putnam and two pikemen were doing their best to trip up the creature with their pikes, its footing still uncertain amidst the rubble. Frem rammed the back of the creature's leg as it made to take a step. He kept pushing. He used his momentum to move the massive leg forward. Overbalanced it. Sent it crashing down again. Frem set his hammer loose on the creature's head again. He pounded away directly atop the largest crack that ran through the creature's forehead. On the second swing, the thing's head broke in two, and it went still. Green blood gushed from the thing's wounds. A natural creature after all, for blood flowed through it.

Then men all saw that the thing was truly dead. And they cheered. "Frem the giant slayer. Frem the monster slayer. Long live Captain Sorlons."

"Fifteen of us left now," said Putnam as he looked down as the remains of poor Trooper Craybin. "And three of us out of commission. Four if you count Sevare. Your orders?"

"Back the way we came," said Frem. "There's nowhere else to go."

"There are still hundreds of elves between us and the rest of the troop," said Putnam. "How do you fix to get by them?"

Frem looked over at Sevare. The wizard sat with his legs crossed. His arms resting on this knees, his red blistered skin bandaged up tight. Still, smoke rose from those bandages. Smoke that smelled like charred flesh. There was no more water to spare to pour over him. He'd just have to smolder away. The wizard's eyes were closed, his jaw clenched. He was baring the pain. That's all that he was doing. All that he could do. He didn't even try to help in the fight with the stone thing. The pain that he was in, he might not even have known what happened.

"I figure that Sevare has got one more good blast of sorcery left in him today," said Frem. "If we give him some time to rest before that's needed. After that, it'll be knife work for us. A lot of it. We keep fighting until the Valkyries take us or until the black elves are all dead. What else can we do?"

"We could try a side tunnel," said Putnam. "Try to go around them. Find another way back to the monastery or to the outside."

"The map doesn't show where the side tunnels go," said Frem. "We'll be steering blind in enemy territory."

"We're doing that now, Captain," said Putnam.

"Aye, so we are. We can't go back," said Frem gesturing toward the rockfall. "Only forward. Best chance we got is to fight our way through to Ezer and the company."

"There's nothing else we can do," said Sir Royce. "Only six of us still have our packs. We don't have enough supplies to make it through on our own."

"Let's move," said Frem. "Pick up whatever supplies we pass along the way. Leave nothing useful behind.

24

JUTENHEIM

OB

The crone's boy stepped up to the foot of the gangway as soon as the seamen lowered it and secured the ship to the pier.

"Speak your piece, boy," said Ob as he strode down the ramp.

"The Angel of Death seeks words with your headman," he said, his voice oddly high for a lad so tall. Not yet a teen, Ob marked him, but taller than most full-grown Volsungs.

"That would be the whippersnapper darkening my shadow," said Ob.

The boy looked confused.

"I'll speak with her," said Claradon from immediately behind Ob. Sergeant Vid and Sir Paldor trailed behind them.

The crone looked Claradon up and down, taking her time about it, and then did the same to Ob. She glanced at the other men, but paid them little heed. Claradon stood patiently.

"A Wotan-son you are, headman," said the crone, as a smile formed on her wrinkled face and she put her yellowed teeth on display. "A religious knight; a nobleman; young, but a leader of men I mark you." She moved closer, a step too close for Claradon's comfort. She reached out and grabbed

Claradon's hand with surprising strength and closely examined his palm, tracing her fingers over the lines in his skin. "An old bloodline has birthed you, I see," said the crone. "Very old indeed. Ancient, one might say. And, I think, you are even more than you seem, and you seem a good deal more than most men."

"Brother Claradon Eotrus of the Karadonian Order, down from the Lomerian northlands, far across the Azure."

"I know of your people," said the crone. "I know them well, I do. Kindred they are to us — as cousins, though far removed. We follow the ways of Wotan here, and that of Donar, and the other Aesir. Same as you, though you call them by other names. You are welcome here, warrior-priest of the Eotrus. You and yours." The crone stepped even closer and she lowered her voice to a whisper. "Now tell me true, is he aboard?"

Claradon's eyes narrowed; he looked confused. "Of whom do you speak?"

"You know who," she said, still in a whisper.

"Speak plain, woman," said Ob, his ears twitching. "Who are you asking after?"

She wrinkled her brow and narrowed her eyes before she spoke again. "Him. The harbinger. The herald of doom."

"Oh, boy," said Ob as he rolled his eyes and shook his head. He turned toward Vid and Paldor. "Get ready boys," he said. "The whole town will be on us any second! They're probably cannibals too."

"Ob!" said Claradon as he grabbed the gnome about the shoulder. "Enough."

"Aboard he is," said the crone. "There is no denying it. I would have words with him, sir knight. If he would honor me so."

Ob looked surprised. "So you don't mean to kill him, the harbinger?"

"Enemies in Jutenheim he will find," said the crone, "but I be not one of them. Of that, you have my word."

Even as she said that, Theta appeared at the ship's rail and stepped down the gangway, the men making way for him. He could not have overheard the whispered exchange with the crone from up on deck.

The crone put her hand on her boy's shoulder and whispered. "That be him," she said, barely containing her excitement. "The great dragon himself. Look at his eyes, see how they bore through you. See the armor, ancient in design. Mark his bearing well. The hammer! He carries the hammer."

The boy fell to one knee, his head lowered.

"Get up, get up!" spat the crone. She pulled him up by the shoulder and looked about in a panic, as if checking if any of the townsfolk had noticed. But what folk were about paid *The Falcon* and her crew little heed, their attentions focused on their own business, much of which was the loading and unloading of cargoes for the various ships in the busy port.

"I am Jutenheim's bone thrower," said the crone to Theta. "The Angel of Death they call me, great lord. There is much of import that I can tell you, and aid that I can offer, if you'll accept it."

"Words, wisdom, and aid are all welcome,"

said Theta. "Has a ship called The White Rose been here?"

She nodded, knowingly. "Here and gone, great lord, but that is only some of what there is to tell. There are too many eyes hereabouts the docks; too many ears. If I linger here, attention will be drawn. Attention that neither you nor I will want. The sun will soon be setting. Visit my house after dusk and we will speak at length. Until then, I urge you to keep your presence and purpose secret and to alert no one with questions about The White Rose. I will send my grandson to collect you when the sun sets. But be warned, the black elves roam freely hereabouts in the dregs of night, working their mischief, and their dark magic. Be wary and go nowhere alone."

"**W**ho does she think you are?" said Ob to Theta as the crone and her entourage walked away.

"The leader of this sorry company, no doubt," said Theta with a shrug. "You must not have impressed her, gnome. Perhaps polish your armor or grow a few feet taller, the better to catch the ladies' eyes."

"You're wrong on that," said Claradon. "She barely took her eyes off Ob, even as she spoke to you and to me. She fancies him for certain."

Ob's eyes widened and he looked at Claradon incredulously.

"Now that you mention it, I noticed that too," said Theta, his tone, matter-of-fact. "Perhaps this be an opportunity for you, gnome. A chance for you to settle down. Jutenheim looks a nice enough place. You and she would make a handsome couple."

Ob looked back and forth from Claradon to Theta, his mouth open, his eyes wide.

"I will not stand in your way," said Claradon. "You've served the Eotrus well all these years. You deserve a fine retirement with a good woman."

Ob paled; sweat beaded on his brow. "Are you, I mean, you must be –"

But then Claradon burst out laughing, and so did Vid and Paldor. Even Theta couldn't hold back a smile.

Ob rolled his eyes and shook his head, though he looked relieved.

"She asked after the harbinger," said Ob after the merriment died down. "Called him something else too. What was it?" he said as he turned toward Claradon.

"The herald of doom," said Claradon. "And that's who she thinks you are, Lord Theta. And she was expecting you. Expecting us."

Theta sighed. "The Leaguers must have spewed their venom from one side of Jutenheim to the other," he said. "They have the Jutens expecting a demon out of ancient legend to show up."

"Mayhap not," said Ob. "She said she was an ally of the harbinger, or words to that affect."

"She offered up her aid without even being asked," said Theta, "so she's either an ally looking to help us, or an enemy looking to trap us. I suppose we'll soon find out."

"So you think we should accept her invitation?" said Claradon.

"I plan to," said Theta. "But we must proceed with caution. Take nothing for granted; nothing at face value. The forces aligned against us are many and are devious — devious beyond common understanding. You've seen some of that on this voyage already, and I expect you'll see more of it before we take the homeward road."

"But if she spoke truly, and she is aligned with the harbinger," said Ob, "does that make her good or evil?"

"Depends on whether she thinks the harbinger is good or evil, doesn't it?" said Theta, annoyed by the question.

"And which is he?" said Ob.

Theta shook his head. "That depends on your perspective, doesn't it? The harbinger of legend stood as Azathoth's enemy. If you consider Azathoth the one true god, all good, all holy, as does the League, then the harbinger is evil incarnate — a traitor unmatched by any in history. But if you see Azathoth as evil, then the harbinger is good. How does the seer see things, do you think?" he said, looking towards the men.

They offered no answer.

"She told us," said Theta. "She follows Wotan, or Odin, as we name him. Odin's followers — the true ones — know too that he stood as Azathoth's enemy in bygone times."

"Some think that Odin and Azathoth are two names for the same god," said Claradon, "just as Odin and Wotan are."

"If she thinks that, than we know not her heart," said Theta. "Not yet, anyway. Let me say this once more, so we have no misunderstandings, and so that I need not say it again, for I tire of saying it. Evil is as evil does, gnome. Judge a man by his actions. By what he does. What he accomplishes. What he fights for and against. By what he holds dear. Those things define him. They mean so much more than any words he might spout and a thousandfold more than appearances or perceptions. We will meet with the seer tonight and we will come to know her heart."

25

SVARTLEHEIM

JUDE

Jude's mouth dropped open when he saw Korrgonn blast the stone creatures to bits. The power he wielded was amazing. Frightful. No practitioner of the Militus Mysterious that Jude had ever seen could throw such a spell. He wondered whether any wizard of the Tower of the Arcane could. Even a Grandmaster?

Mayhap Korrgonn was a god.

Or a demigod or some such. Or maybe Jude's knowledge of magic and wizards and gods was woefully wanting.

Par Brackta appeared beside Korrgonn. Ginalli with her. They stepped between Korrgonn and the horde of black elves that rushed toward him.

Jude didn't expect that.

Not from Brackta. Not from Ginalli. He wanted to call out to her. To tell her to get away from there. No — he wanted to run to her and pull her away. To save her. But he knew that he couldn't. That he shouldn't. In his heart, he'd hoped that Brackta wasn't really one of them — a Leaguer. That she'd just fallen in with them without knowing what they were really about. But she threw herself in harm's way to shield Korrgonn — who didn't appear to need shielding. Why risk

herself for nothing?
 Was she a hero?
 A reckless fool?
 Or a true believer, stepping in to aid the son of her god, be he in need of that aid or not?
 Jude didn't like his own answers. He figured that she was a believer. Simple as that. She'd never given him reason to think otherwise, her affections notwithstanding. Yet he carried hope. Hope that crumbled before his eyes.
 Ginalli was a blowhard. A professional liar. A cult leader. But he surprised Jude earlier in the battle. He'd thrown his share of magics at the elves. Deadly stuff. The man was more than bluster and bravado after all. He had substance. That surprised Jude. But courage too? Had to be, for there he went, right at the elves. There was more to the Leaguers than Jude had supposed. Mayhap a lot more. That made them all the more dangerous. And that became clearer every day.
 From where he stood, Jude couldn't see Brackta's face. Didn't know whether she was afraid. She had to be. Hundreds of black elves raced toward her in the dark, weapons to hand, out for blood. Already awash in it. Who knows how many of the expedition had already fallen to their blades? But Brackta stood firm. Weaved her magic, Ginalli alongside her. Her arms and hands moved in strange patterns difficult to watch. Unintelligible arcane words spat from her mouth. After a few moments, from the palms of Brackta's hands erupted yellow flames — a continuous stream of fire as if from a dragon's maw. From Ginalli's hands came green fire, much the same.

Even back where he stood, Jude felt the heat from those flames. He lifted a hand to shield his face. The blasts of mystical fire roared down the tunnel, side by side.

They engulfed the elves.

Incinerated them where they stood. Those fires were so hot, so powerful, that few of the elves even had time to scream.

When it was over — when those flames fizzled out, nothing moved in the tunnel for as far as Jude could see. Ash was everywhere and a burnt odor wafted through the tunnel. The smell of fiery death. It planted itself in their clothes, their hair, their very pores.

The Leaguers cheered. Happy for the victory. In awe of the wizards' powers. And truth be told, in fear. Wizards always were frightful things. Wizards that could kill a whole company at a time, were all the more frightful. But that kind of power always came at a price.

Brackta staggered toward the back of the line of troops, her face filled with pain. She held her arms up before her to avoid touching anything. Smoke drifted off her body. Her skin was red as if sunburned. Her steps, unsteady.

She headed for the rear of the troop, no doubt to give the elves at that end the same treatment. She passed by Jude. Their eyes met for a moment. Jude's gaze lingered, but hers did not. Was that a hint of a smile that she gifted him before she looked away? Or naught but his imagination? A bit farther down the tunnel, she staggered and fell. Then dropped face first to the tunnel floor.

Donnelin's hand clamped down on Jude's shoulder, as if to hold him back. Jude wanted to run to her side. Had the priest not grabbed him, him may well have, and damn with the consequences. He wanted to help her up. Bind her wounded arms. See her to safety. Comfort her. Hold her close. But that would give away that there was something between him and Brackta. That would be dangerous for the both of them. No good could come of it. Ginalli or Thorn might mark her a traitor.

The Shadow League didn't suffer traitors.

Ginalli also moved toward the rear, his hands burned. Held before him, they were red, and blistered. Both his arms shook. His face was scrunched into a mask of pain. But he trudged on. He did not falter. He passed by Jude and Claradon without even a glance. No one had noticed that they had slipped their bonds. Or else mayhap no one cared. Happy for two more sword arms to help them against the elves.

Jude saw his chance. He and Donnelin were near the very front of the troop and no men were close to them. Smoke from the flame strikes filled the tunnel, making it much darker than before, and difficult to breathe. Five steps from a torch and all was black. Jude scooped up a cloak from a fallen Sithian and draped it over his shoulders. Donnelin did the same, and grabbed a helmet for each of them. Both made sure to stay as far from the nearest torches as possible.

Only Korrgonn, Mort Zag, and about twenty soldiers stood between Jude and the end of the League's line. Nothing moved in the tunnel beyond, except for the fluttering of scattered fires fueled by what little was left of the black elves. With no more opponents to fight, Korrgonn turned back toward the others, Mort Zag beside him, scorched and battered. Old Big Red had lost track of Jude and Donnelin in the chaos of their flight through the tunnels. Mayhap he figured them dead; mayhap he forgot about them, or mayhap he no longer cared.

All the men turned from the ashen tunnel and headed back the other way.

Jude and Donnelin walked along in line with all the others, helmets on their heads, their cloaks pulled tight, covering over their shirts and shirtsleeves as best they could since they didn't match the Sithian uniform. Jude walked hunched over and faked a limp. Donnelin pretended to help him along, the two of them moving slower than the rest, but not so slow as to attract unwanted attention. Man after man passed them in their urgency to get out of that acrid smoke and away from the end of the line. No one wanted to be rear guard when the elves came at them again.

Luck was with Jude. Korrgonn blustered past. Mort Zag on his heels. The makeshift disguises plus the darkness was enough to hide them. After another dozen men passed them in the smoky darkness, they were in the clear. They were at the end of the line. They slowed and let the last men pass out of sight, then turned around and moved through the tunnel with purpose. Along the way, they passed a couple of Sithian stragglers who paid them no heed when they saw that they were headed the other way. Proud men; injured or no,

they didn't ask for help.
 They made it to the line of charred elfin bodies, another few steps and freedom was theirs.

26

JUTENHEIM

OB

The crone's boy and his wolf led Theta, Claradon, Ob, Artol, and Dolan through the darkened streets of Jutenheim as a thick fog rolled in and blanketed the town.

"I see no one about; no one at all," said Ob. "Are the slackers all in their cups already? The sun has barely set."

"Every door and every shutter is closed," said Dolan.

"So too are the curtains drawn behind the shutters, best as I can see," said Artol. "The place is locked up tight. Whatever goes on out here at night, they don't want to see it."

"Or to be seen," said Ob.

"It's the curfew," said the boy, as if that was all that need be said.

"What curfew and why?" said Ob. "Something to do with the stinking elves the seer spoke of? That was naught but a fiction, wasn't it?"

"The curfew keeps us safe from them," said the boy. "Safer, anyway. We never go out at night, except just at sundown, and even then, only when at great need."

"All for fear of elves?" said Claradon.

"Not elves, my lord; black elves out of

Svartleheim. If they catch you out at night, they truss you up, and carry you screaming down to Thoonbarrow, never to be seen again. They cook folks down there — in their great ovens, eat them whole, way down deep in the earth. That's where they live, you know – in the earth; in the deep caves."

"Of course they do," spat Ob. "I knew there'd be cannibals somewhere hereabouts. I said it, didn't I? No doubt, they've a special taste for gnomes; probably a whole recipe book for cooking up my kind in stews and soups and such. Oh, and I bet they have an ancient grudge against old Mister Fancy Pants here too. How could we expect any less? All of Midgaard is out to kill us, why not folks down here too? Thank you Mister Harbinger of Stinking Doom for making this trip such a pleasure. Thank you again."

"They take the eyes," said Theta, his tone deadly serious.

"What say you?" said Ob.

"The Svarts," said Theta. "Best not to joke about them — for somehow they know it if you do. Eyes are a delicacy to them. They'll eat anyone but they do prefer gnomes and dwarves over all others. Why, I cannot say. What I do know, is that when they capture you, they make sport of you. When they tire of the torture and begin to grow hungry, they pluck your eyes out — right out of their sockets, first one, and then the other. And they do it while you're still alive; make you watch as they eat the first one. Then they go for the teeth. Tear them all out, one by one with long pliers. Scream all you want. Beg all you want.

They won't stop until they're done. Then they take the tongue, then the toes. They have no mercy, the Svarts; none at all. The flesh they eat, but what they do with the teeth, I've never understood, and no one has ever lived to tell." Theta paused and let his words sink in.

Ob paled, his skin turning white as a ghost. Sweat beaded on his brow despite the chill in the air. He opened his mouth as if to speak, but the words caught in his throat.

Then Theta spoke again, his tone just as serious, just as dark. "So you best keep your eyes fixed to purpose and your teeth together, gnome, lest you risk losing them both."

After a moment, Artol roared with laughter, the sound echoing through the night.

Claradon put a hand to mouth to hold back his own snickers.

Dolan looked confused by the whole exchange. The crone's boy looked about in a near panic, fearing the noise would draw unwanted attention.

Theta smiled at the gnome, just for a moment, then turned his attention back to their path.

Ob shook his head, rolled his eyes, and grumbled, but chose to keep quiet for a time as they walked along.

"You guide us after dark," said Theta to the boy. "Don't you fear the Svarts?"

"Night is the only time that you can speak to grandmother in secret, and that is the way she wants it. We're in dark times, says grandmother, and we must keep things close, lest Wotan's enemies assail us — whatever that means. Besides, Trak and I know these streets as good as anyone. We can outrun the black elves if we need to, can't we, girl?" he said, patting his wolf. "We've done it before."

"Seen the black elves, have you, boy?" said Artol.

"From a distance," said the boy. "They move like rabbits, fast and low to the ground, but they howl like the banshee. Sometimes there are flaming skulls that roam the streets with them making a racket; they float about by dark magic. I've never gotten too close though; don't want to get pulled down to Thoonbarrow."

27

SVARTLEHEIM

JUDE

On the verge of freedom, Jude hesitated and started to turn back.

"Don't look back," said Donnelin. "She's alright. Others were seeing to her. She's too important to them; too few wizards left; they'll not leave her behind."

Donnelin had read his intent. He wanted to run back down that tunnel, scoop up Brackta, and carry her along with him. He knew at that moment that his feelings for her were real. Not just an act to win his escape. Or at least, no longer an act. But he had to leave her. He didn't know that she would turn away from the League to run off with him. She never said or implied that she would. More than once she remarked that she wished that she could let him go, but that she couldn't, and she refused to be drawn into further discussion on the matter.

He left her lying injured on the tunnel floor. Didn't go to her. Didn't help her. Didn't do anything. A woman. One that he cared for. Perhaps even loved. And he left her in pain. Suffering.

What had become of his honor?

In love with the enemy. She may have even

played a part in his father's death. She said that she didn't. That she knew nothing of it. But where did the truth lie? Jude didn't know. His head was spinning. He knew that she wasn't seriously injured; only the effects of using too much magic in too short a span. He'd seen that happen to her before, when she fought with the Leviathan at Dagon's island. He saw the welts on her hands after that battle. The blisters on her arms. The scorched flesh. He knew that she'd recover soon enough. Still, how could he turn his back on her? It was wrong.

"This is the chance we've been waiting for, boy," said Donnelin. "Snap out of it and let's move." The priest pulled on his arm to get him moving, but he resisted.

"Maybe she'll come with us," said Jude.

Donnelin's good hand lashed out and slapped Jude across the face. "Lovesick pup."

Jude stepped back. More shocked than hurt, his eyes wide.

"You can't get her now, if even she would come. They'd spy us out for certain. They're looking for us by now. They're going to kill you. You know that, don't you? They want your blood for some vile ritual. Think you they'll leave you any when they're done? They won't. Let's get clear while we can."

Donnelin's words rang true. Jude was no fool. He'd come to the same conclusion long ago. But he held out hope that Brackta would save him in the end. But he also often wondered, if making him think Brackta cared for him was the League's plan all along. That her feelings for him were nothing more than an act. A means to an end. He didn't think that. But the fear of it was always near to his thoughts. He had to leave her. The risks were too great.

"You're right," said Jude. "Let's get clear." They ran down the tunnel side by side. Jude marveled at how well the old priest navigated the treacherous footing in that tunnel of burnt corpses. He had an easier time than Jude did, and had no trouble keeping up.

They went a hundred yards in, close to the point where they'd been encamped during the first part of the battle. There was no sign of pursuit.

Then an elf scurried out of the shadows, curved sword slashing. It caught Jude off guard. The Svart's first strike sent Jude's elfin blade flying from his hand. Jude blocked the elf's next thrust with a torch he'd picked up, though he was loath to do it, for fear that it would go out and plunge them into darkness. As the elf came in, Donnelin stepped in front of Jude and slammed the elf's sword aside with a Stowron staff he'd salvaged. The elf's blade went flying from its hand. Donnelin's next swing, quick as lightening, hit the elf in the neck. It crumbled, and a third strike to the side of the head finished it. Jude looked to the ground to pick up the elf's fallen sword or his own, but he didn't see them, and could waste no more time looking.

"We have to move," said Donnelin.

Then two more elves came at them out of the darkness. Jude swung the torch back and forth, holding them at bay. Donnelin swung the staff, awkward though it was to wield such a weapon one-handed, yet Donnelin did it with surprising skill.

By the time Jude's kick sent one elf to the ground, the air (and the fight) knocked out of it, Donnelin had already dispatched the other two, his staff whirling around faster even than the speedy elves could evade. Jude planted his foot on the elf's sword arm and dropped his knee onto the middle of its chest, all his weight behind it. He heard the thing's ribs crack, a sickening sound that made Jude want to puke. Better that he supposed than stuffing the torch into the elf's face, which was his first impulse, but he couldn't take the chance of losing the torch.

Jude grabbed the black sword from the elf, and the moment he grasped it, he felt its alien aura. The thing was ensorcelled with elfin magic. All his instincts told him to drop the blade, and to cleanse his flesh by plunging his hand into the torch's fire. He resisted that insanity, and instead thrust the blade up under the elf's chin, all the way up into its brain, putting it out of its misery.

Jude grabbed the torch in his off hand and rose. The elfin blade tingled in his hand. It made his whole arm tingle with a strange feeling like when a limb falls asleep. He swung it side to side a couple of times to get the feel and balance of the blade and to stretch his muscles, but the tingling didn't go away. If anything it got worse. Jude had no time for that.

They moved down the tunnel again with speed. They came to a spot where the tunnel widened. Two more elves came at them from the shadows. This time, it was Jude that dispatched them. The elfin blade dancing to his commands. And more. It moved of its own accord and to good affect. The thing had weighty magic to it.

And then a figure blocked the tunnel up ahead. Several of them. Tall figures. Men, not elves. Leaguers.

"Down a side tunnel?" said Donnelin.

"They've already seen us," said Jude. "Blast them, if you can."

Donnelin's arms waved, the fingers of his one hand gestured, and strange words passed his lips. Words of the Cleritus Mysterious, that ancient mystic language of the priests of the Aesir.

A white light emerged from Donnelin's chest and hung in the air before him, humming and crackling with electricity. Barely a moment later it expanded to the full width of the tunnel, with a thickness of no more than an inch or two, opaque in its whiteness. The men up ahead scattered, diving to the tunnel floor, turning and running, crouching low against the walls. One man stood tall, his arm outstretched.

Donnelin's sorcery shot toward the Leaguers. An instant before it reached them, a shimmering blue barrier appeared.

Donnelin's blast crashed into that barrier. When it hit, a sound like a thunderclap rang out. Sparks flew everywhere. Some rained down on Jude. They sizzled as they settled on his clothes and armor. They burned any bare skin they touched. Then the magic, both the white and the blue, fizzled out and was gone.

The Leaguers charged.

Donnelin reached for his staff, but he was off balance, drained from throwing the magic, and shocked that it had been countered.

"Back whence we came," said Jude. As they turned, they saw a huge figure looming in the shadows just beyond the light of their torch. They hadn't heard its approach. A shaggy red figure.

Mort Zag.

He stood there with a grin on his demonic face, his huge sword in his hand.

"Going somewhere, Eotrus?" said a gravelly voice from behind him. Ezerhauten. He was the one that had countered Donnelin's spell. How a mercenary commander could do such a thing, Jude knew not. He had many men with him. Sithians and stowron alike. The survivors of the expedition's vanguard.

"Put down your weapons," said Mort Zag. "Or we'll kill you where you stand."

Jude tightly gripped the elfin sword in his hand. He'd not be a prisoner again. He'd not submit. He'd not allow them to sacrifice him on some unholy altar to their demon god. He knew that was coming. It didn't take a genius to figure that out. Better to die fighting. A sword in his hand.

Donnelin sensed his intent. "No!" he said just as Jude launched himself at Mort Zag, sword swinging.

28

THE CRONE'S COTTAGE JUTENHEIM

OB

As Claradon and the group approached the Crone's cottage, there were no elves, no floating skulls, or dark magics in sight. The cottage looked much like the crone: larger and sturdier than you'd expect, but overworn from long years, though the shrubbery around it and along the stone walk was well tended and pruned. No doubt, she fiddled with it while she lurked in the garden, spying on the townsfolk as they went about their daily toils. Her home featured walls of thick weathered stone, mortar cracked and crumbling; the slate roof much the same. Windows, small and speckled with soot, glass intact, though the shutters were old and checked. Smoke wafted from no fewer than four chimneys fueled by the large woodpile that huddled against one side of the house. A heavy door, thick and solid, framed the entry.

The cottage was warm and smoky, the wood, an unfamiliar type. The air was heavy. It smelled of incense, stew, herbs, wolf, and pee.

The crone waved them in but did not speak until the boy closed and locked the door behind them.

"You honor me with your presence, great lord," said the crone, her voice slipping from confident to crackling with nerves, and back again. "Come and warm yourself by the fire. Come, come."

Theta's eyes scanned the place before he moved from the doorway. Most of the crone's home was one large room, high ceilinged and stoutly built — designed to weather the ocean winds and Jutenheim's long and frigid winters. The place looked old – ancient, just like the crone. A hearth dominated the center of the room, cast iron cook pots hanging above and piled around it. Along the side wall stood another great fireplace of weathered brick; a low table sat near it; worn and frayed sitting cushions adorned the stone floor. Off to the back of the place, farthest from the front door, were more rooms, presumably the bed chambers, two or three in number.

No one but the crone was about.

Theta sat across from the crone; Claradon and Ob near them. The others took seats by the central hearth where the boy offered them an herbal tea, sourdough bread, and generous helpings of a thick beef and vegetable stew well flavored of onion, herb, and garlic.

"Seek The White Rose, you do," said the crone, "but it's not the ship that you want. Not its captain. Not its cargo. Not its crew. It's the thing that lurks aboard that you seek – the creature that they transport. That's what you're after, great lord, is it not?"

Theta nodded.

"It's a thing of terrible power," said the crone, "as I'm sure you well know. And of great evil.

Though it might choose to wear the face of a man, it is no man, never was, and never will be. It is a thing."

"You saw him?" said Theta.

"I did not see it with these tired eyes, thank Odin, but I felt it. I felt it the moment I approached The Rose. Even before that, when it was still far out at sea — I felt something — something powerful, something odd, unnatural, dangerous. Something headed toward Jutenheim aboard an accursed ship filled of blasphemous men. That's why, when it came into port, I had to go see for myself. I wanted to mark the thing, to name it. Perhaps even to confront it. What a foolish notion that now seems. Before I felt its true power, the full force of it, I dreamed of driving it off, of banishing it, of sparing Jutenheim of whatever evil it came here to wrought. But when I got close, I knew that I was overmatched. That any seer, wizard, witch, or warlock of mortal make was no match for that thing. So I withdrew, cloaked myself as best I could, and stood silent and still – just an old crone hanging about the wharf, looking and snooping as the day wore on. I saw enough, I did, even from a safe distance. Enough."

"And so too, when your ship approached, I felt a great power – though one of a different nature. But even for you, great lord, I fear that the thing that travels on The Rose will be a foe hard to defeat. Mayhap impossible to defeat. There's an age to it. It's an old evil. Older than I can say. Older than I can imagine. Something that was ancient when the *Dawn Age* was born. Something that came before – even before you, great lord. Before anything."

"A Lord of Nifleheim," said Theta, his voice stern and serious. "Korrgonn, the son of Azathoth is what he is called. He seeks to bring his father forth from Nifleheim, to restore his kingdom, and to subjugate all of Midgaard. I am to stop him. Which way did he go?"

The crone stared back at Theta as if confused or in disbelief of his words. When he offered no more, she looked to his companions but their faces yielded her nothing.

"They went up the cliffs, great lord, those men from The Rose, and the Nifleheimer that you named. They sought help from the monks. The monks of Ivald."

"Ivald?" said Theta. "You mentioned black elves and now you mention Ivald. Is that the name, or is it Ivaldi?"

"Ivald is the only name we know them by," said the crone. Do you—"

"Tell us of them," said Theta. "All that you know."

"They've been there, in their monastery atop the cliffs, before Jutenheim had a name. When our forefathers first settled here, that monastery was already there. It was already old. Some say, far back in olden days, it was an outpost of Thoonbarrow, of Svartleheim. A castle of the black elves. A rare foothold for them on the surface of Midgaard – exposed as it is to the cleansing light of day; a light that they shun, even at great cost. But if ever that were true, the monks took the castle from them in times long past. Long before my people settled here."

"Would the monks help Korrgonn and his ilk?" said Theta.

She shrugged. "We know almost nothing of the monks. They are a secretive lot beyond all imagination, but they mind their business and cause us no trouble, so we leave them be and they us. They speak to no one. They rarely leave their monastery. Only now and again do they venture forth to purchase goods that they have no other access to. Even then they are careful to speak no more than needed to buy their goods."

"They are ordinary Volsungs by appearance, though they hide their faces beneath deep cowls whenever they are about. If they knew who your Korrgonn was, I can't imagine that they would help him. But I may be wrong, for if but a week ago you asked me whether the monks would open their monastery to a shipload of foreign men, I would've told you that you were daft. That it was unlikely even for a single visitor to gain entry to that place; impossible for a whole troop of men; a troop of soldiers no less. But let them in, they did. Why they did that, remains a mystery — one that I would have solved."

"There were wizards amongst them what came off The Rose. Sorcerers that stunk of chaos magic, the dark arts, and worse; they dripped of it. The disturbance to the ether that their presence wrought made me dizzy as they passed; the tendrils of black — so deep, so dark, and the crimson red, all swirling together in an unholy dance of the nether realms. Dark wizards they were. Dark. Dark. Dark and foul." With those words, the crone spat a wad of phlegm into the fire, a look of disgust on her face.

"And amongst their company traveled two creatures even worse. Two creatures the like of which I have not seen before and hope never to see again. One had the form and features of a man of giantish size. At first, I thought him an ogre, but on further inspection, he was something even less common, something even more cruel." She leaned closer toward Theta and lowered her voice almost to a whisper. "He was made of stone. Stone, I tell you. Not flesh, not blood, but the cold stone of the earth. They tried to conceal his nature beneath cowl and cloak, but spied him out I did. Such a thing could not pass through here without my notice."

"A golem that thing was. They are—"

"I know of golems," said Theta. "What of the other?"

"A beast of the nether realms. A creature that has haunted my dreams since I was a wisp of a girl. A red giant of Fozramgar."

"A demon?" said Theta.

"Aye, my lord," said the crone. "A creature of Helheim."

"You're talking fangs, claws, wings, and such?" said Ob. "Fire and brimstone and all that?"

The crone nodded. "I would not have believed it, had I not seen the thing myself. It too moved in disguise, but I marked its nature, I did. Marked it well."

"And Korrgonn went with all of them into the monastery?" said Theta.

"He did, along with many others. Count them,

I did not, but I'd mark their number at two hundred men. They marched a grand procession up through the streets of town, and up the steep paths to the monastery near the top of the rock. A treacherous journey up those cliffs."

"How did they know to go there?" said Ob.

"Darmod Rikenguard told them of the monastery. He's the best guide in Jutenheim, he is. And a good man."

"Guide to what?" said Ob. "One lousy trail up the rock? I heard the island is nothing more than that beyond this town."

"Ha," laughed the crone. "Jutenheim is much more than rock, little man. And so large that to call it an island makes little sense. There are vast tracks of land in the interior. Lakes, cold and deep. Swamps, dark and deadly. Plains of grass as far as you can see. And mountains and hills aplenty. Mountains, with caves pitch black and bottomless, and great peaks tall and deadly. Creatures old and evil lurk in those depths. Things left over from the Dawn Age. Things best left alone. Those things would eat you for a snack, little man. Supper for them, ha ha!"

"This town, great lord, is just one tiny corner of Jutenheim though perhaps it be the only corner in which men can live in peace, if even only during daylight hours."

"Where in the interior were they headed?" said Theta. "Another town?"

"This be the only town," said the crone. "Save for a few tiny villages that hug the rocky coast. No one lives in the interior. No men, anyways."

"What does live there?" said Claradon.

"Lugron. Giants. Ogre. And worse. Much worse if the legends be true. I haven't ventured there myself in many years — it's not a fit place for anyone, especially a woman older than dirt."

"We'll need a guide," said Theta. "Who is next best?"

"No need for next best," said the crone. "Hire Rikenguard, they did not. Wouldn't pay his price. Instead, Rothmar Blacksmith led them up the rock, he did, and then came straight back. Owed them a debt he did — for they saved his infant boy from the black elves."

"So they're doing hero stuff now, are they?" said Ob. "That don't square with what we know of them."

"A knight, tall and broad as you, great lord, was amongst them. It was he that saved the lad."

"Tell me of this man," said Theta.

"Frem Sorlons was his name. Wore a dragon crest upon his breastplate, he did. Many soldiers amongst them from The Rose wore the same."

"Sithians," said Ob. "The same ones what ambushed Jude. At least we know we're on the right trail."

"Did you speak to any others amongst them?" said Theta.

"One called Putnam, a plug of a soldier. And Par Sevare — a sorcerer, less dark than some, but darker than others. The leaders of the troop, I steered far clear of, owing to the evil amongst them of which I spoke. There was much that I wanted to know, to ask, to learn, but if I did, they might mark me as a threat — and that would get me dead. Old I be, but I'm not done with this life yet, so I steered clear. Mostly, I watched them from afar, and I asked after them once they were gone. I learned what I learned, as I've just told you. Go after them, you will?"

"Korrgonn must be stopped," said Theta. "Did they leave any men behind in Jutenheim town?"

"Not a one or I would know," said the crone. "Soon after they went up the cliffs, The Rose pulled out of port. Off west she went, to what end, I cannot say."

"How long ago did they go over the cliffs?" said Theta.

"Three days it will be, tomorrow, come dawn."

"Aargh, that long," spat Ob. "They're much farther ahead than we hoped."

"Too far ahead," said Theta. "Your lad can lead us to Rikenguard's home?"

"First thing in the morning, if that be your wish," said the crone. "You may stay here this night if it pleases you, and get an early start."

"We cannot wait," said Theta. "We will go now. Let's move," he said to the men as he stood up.

The crone's mouth dropped open and her eyes went wide. "My lord," she stammered, "it would be much safer to wait until morning. At night, when the fog is thick like it is tonight, Jutenheim is very dangerous; very dangerous, indeed."

"So am I," said Theta. "Thank you for your help."

"He's only a boy. Please. He's all I have."

Theta paused and turned back to the crone, his expression softening. "We will see the boy safely home this night, or in the morning if need be. Worry not, seer, for he is under my protection."

Her face still in a panic, the crone nodded and thanked him. As the others filed out, the crone rushed forward and put a hand to Theta's elbow. "A private word, great lord, before you depart," she said, her voice, a low whisper. "A moment; a moment only do I need, and you will find it of value," she said, as he seemed ready to pull away.

Ob overheard; his gnome ears far more sensitive than those of the Volsungs. He looked to Theta, as if to ask, "Should I stay?" but Theta gave him the nod to depart with the others. That wasn't the answer that Ob wanted. He thought that the whole business was suspicious and wanted to hear whatever more the crone had to offer. The moment the door closed behind him, he pressed his ear to it. One look, and a wave of his hand, and Artol stepped behind Ob to block the crone's boy's view, even as Claradon and Dolan engaged him in conversation.

The door was thick and dense, and the wind was howling through the streets, the fog billowing about, but Ob was able to hear much of what was said. He wished he hadn't. It made his blood run cold.

"Your Nifleheim Lord was not the great evil of which I spoke," said the crone.

Theta's look grew grim and grimmer still. His steely eyes bore into the old woman, and she turned her gaze away, though she continued to speak. "I sensed the Nifleheimer too, of course," she said. "His power is great and fearsome; far beyond that of any mortal. At quick glance, he is like the wizards and warriors that follow him, only a thousandfold stronger. Dark energies hover all about him; black tendrils, thick, quick, and probing — the stuff of the Nether Realms; magic unseen by all except those with the sight. I saw all that, but that is not what I was warning you about. I was speaking about another."

She paused, as if waiting for Theta to acknowledge what she said.

"Explain," said Theta. "Quick and clear. I have no patience for suspense or theatrics."

"Who or what it was, I cannot say. But it was a creature of power far beyond anything I've ever felt. The Nifleheimer was nothing next to it, like a child. It felt old; ancient. So ancient, it was unimaginable."

"What did it look like? What was its name?"

"I thank the gods that these old eyes never fell upon it, for if they had, surely I would have been struck blind, or dead, or worse. I only felt it, great lord. But it was there. It was real. It was amongst them."

"Are you certain that it was not Korrgonn that you felt?"

"I am certain, great lord. Be wary for that thing has no match in all Midgaard. Even the gods might not be its match."

29

SVARTLEHEIM

JUDE

"You're lucky you're not dead," said Brother Donnelin as he sat on the tunnel floor beside Jude Eotrus. Jude was flat on his back, his forearm draped over his brow.

"What hit me?" said Jude.

"Ezerhauten. He could have killed you easy enough. They still want you alive, thank the gods."

"Did I get in any licks?" said Jude.

"Not a one."

"You could have lent a hand," said Jude.

"And I'd have gotten dead for it. Then I'd be of no use to you going forward, and my help, I believe you'll need."

Jude sat up with effort, his head pounding. They were back at the spot where they were camped during much of the battle. No side tunnels, a wider and taller space than elsewhere nearby. Men were all around them. Some wounded, sitting or laying down, some being tended to by their fellows. Some were dead. Not many were standing. "How many are left?"

"That's what Ginalli is trying to figure out," said Donnelin. "They've got men scattered all over the tunnels. They're trying to gather everyone back together and take stock. I figure that they lost no less than half the company. Probably more."

Someone stopped beside them, their shadow hanging over them.

Glus Thorn.

Ginalli was a step behind him.

"You have value to us, Mr. Eotrus," said Thorn. "Your priest does not. Next time you try to escape, the priest dies. Slowly. Try again after that, and we'll take one of your arms off. We have a use for you. But we can leave a few pieces behind if need be." Without another word, Thorn turned and strode away.

30

JUTENHEIM

OB

The crone's boy was all nerves, but he and his wolf led the group straight and true to Darmod Rikenguard's house, the fog and the black elves be damned. All the way there, a baleful howling hung on the wind. It followed them, dogging their every step. Whether a natural sound created by the southern wind as it roared through the town's narrow alleyways, or the call of some creature or spirit, none amongst the company could say for certain, though the boy mumbled of restless ghosts that he called, the banshee. The moans came at once from this direction and from that, seemingly, from all around, even above them. But no matter which way the men turned, they saw no one – friend or foe, and ultimately, and in truth to their surprise, reached their destination unmolested, only their frayed nerves to plague them.

At Rikenguard's house, hanging on the knocker was of no use. Not until they mentioned The White Rose would Rikenguard dare even open his peephole.

"We need a guide," said Theta when Rikenguard finally appeared. "We're following the men off The White Rose."

Rikenguard looked Theta up and down, and eyed each of his companions in turn as best he could through the narrow slit before he unlocked and swung wide his door. He and his sons stood there, braced, each armed to the teeth, armor hastily strapped on, weapons held like they knew how to use them. Darmod Rikenguard was a very tall man, even for a Juten — and broad and thick of shoulder, arm, and chest. His eldest sons were leaner of limb and torso but nearly as tall. It was not often for men to darken his door that were as tall or taller than he, but Theta and Artol were.

Rikenguard ushered the men in from the night, though his sons stood wary, weapons close at hand.

"You know better than to be out after curfew," said Rikenguard to the crone's boy, his voice, deep; his Juten accent, strong. "Why not wait until morning to come here?"

"Grandmother said I should bring them straight away," said the boy, though his voice carried little resolve. "Their business can't wait, they claim."

"It never can," said Rikenguard. "Everyone is always in a great rush when they come to see me. No doubt, you want to follow them others over the cliffs. Rush headlong into death with them."

"What do you know of where they were headed?" said Theta.

Rikenguard motioned the men toward seats at the big table. He sat at one end, in a chair bigger and fancier than the others. "First, tell me true," said Rikenguard. "Do you call them folks from The Rose friends or foes?"

"Which do you?" said Theta.

"Neither," said Rikenguard. "Strangers they were, just as you are. They sought to hire me to guide them over the rock and down into the valley beyond. They wouldn't pay my price and that was that."

"What is your price?" said Theta.

"Eight thousand pieces of silver, or the equivalent."

Theta and the others exchanged glances.

"One can hardly blame them, laddie," said Ob. "That's a princely sum."

"Aye, but that's my price. I'll risk my life and that of my sons for nothing less."

"Did they hire another guide instead?" said Claradon.

"Darmod and sons are the only guides over the rock," said Rikenguard. "I told them, and I'll tell you the same — there's a hundred men what can guide you up the cliffs for a look-see, all fair and square and smiles aplenty, but only a few what will take you down into the valley. And them few will strand you there and be off with your coin the moment that you turn your backs."

"Thieves?" said Ob.

"They are not bad men at heart, but they know that anyone what goes over the rock, other than me and mine, does not come back, so they figure, why not make some profit off men what soon will be dead anyway."

"Just how dangerous is this valley of yours?" said Claradon.

"If the beasts don't eat you," said Rikenguard, "the snakes or spiders will poison you, or the fever will burn your brains. Make it in far enough, and the Lugron will make sport of you for a goodly time before they feast on you bit by bit, keeping you alive through it all for as long as they can."

"Yet you travel there freely," said Theta.

"Not freely, sir. I've lost several friends and kinsmen over the rock down through the years, including one son. I don't go there lightly, not lightly at all, but I have skills that other men do not. And I've got brains where most have mush. I know what's what over there, and where's where, and that makes a heap of difference.

"We aim to follow them," said Theta. "Will you guide us?"

"If you pay my price, I will, but know well, that you'll not find them men alive. It'll be three days already that they've been over the rock. By now, you'll find only a trail of corpses and gear, and not much even of that."

"We were told that they were two hundred men, and well equipped," said Theta.

"It won't matter. I expect that most of them are dead already. Probably all the rest will join them before we catch up. If they're good and lucky, and stay in one spot, it may be that a few of them are left when we get there, but I doubt it. That's the way it is, like it as not. I get paid either way, whether they are dead or not. Half before we leave; half when I bring you back."

After coming to agreement on payment terms, Theta said, "What think you of the men you met from The White Rose's company?"

"A strange mix they were," said Rikenguard. "Some of the strangest I have ever seen, and I have seen many, for many come to Jutenheim seeking many things — nearly all of which exist only in song and story or their muddled imaginations. Hunters, adventurers, zealots, dreamers, and dumbasses. Mostly dumbasses."

"And the men off The Rose?" said Theta. "How do you mark them?"

"Zealots, killers. . . and dumbasses," said Rikenguard.

"Ha, ha," went Theta. "We are of like mind about them it seems. Name me the ones you met, if you will."

"The priest, Ginalli, is their headman. Soft hands, sharp tongue, too large an ego, too small a brain. The one who tracked me down was called Putnam — a bald man, short and thick. I mark him a veteran by his manner and his gear. Several other soldiers were amongst them. Hard men. Killers. The only other one what spoke to me was a tall, lanky fellow with a gravelly voice. Had a dragon crest on his breastplate and a scarred face — his armor all fancy and angled with dents and gouges aplenty. He's killed his share and then some, that one has, I'd wager.

"The soldiers, I mark as mercenaries. Dragon Crest was probably their leader, all paid by the priest's coin. The priest — he's a dangerous one as are all men on religious quests. A zealot, I name him. And a dumbass."

"We must leave by midday," said Theta. "I must catch them before they get where they're going."

"Midday of what day?" said Rikenguard.

"Today."

"Impossible. There are supplies to gather; equipment to prepare. We can't even begin until dawn."

"We will bring much of what we need off our ship."

"You won't have the right gear. It will take—"

"Procure it tonight."

"The curfew—"

"My men will escort you and yours safely to wherever you need to go. If any black elves cause trouble, we'll deal with them."

"Will you now?" said Rikenguard. "They are not be trifled with. They have—"

"I know well of the Svarts," said Theta. "And will deal with them if they deter us."

"The price will be—"

"We'll pay half again what we already agreed to," said Theta. "But we must depart by noon, if not earlier."

"Do you know where in the interior they are headed?" said Rikenguard. "They would not tell me when I asked."

"A temple of some kind," said Theta. "Something old. Ancient."

"The monastery is ancient," said Rikenguard. "It sits atop the cliffs."

"We'll check there first," said Theta, "but I do not think that we will find them so close at hand."

"Why not?" said Rikenguard. "We already know they went there."

Theta didn't answer.

"He works in mysterious ways," said Ob. "Best not to ask any further."

And Rikenguard did not.

31

SVARTLEHEIM

FREM

Frem stood before Korrgonn, Glus Thorn, Ginalli, and Ezerhauten at their makeshift command post.

"The elves pulled out," said Frem. "It was clear sailing all the way through to you. But they were busy afore they fled. They didn't leave a single sword, torch, pack, canteen, nothing. Every body we came across was stripped of all but the clothes. They even took most of the armor."

"We found the same," said Ezerhauten.

"There must have been hundreds of them to do that so fast," said Ginalli. "Why break off their attack?"

"They used the females and children as scavengers," said Thorn. "It was hundreds of them that picked the bodies clean."

"If that's so then they've thrown all that they had at us," said Ginalli. "Then we've won."

"Maybe," said Ezer, "but they came at us quick. More than likely, there are more of them farther afield."

"You think they'll attack again?" said Ginalli, his eyes wide.

"Plan on it," said Ezerhauten.

"I agree," said Thorn. "We must move with caution, but speed."

***

"**A** half hour of rest is all we get after beating back the black elf horde from Helheim?" said Sevare, his voice hoarse and weak as the group started moving again. "I'm dying here," he said as he held up his bandaged arms.

"If we stayed put and they hit us again, we'd all be dead," said Putnam. "Getting out of there and quick is what we had to do."

"If they hit us when we get farther in, it'll be worse," said Frem. "We know that ground back there; we don't know what's up ahead."

"So we're dead either way," said Sevare.

"They need time to regroup," said Frem, "especially if they're pulling in more elves from farther out. If we can keep ahead of them, we have a chance."

"Unless we're walking straight into their stronghold," said Putnam.

"There's that," said Frem.

32

MONASTERY OF IVALD, JUTENHEIM

OB

"I don't think anyone's home," said Ob as Artol thumped on the monastery's door with his hammer and shouted for someone to open up. Nearly the whole of the Eotrus expedition was behind him, arrayed in defensive posture behind the rocky cover that the clifftop offered. Despite the chill in the air, sweat beaded on the men's brows from the hike up the steep trail from Jutenheim Town. In some spots, they had to resort to climbing, but Rikenguard's knowledge of the area kept them clear of loose rocks and the most treacherous spots. The whole company made it there safely. All the Eotrus men were there; so was the squadron of House Harringgold's soldiers led by Sir Seran, and the Malvegillian archers under Glimador. Captain Slaayde was with them, along with Tug and a few picked sailors, including N'Paag (the First Mate), and Captain Graybeard.

"Solid iron and thicker than a Lugron's head," said Artol of the door. "If no one inside opens up, it will be no easy feat to break through here. I see no windows save for slits high up."

Dolan ran up to the others. "No other door that

I can find, and no windows in reach; too narrow, anyways. The place is built right into the rock; the seams smooth at all the edges — even a mouse couldn't squeeze in."

"Have you any way to get us in?" said Ob to Rikenguard who stood nearby with two of his sons. "Any influence with these people?"

"I've been hereabouts a hundred times at least, but I've never been inside. Only seen the doors open a few times, but even then, the monks were vigilant about letting none but their own inside. Very odd that no one is about, though. Some few of the monks are usually out and about working on things or tending their gardens. Never seen the place deserted before."

"They saw us coming and decided to lock the place down," said Claradon.

"So do we break it down?" said Ob.

"There's probably a hatch up top," said Dolan. "If there's no other way, I'll climb it."

"It's straight up, laddie," said Ob. "No man can scale that."

"We brought along our climbing gear," said Dolan. "I can get up there if need be."

Claradon looked to Theta, to seek his advice, but the big knight's attention was fixed on runes carved above and around the door. He studied them closely and ran his hand over the patterns, gently touching the olden, iconic script.

"Can you read it?" said Claradon.

Theta paid him no heed.

"Lord Theta," he said loudly after some moments; that finally drew his attention. "Do you know what the runes mean?"

"This is, or was, the stronghold of Ivaldi —— a great king of the Svarts in ancient days, back even unto the First Age," said Theta, though he seemed to be speaking more to himself than to the others. "That is his sigil," he said, as he stretched and ran his hand over the rune at the center, above the door. "Perhaps he settled here after the fall of Azathoth, or perhaps even then he dwelt here; who knows; the Svarts were always secretive, their comings and goings unknown to any but their own. Ivaldi's sons were great smiths — some of the greatest that Midgaard has ever known. They worked in metal and magic. Blended them together in ways rarely replicated by any other. The spear that I once carried – the one with which I struck Bhaal down and cast him back into the abyss – was made by Beckir and Birkir, the eldest sons of Ivaldi. This place is something that I did not expect to find here. There may be much of value inside. Much besides all that we seek."

"How would you advise we proceed?" said Claradon.

"Break the door down," said Theta. "And be ready for anything."

"Agreed," said Claradon.

"You men," shouted Artol to the troops, "find us a log. We're to make a ram and batter this door in."

"This thing is solid," said Ob to Theta and Claradon. "Unless we get lucky and the door isn't barred from within, we'll be delayed here for hours at least."

"Time we can't afford to lose," said Claradon.

"Maybe the lock will be brittle with age," said

Ob. "A few good hits and it'll snap."

"Not metal forged by the Ivaldis," said Theta. "To get past their handiwork quickly, brute force alone will not do. Stand aside."

The men moved away from the door even as Theta pulled his hammer from his belt. The runes engraved in the hammer were not unlike those around the door; similar to them in form and style; perhaps even of the same script, but created by a different hand.

Theta firmly planted his feet and hefted the hammer. "Best you step back farther," he said to Ob, Claradon, Artol, and Dolan, who lingered a few feet from the door. Ob rolled his eyes but moved clear with the others, giving Theta and the door nearly twenty feet of lonesome. Theta grunted as he swung that giant maul, and when it struck the iron door there was a great flash of light and sparks, and a sound akin to a thunderclap, painful to the ears. A half inch deep imprint of the hammer's head lay in the door, centered on the lock, but the door remained closed. Theta put his shoulder to the door and pushed — and the door swung inward. Metal clanged to the stone floor as pieces of the door's lock or bars fell to the ground.

Gasps of surprise came from all around. Theta immediately took up a defensive stance and peered inside, but no one seemed to be about.

"Nice trick, Mister Fancy Pants," said Ob. "I've seen my old pal, McDuff, do the same, more than once. You've got the knack, I'll give you that."

33

SVARTLEHEIM

FREM

Moag Lugron was on point, as usual. Frem preferred to have two men out front, to watch each other's backs and such, but where Moag was concerned, and given the tight confines of the tunnel, he worked better alone. Moag was a ghost: quieter than air on a breezeless day, and stealthier than the best Hand assassin. He was short for a Lugron, but even thicker built than his fellows, yet all the more agile. He wore very dark colors, head to toe, and spread cavern dust over his clothing and face to better obscure him from sight. Frem ordered him to keep close, within sight and sound of the Pointmen at all times. Moag had a mind of his own, and interpreted orders rather loosely. He was probably too far out, but Frem couldn't tell. Strictly speaking, Frem couldn't see him, though he knew he was there. Somewhere. Every once in a while, Frem caught a glimpse of movement out beyond the edge of their torchlight, so little and so fleeting was that motion, that if Frem didn't know Moag was out there, he'd have dismissed what he saw as a trick of light and shadow. Twice along the way Frem heard a grunt or groan only to come upon a dead elf some moments later. Moag was picking off their scouts and lurkers. Even the elves couldn't see him coming. Frem wasn't easily impressed, but that impressed him.

After a time, they came upon a good-sized cavern. Originally, much of that cavern may well have been natural, but the elves had added carvings and friezes along the walls, in bands high and low, and statuary placed in pockets cut into the walls. They depicted black elves, various animals, and assorted monsters of myth and legend. At the center of the hall was a great round well, bucket and pulley system in place. The floor was polished stone, with joints carved into it, a strange hexagonal pattern that made it look tiled. The pattern of those joints produced a strange blurring effect that made it uncomfortable to look at. When one did, you tended toward dizziness and nausea.

The most notable feature in the cavern was directly across the way from the mouth of their entry tunnel. A great stone arch, twelve feet tall, intricately and exquisitely carved with runic symbols all about. The shape of the arch was that of a great eye, oddly formed. Not the eye of a man, was it, but rather, the eye of a black elf. Through that eye was the only exit from the room. Frem recalled that the monks spoke of that place. The Eye of Gladden they called it. Who or what was Gladden, Frem had no idea.

Moag appeared, knife bloodied. Frem saw two elf bodies on the ground, one near where they entered, another near the great eye. Moag had a strange look on his face. As if he'd eaten something foul and was about to puke.

"One was old," said Moag. "The other, a child. I didn't know. Not a child. I wouldn't have. . ."

Frem placed a hand to Moag's shoulder. "There will be time to think on this when we're outside," whispered Frem into Moag's ear. "For now, you must put it from your mind."

"Aye, Captain," said Moag, nodding.

Frem turned to the Pointmen. "Royce, Carroll, Borrel, and Torak — stand at the eye and hold it. Ward — check for water in the well, but don't drink it. The rest of you fan out and check for secret doors or hatches in wall and floor. And keep quiet."

The water was clear, fresh, and icy cold. Once they were convinced that it was safe, they drank their fill and topped off their canteens.

"One way in, one way out," said Putnam. "A good place to camp, but too close to where we fought them."

"We won't be camping, unless Ginalli and the wizards are truly dense and daft," whispered Frem.

Korrgonn, Ginalli, Glus Thorn, and Stev Keevis stood before the Eye of Gladden.

"I can read but fragments of this," said Thorn.

"I know it not at all," said Ginalli. "My lord, do you know these runes?"

"A script of the Svarts," said Korrgonn. "But its meaning is unknown to me."

"I can read it," said Stev Keevis.

Ginalli turned to him, a surprised expression on his face.

"The Eye of Gladden, say the runes, the bold lettering across the very top. Farther down it says, Welcome to Starkbarrow, Fourth Hive of Ancient

Svartleheim. Hail to its First High King, Ivaldi, the First of His Name; Hail to the Sons of Ivaldi, the Makers of Wonders; and Hail to the architect of the realm, the High Magus Gladden."

"That's all?" said Ginalli. Does it say nothing more?"

"I thought it quite a lot," said Stev Keevis.

"Were you hoping for a riddle?" said Ezerhauten. "Or some dire warning of death if we dare pass its threshold? I think we got that message already."

"I was hoping for something useful," said Ginalli.

A soldier ran up to the group. "Black elves at our rear, my lords. A large force. Even now they mass behind us."

Thorn growled. "I had hoped to outpace them. This is a violation."

"This cavern seems quite defensible," said Ginalli as he glanced around.

"It's a death trap," said Ezerhauten. "If they breach the entry in numbers, we'll be overrun. We must move from here. If we can't outrun them, we fight them in the tunnels, same as before."

Moag appeared. "This here tunnel splits into two, not long past the Eye. One, the same as the other, but they go opposite directions.

"Commander," said Thorn. "I want your Pointmen to hold them here while we make our escape. We need ten minutes at the least. Can you give us that?"

"Better that the Lugron hold this place," said Ezerhauten.

"Only your best have the skills needed for

this," said Thorn.

"Give us one of your wizards," said Ezerhauten.

"This is not a negotiation," said Thorn. "You have a wizard. Use him."

"He's spent," said Ezerhauten.

"As are ours," said Thorn. "Will your men hold the hall or not?" he said, his voice menacing.

"For as long as we can," said Ezerhauten.

"You mean, for as long as Captain Sorlons and his Pointmen can," said Ginalli. "You will remain with us, Commander."

***

"They will run us down," said Putnam.

"We can't stand and fight again," said Ezerhauten. "We don't have enough men to face an assault even half as fierce as the last."

"I'll not stand to the last man to protect the priest and his Leaguers," said Frem.

"I don't want you to," said Ezer. "Hold them a few minutes, as best you can. Then lead them down the tunnel to the left; we're taking the right. I'll have our tracks covered as best we can."

"So we're on our own?" said Putnam.

"The left passage may well lead to the outside," said Ezerhauten, "and the right to certain death. Or the reverse. Or both may meet up again after a short ways. Who knows? Your chances are not much worse than ours. I don't think we have much of a choice in this — as

Putnam says, they'll run us down. You men can move with more speed on your own."

34

MONASTERY OF IVALD, JUTENHEIM

OB

"He will not speak," said Artol as he stood with Theta, Claradon, Ob, Dolan, and Par Tanch outside one of the monk's rooms — the only man they found within the monastery.

"What happened to him?" said Claradon. "He looks half dead."

"Sliced by a heavy blade across his abdomen," said Artol. "Two days ago I would guess; possibly three. It may be infected as he has a fever. It's bad, but with proper care, he might yet live. He's also got a broken arm, lost a few teeth, and maybe some broken facial bones."

"Apparently the monks and the Leaguers didn't get on too well," said Ob.

"There are droplets of blood on the floor," said Theta. "Follow them," he said to Dolan. "Let's find out where this battle took place."

Dolan was off in an instant.

"Where could they all be?" said Claradon. "Rikenguard thought that there were a few dozen monks at least."

"It wouldn't make sense that they all went over the rock into the valley with the Leaguers," said Artol.

"Maybe Korrgonn killed them," said Claradon.

"There would be bodies," said Theta. "And a lot more blood. No one would've cleaned it up."

"I wager that they're hold up in some hidey hole, hoping that we go away," said Ob.

"Or waiting to ambush us," said Artol.

"Let's do another sweep through this place," said Theta. "We may have missed something. Keep the men together; no one goes off on their own in case the monks or the League does try to jump us. Artol — see what you can get out of him, but do not harm him."

"I wouldn't think of it," said Artol, a wounded expression on his face.

35

THE ABBOT'S CHAMBER MONASTERY OF IVALD, JUTENHEIM

OB

In the abbot's chamber, Ob held a stack of parchment and quickly scanned each sheet, while Claradon and Theta searched the rest of the room.

"Ledgers, planting schedules, and miscellaneous ramblings about nothing of consequence," said Ob. "There's nothing here of use to us."

"What of these symbols engraved on the wall, and those we found in the sanctuary?" said Claradon.

"Svartlescript," said Theta as he approached and took a closer look. "Runes from the *Age of Myth and Legend*. They confirm that this is the fortress of Ivaldi, just as I thought. But he and his are long since gone; the monks have been here a long time. Little of the Svarts remain, save for the carvings. Wait—" he said as he peered closer at the wall. He pressed his hand against a curious crack in the masonry — one that ran straight and true. When he did, there was a click and a small panel opened in the wall revealing a hidden cubby behind. Filled of scrolls, parchment, and small sacks it was. Theta examined the contents.

"More Svartlescript," said Theta as he perused a sheet of parchment, "but this is newly written."

"Can you read it?" said Claradon.

"The dialect is unfamiliar to me," said Theta, "but I can understand most of it. They are messages."

"From who to who?" said Claradon.

"Love letters between the black elves and the trolls, I bet you," said Ob.

"This one is from a Svart king called Throonbilg biln Mac-Murth to an abbot called Brother Krisold," said Theta. He quickly scanned the pages. "They are in order from oldest to newest. Always from Throonbilg to the abbot, but the abbot changes over time. Some of these go back hundreds of years — many hundreds of years — the parchment preserved with oils and essence of elmwood. Treaties they are. Confirmations of alliances."

"So the black elves and the monks are in league?" said Claradon.

"And have ever been, it seems," said Theta. He lingered overlong over another document.

"What is it?" said Ob. "Spill it. Good or ill, we've a right to know."

Theta looked up, but paused, as if considering whether to respond. At last he did. "It speaks of mutual vows of servitude to the great lord."

"Not Azathoth, is it?" said Claradon.

"No," said Theta. "They speak of him as if he's a living man, as if they have direct contact with him." Theta paused again on one page, seemingly reading a passage over and again to himself.

"You found it," spat Ob. "Tell us. Who is their lord?"

"Uriel," said Theta. "They are followers of Uriel the Swift."

"Who is Uriel?" said Claradon.

"One of the damned," said Theta.

"Of course he is," said Ob. "No doubt he's an old enemy too, with a score to settle with you?"

"Ages ago," said Theta, "one of Azathoth's arkons was called Uriel. He was one of those that rose up against Azathoth. A rebel. A traitor to his god. One of those that aligned with the Harbinger of Doom. The one I'm so often accused of being."

"But that all happened thousands of years ago," said Claradon. "He couldn't still be alive."

"Some say the arkons of Azathoth were immortals," said Theta.

"What say you about that?" said Ob.

"I say it all falls into place," said Theta.

"What does?" said Claradon. "What does this mean for us?"

"It means that Uriel guards the Temple of Power that the League is seeking. And that the monks and the Svarts are his minions. That means, whether they know it or not, both the monks and the Svarts are on our side. And that means we're not alone in this any longer. We can ally with them — if we can get them to believe our purpose."

"An unexpected boon this is," said Claradon.

"Except that them monks are probably all dead thanks to the Leaguers," said Ob. "And if we run into any Svarts, they'll probably try to kill us straight away instead of sitting down to tea."

"Either way," said Tanch, "somehow, it will all come to shit. It always does with us."

"Now let's see what's in them bags from that hidey-hole," said Ob.

Theta tossed one of the bags to Ob. Ob opened it, peered in, smiled, and dumped a handful of gold coins and gemstones into his palm. "A king's ransom. And several more bags filled of the same, it looks like."

"We should put it back," said Claradon. "The Eotrus are not thieves."

"Of course we're not," said Ob. "But dead men can spend no coin, and I've a feeling that the monks are just that."

"And if they're not?" said Claradon.

"Then it belongs to them," said Ob. "We'll turn it over."

"One at least is still alive," said Theta.

"We'll leave him a goodly share," said Ob, "though I doubt that he even knows this loot exists."

"Fair enough, I suppose," said Claradon. "If we don't run into the other monks, then on our way back through here, we'll check if any of them have shown up, and give them what's theirs. If not, we keep it."

"Agreed," said Ob. "Any objection?" he said looking to Theta.

"If the monks are truly dedicated to our cause," said Theta, "and they be dead, it's fitting that we put this coin to good use. And good use for it we may have before this quest be done."

"These are the end times," said Tanch as he stared off at nothing.

The others exchanged concerned glances.

"What's your trouble, Magic Boy?" said Ob. "You've been acting nuttier than usual ever since Evermere Bay."

"All this is going away soon," said Tanch, still with that distant look, his eyes glazed over. "It's all coming to an end."

"What's coming to an end?" said Ob. "Make some sense, man."

"Soon nothing will make sense," said Tanch. "These are the end times," he said as he walked out the door, nearly bumping into Dolan who was arriving.

Dolan stepped into the abbot's room. "The blood trail leads to a door in the deepest level. Stone tunnels lie beyond for as far as I could see. A smell of death comes from down there."

"Could the temple of power be under the mountain?" said Claradon.

"Perhaps," said Theta. "Or perhaps the monks led the Leaguers there to entrap them. Like the gnome says, we won't know nothing until we get our behinds down there to see for ourselves. Get the men ready. We're going into the tunnels. We'll need torches. A lot of them."

***

"I cannot guide you through these tunnels," said Rikenguard, "for I know nothing of them. Until this morning, I didn't even know that they existed. The surface world is where my expertise lies. You don't need me any longer. I trust that you will pay me for leading you up here, and that we will part ways on good terms."

"We still need your services, laddie," said Ob. "There's a goodly chance that the men we're following used these tunnels as a shortcut, to get themselves to where they're headed. If that's true, then there's an exit from these tunnels on the other side of the cliffs – somewhere out there, in your valley. Once we get there, we will need you. I know skulking through the deep dark is not what you signed on for, but will you see this through with us?"

Rikenguard took his time considering, and then he said, "All my life I've lived at the foot of these cliffs and never suspected that there were tunnels that ran through them. It's got my curiosity up, it has, and I don't mind saying so. At our core, me and my boys are explorers and adventurers. Heading down into that dark may be quite an adventure – one that I'd not soon pass up. So I'll be going with you, I will, and my boys too."

36

SVARTLEHEIM

FREM

"We make our stand at the eye," said Frem as the rest of the company rushed past the arch. "Within the passage." He turned to Sevare.

"One blast only," said Sevare as he held his arms away from his sides, as if the merest touch caused him pain. "And if I'm not dead, you'll be carrying me." His hands were bandaged, his arms heavily so, all the way past the elbows. The white cloth was splotchy red from blood that seeped from the wizard's wounds.

Par Rhund and Par Brackta were the company's rear guard. Before entering the cavern, each threw some powerful sorcery back whence they came, which rocked the whole cavern. The screams of the elves filled Frem's ears. Frem felt sorry for them at that moment, hearing their terrible suffering. Trapped in the narrow confines of the tunnel, they had no chance. After all, it was the Lomerians that were the invaders here, a large armed forced passing through the elves' tunnels. They had a right to defend themselves, their lands.

The smell of burnt flesh assaulted Frem's nose. Rhund and Brackta dashed through the Eye of Gladden and by him without a word or a glance.

Twenty four men stood behind Frem — all that remained of his Pointmen, plus several men from 2nd and 4th Squadrons, and Ma-Grak Stowron. Ma-Grak refused to join up with the surviving remnants of the other Stowron squadrons. He said that all his tribesmen met their end fighting alongside the Pointmen, and that he would do the same. Scrappy fellow. Brave as they come. With skills too. Better even than most of the Sithians. Frem was glad to have his sword. But he didn't trust the bugger in the slightest. Something about all the Stowron just wasn't right. Something in their eyes. They felt alien. Much like the black elves. In fact, superficially, they resembled them, though they were much the taller, their eyes and features more human.

After the wizards' blasts, the elves took their time about coming forward again. Who could blame them? They'd lost untold hundreds of their fellows. Probably a few thousand all told by that time. They probably had little stomach for more battle. Their pause gave Frem some minutes to prepare. The Pointmen would use the same tactics as before, switching their spent men for fresh, using what few pikes they still had in the second row. Standing their ground. Holding a shield wall until the bitter end.

The minutes went by and Frem began to worry that the elves knew some way around them. That they'd soon appear both in front and behind. That would likely mean the end of them.

After a goodly time, as much time as the Leaguers had asked for, the elves showed their faces.

They came on in a rush.

A full-out charge. Shouting their war cries. Thank the gods, not one of the stone creatures was with them.

Frem was ready for them. He expected a charge. That's what he would have done, given their position. Sevare was by his side, both of them behind a wall of wood and steel shields.

"Hold until my mark," shouted Frem to Sevare, as the wizard's fingers weaved this way and that and he mouthed his forbidden words of olden sorcery. Frem waited, and waited still. Waited until the first of the elves were on them. That was the plan. Sevare designed his spell to go off at the very center of the chamber. It would explode outward in a hail of fiery death that extended from one side of the cavern to the other, but not one single step beyond, thus safeguarding Frem's own men. Battle, being chaos and craziness, not much ever goes as planned.

That time it did.

A blue sphere appeared in Sevare's upraised palm. It sped over the heads of the elves. Grew in size as it flew. Exploded the moment it reached the very center of the cavern — a trip that took no more than a heartbeat or two.

The blue sphere expanded outward in all directions. There was no pressure to it. No blast wave. Just the numinous blue energy that rained down on everything in the cavern, covering it like a cloak. A lethal shroud that destroyed all life that it touched.

A hundred elves collapsed simultaneously around the cavern, falling dead in mid-stride.

Those at the front crashed into the shield wall, but they were already dead when they struck it. Not a moment later, a beam of blueish white light shot from Sevare's fingertips and blasted clear across the cavern, and through the tunnel opening on the other side. There, more elves were massed. That magical beam blasted straight through their ranks, carving through the elves like a knife through butter. It dropped them by the score, the magic flowing down the tunnel until it fell out of sight. All the elves were down. Bodies writhing and voices screaming told that not all were dead. But they were all out of action. Not one in sight was left on its feet.

Torak and Wikkle Lugron scooped up Sevare as he fell backward, his eyes closed, consciousness already fled. The Lugron had damp cloths wrapped around their own arms to protect them from the heat the came off the wizard. Ward quickly wrapped a damp blanket around the wizard's arms, which steamed and smoked on contact. As one, the whole squadron turned, and raced down the tunnel toward the left, making no effort to hide their passage. They wanted to be followed, assuming that there were any elves left to follow them. Somehow, they knew that there were.

Frem was the last, Putnam by his side. He waited some moments; he knew that he could catch up. When he wanted to be, Frem was fast.

And then he saw it.

Movement in the far tunnel. More elves coming up. Ignoring their fallen comrades. Those elves were determined to kill the intruders, though it cost every one of them their lives. And so, the chase was on.

37

MONASTERY OF IVALD, JUTENHEIM

OB

"A lot of men came through here recently," said Ob as he squatted and studied the dust in the large chamber with the door to the tunnels that Dolan spoke of. "Heavy boots and leather shoes. The Leaguers and the monks. The monks followed after. A few score of them at the least."

"More runes," said Claradon as he pointed to characters carved above the door.

"It says, Svartleheim," said Theta. "The realm of the black elves."

"I thought that was a mythical place," said Claradon.

"Whatever underground territory the Svarts control, or claim to control, they name Svartleheim," said Theta. "It means no more than that. Open it," he said gesturing at Dolan.

Dolan pulled the door open; Theta stood before the opening, shield raised protectively before him. At once through that portal wafted the unmistakable stench of death carried on air both cold and dry. The place was utterly dark. The only sound, a breeze that whistled through the passages; an eerie sound that grated on the nerves.

"What do you see?" whispered Ob to Theta.

"Next to nothing. It's too dark."

Someone brought up a torch and Theta raised it high. The light revealed a stone tunnel, generally round in shape, the ceiling seven feet or so high.

"A natural tunnel?" said Ob.

"A lava tube," said Theta. "But it has been modified: widened by a few feet at least. They added braces and pilasters to strengthen it; there must be sections of weak rock. We'll need to be cautious.

"Wonderful," said Ob. "Lava tubes mean this whole place is built on a volcano. They are almost as much fun as dragons. You like dragons, Theta?"

"Broiled over an open flame is the best way to eat them," said Theta, his face betraying no emotion.

"You're kidding, right?" said Ob.

"This volcano will give us little trouble, I think," said Theta. "The air is cold and not tinged of brimstone. The mountain may have no fire in its belly, and that will make our passage all the easier."

"I don't know exactly why, but it feels . . . large," said Ob. "As if the tunnels go on for a long way."

"I expect that they do," said Theta, "otherwise there would be little sense to widening the tunnel. We need to make certain we've enough torches and oil. As much wood as we can carry. If we're caught in there without light, we're finished. And water too. Make certain we've got all that we can manage and still move with some speed."

"That will take more time," said Ob.
"Aye, but it's necessary," said Theta.

***

Theta, Claradon, Ob, Tanch, and Dolan stood nearby the door to Svartleheim as the men made their final preparations to enter the tunnels.

"I hate caves," said Tanch. "The living shouldn't dwell in caves. Claustrophobia, you know. I hate climbing too, but caves are worse."

"Gnomes are natural spelunkers," said Ob. "Stick close to me and you'll be alright."

Artol walked up to them. "The monk is dead," he said. "The fever was worse than I thought."

"Did he speak?" said Theta.

"In the end, the fever loosened his tongue, but his mind was scattered. Mostly, he babbled to himself; he would respond to no questions. In his delirium, he seemed to think I was his master. He said that they failed and begged forgiveness. Nothing more.

38

SVARTLEHEIM, JUTENHEIM

OB

The tunnels were cold. The kind of cold that chilled you to your core; the kind that made your bones hurt and your teeth chatter. The kind that made your snot freeze up right in your nose. Ob had felt that kind of cold many times before, though rarely underground, and never except in deepest winter during the coldest years. Why the Jutenheim tunnels held such a chill, Ob didn't know, and he didn't much care — so long as he and his got through to the other side in one piece.

Assuming that there was another side. For all he knew, the place was a deathtrap. Mayhap the monks led the Leaguers down there to put an end to them all, for reasons of their own. That would account for the smell of death that polluted the place, and the wounded monk, and the deserted monastery.

Or else, perhaps the temple of power, the one that old Korrgonn had been searching for, was buried down deep in the tunnels, instead of somewhere in the valley beyond the cliffs. Maybe the Leaguers convinced the monks to lead them down there, to show them the way, and then killed them, one and all — except for that one sorry fellow that crawled back up, bleeding all the way.

Or else, maybe something different happened. Maybe something that Ob couldn't anticipate. Who knows? That's why they were going through these tunnels. To find out. To learn the truth. And ultimately, to stop Korrgonn. To put him down, somehow. How they would do that, Ob had no clue. But he figured, old Mister Fancy Pants would find a way. That fellow usually did.

The gnome's breath wafted before him, illuminated by the hazy, crackling yellowish light produced by the torches the men carried. The torchlight notwithstanding, the tunnels' environs gave everything a dull, grayish blue cast. Shadows cavorted all about with the slightest movement, dancing on the tunnel walls like frenzied demons.

The air grew dusty due to the company's passage; the men near the rear had it the worst. At the front, the air was clean, and surprisingly light, except for that tinge of death that crept towards them from somewhere far up ahead. The promise of finding the source of that smell haunted their every step.

The whole place was eerily quiet. Every sound, however slight, bounced off the walls, and came back again — echoing two, three, sometimes even four times before fading away to nothing. But the echoes of loud sounds were truly disturbing – for the tunnels amplified them by craft unknown — the first echoes louder than the original sounds that birthed them. Those echoes made the men's throats rumble, their ears vibrate, their nerves fray.

Taken together, those things created an eerie, unnatural feeling about the place.

In such a place, a man's mind could conjure all sorts of terrors, could imagine all sorts of unlikely things. More often than not, those bogeys were far worse than what reality provided.

Fear.

Fear of the unknown — a formidable enemy that rarely retreated, and no matter a man's will or resolve, could not be forever banished. Not by common men. Nor by lords or knights, wizards or warriors, scholars or scoundrels. Not even by heroes. Maybe by such as Theta, but there was no accounting for him, nor his kind, whatever they were, whatever their nature. Outliers. Wild cards. Enigmas.

Ob had done battle with fear many times; every soldier has; the old ones more than the young. He expected to battle it again that day. He'd spent a goodly time in deep caverns; he was used to such environs. He could operate within that place as an expert. But the men with him could not. He didn't know how they would manage. He'd seen men panic in caves — good men, brave men. He seen them lose their nerve in the deep dark; get themselves lost, hurt, or just plain dead.

The Harringgolds, the Malvegils – every man amongst them was untested in such places. And few amongst the Eotrus had caving experience. Ob would have to watch them closely. Lend a hand where needed, an encouraging word from time to time, and maybe a kick in the butt, wherever it would do some good. The burden to get them through to the other side lay as heavily on him as on anyone, Theta included.

And Ob knew it.

The trouble was, he was tired. His old bones were weary. In need of a long quiet retirement. He figured he'd earned it, for all his service to the Eotrus. For all those years. The blood. The sweat. And even some tears.

The long sea voyage and all the perils they'd faced along the way had taken a lot out of him. More than he expected. Maybe more than he could spare. He had dreamed about retirement for many years. For decades even. He started talking about it, thirty, maybe forty years prior. But it never happened. And he was rather certain that it never would. So long as he staved off serious illness or crippling injury, he'd keep on soldiering. It's what he knew. It's what the Eotrus knew. It was the way of things on Lomerian's borderlands.

A world that didn't need soldiers – adventurers like Ob – was a world that Ob wouldn't know how to live in. And strange to say, he might not even want to.

Tired or no, he would do what he had to do. He always did. Such was his nature.

39

SVARTLEHEIM

FREM

Against Putnam's advice, Frem decided to maintain position as the squadron's rear guard. He figured that they'd be attacked for certain from the rear, and he was best equipped to deal with that, his armor being the heaviest in the squad. He had Sirs Royce, Lex, and Ward with him for the same reasons. The black elves's weapons were strong and sharp, but too light to be of much use against good Lomerian plate armor. Ma-Grak Stowron also chose to stand with them near the rear. He was eager to kill more elves, but Frem wondered if he had a death wish. Putnam was up front, in command of the unit, Moag Lugron out on point.

The tunnel headed generally downward, which Frem figured was a good sign. He'd heard that the valley floor beyond the cliffs was about five hundred feet below the clifftops. Frem's best guess was that the Eye of Gladden was about three hundred to four hundred feet down from the clifftops, so they still needed to descend another hundred to two hundred feet just to reach the ground, farther still because the monks said the tunnels continued under the swamp and came up farther out in the interior. Frem figured the tunnels went down for at least a hundred feet below that swamp and then for miles inland. It was going to be a long, dark walk.

To conserve their light, they kept only two torches lit along the line: one near the front, one toward the back. It wasn't much, but it was enough to keep them moving. Things got hard when the tunnel steeply dropped off. They had to climb down a rock face that sloped at a forty-five degree angle. Frem put his back to the rock and walked, climbed, and slid his way down. He didn't care for climbing. Never did. He was too bulky for it. All the more so due to his heavy armor and gear.

Climbing in the dark, well, that just made it all the more fun. In the shadowy light that the torches cast on that slope, the stone looked grayish blue. Dull it was. Dusty. Solid in the main, but with loose shards of small size scattered about its surface. Hand and footholds aplenty.

He couldn't see the bottom of the slope; only the light from the torches enabled him to gage how much farther down he had to go. All the while, he wanted to go slow, to move carefully and purposefully, and thus minimize the chance of slipping and sliding down into the men in front of him, potentially sending them all tumbling to their deaths. But at the same time, he needed to go fast. The steep slope dramatically slowed down their progress, presumably giving the elves the opportunity to close the distance between them. What if the elves showed up atop the slope before he reached the bottom? They could throw stones at him and the others. Batter them or knock them off the slope. Rain arrows or who knows what down on them. He had little cover on that slope. They had to reach the bottom for the elves showed up. Of course that's when he heard them.

The elves had arrived. They were up top. Probably looking down on him even as he looked up. He couldn't see them. Everything above him, out past about ten or twenty feet, was nothing but black, even though he knew he'd descended at least a hundred feet. Distance was hard to gage in the darkness. He may well have gone down twice that amount, all the while dreading the thought that the slope might get steeper. Leaning on his back and inching down was tiring, stressful, even frightening, but it was doable. If it suddenly grew too steep for that, and he had to turn around and search for handholds as well as footholds, he figured that he was done for. It wasn't going to get that bad, he told himself, for the men below him were still moving.

Then he looked up to see a boulder plunging toward him.

40

SVARTLEHEIM, JUTENHEIM

OB

Dolan was a few steps out in front of Ob as they made their way through the tunnel. Ob held a torch, though he sorely wished that he didn't need it.

As a gnome, his eyes were good in the dark — better than most any Volsung's. And so were Dolan's, for the boy had elven blood. How much of it, Ob didn't know for certain and Dolan wasn't much for sharing. But he had the almond-shaped eyes, the pointy ears, the straight black hair, the lithe build, the high cheekbones. Any fool could see that he was of the (elven) blood, though the characteristic features were less pronounced in him than in a full-blooded elf.

Ob knew that elves could see in the dark nearly as well as gnomes. But that wasn't good enough. Not for either of them. Not in that place.

Those tunnels were just too dark.

And so Ob carried the torch. Clumsy things they were, torches. The light they cast didn't carry far enough. Worse, they sputtered, making all too much noise. Attracting unwanted attention. And they dripped sparks and ash, making them dangerous tools indeed. The only good part was, they could double as a weapon in a pinch: you could hold things off with the flame, or else use it as a one-off club, though you'd likely lose your light after a single blow.

The real trouble with torches though, is they kill your night vision. They wipe it out completely. That's why Dolan was up front, Ob carried the torch several feet behind. That enabled Dolan to make use of the light that the torch gave off while preserving his night vision.

Still, he couldn't see very far — fairly well out ten feet and less so out fifteen, but nothing beyond that. It was like being half blind. In a dangerous scenario, that did not serve you well. In close quarters combat, it made you all too vulnerable. Hopefully, your opponent is similarly handicapped. But Ob knew enough about the Svarts to know that they had no such deficit. If the stories were true, they could see in the dark as well as a man could see in the light. And that gave them a great advantage in the deep dark of the underground. No doubt, there were other dangers lurking in the tunnels; some, perhaps worse than the Svarts. If anything was lying in wait out there, they'd be right on top of it before Dolan spied it out. The thought of that sent shivers up Ob's spine.

But Dolan, he took it in stride. The peril of their situation didn't phase him. He showed almost no hesitation, and not a hint of fear. When Ob first met Dolan, he would've chalked up that attitude to simpleminded stupidity; that the boy didn't know enough to be afraid. But now that Ob knew Dolan well, he knew that he was not nearly half as simple as he pretended to be. He was brave. Loyal. And he moved like a ghost – far more silently than any gnome ever hoped to move — and they were the most silent of all the peoples. And Dolan was tough; tough and sturdy as they come. Out in front, on point, there was no one that Ob would rather have at his side. Theta chose his companion well. And Ob was proud to serve with him.

Ob knew that eventually they'd stumble into something ugly. And being out in front, he and Dolan would get hit first. Hopefully, they didn't fall into a pit, have the roof cave in on them, or get pulled down by a bunch of cave dwelling crazies. Ob didn't care for taking the point in such a place, but he knew full well that he and Dolan were the best equipped for it. They could pass silently where the others could not.

Dolan halted and spoke in a whisper. "How far back are they?" he said of the main group, though he didn't turn around. "Can you still see them?"

"No," said Ob as he looked back whence they came. "After that last twist in the tunnel, and diving down the way that it did, they're out of sight — even the glow from their torches. But they're not far back. I'd wager, in a straight run, they're not more than thirty or forty yards from us."

"That's too far to help us and too close to keep us out of trouble," whispered Dolan. "If we get jumped, they may not be able to get to us quickly enough. But we're more likely to get jumped with them making all that racket."

"You're right, laddie," said Ob. "But those lads

are moving as quiet-like as any man in armor can. It's this place. The echoes—"

"Then we should pull farther ahead. Far enough so that we can barely hear them. As long as we stick to the main passage we won't lose them and they won't lose us. But anything we creep up to, won't hear them first. If we give ourselves away, well, then so be it. I just don't want them giving us away. We're out on our own here."

"I can't argue with that logic, boy," said Ob. "But my instincts tell me that we should stay closer to the others, rather than farther off — even if it means we give away the element of surprise."

Dolan nodded. "I'll defer to you, Mister Ob."

They remained there for a few moments waiting for the glow of the main group's torches to creep into view. When it did they began to move but kept their pace slow and steady, Ob signaling Dolan each time the glow behind them faded.

And then suddenly Ob's torch went out.

It didn't fizzle or pop, fade out, or burn down to a nub. It instantly went out; not even glowing embers left behind.

41

SVARTLEHEIM

FREM

It only took Frem a moment to realize that the boulder the elves pushed over the edge wasn't just hurtling down the rocky slope at random, it was headed straight at him. Frem swung to his left, fast as he could. Pressed his body and face tightly up against the rock.

The boulder whizzed by his head. So close was it, he felt the breeze as it passed. He felt it even more than he saw it, it was so close. He tucked the back of his head against the slope, thankful for his helmet, and kept moving. Most of the men below were moving faster. Pulling away from him. They wanted to get off that slope just as much as he did. Frem was close to being out on his own, in a spot from which it was nigh impossible to fight. He had to get out of there. The next rock bounced on a little outcropping above his head and arced directly over him. It must have weighed twenty or thirty pounds. As fast as it was moving, if it had hit him solidly, he'd have been done for.

While he was still thinking about that, a stone smashed him atop the helmet. A small one it was, thank the gods. It startled him; made him almost lose his footing. Made a huge clang as it deflected off the metal, but in truth, did him no harm. Then he saw a hail of stones start to rain down, several at a time. The little buggers must have lined up atop the slope, shoulder to shoulder, and started tossing every stone that they could put their grubby hands on. Frem slid down a good ten feet on purpose, to bring him close to another outcropping. He ducked behind it even as another stone bounced off his shoulder plate. That hit felt like a battle hammer had blasted into him. His arm wasn't broken, so he ignored the pain, just as he'd been trained to do. He ducked under the outcropping.

Clang went the rocks as they hit someone's armor.

Bang.

Clang.

Men yelled in pain.

They cursed.

One screamed. His voice trailed away as he fell to his death.

But after a few moments it was over. Frem figured that the elves ran out of loose rock. There was only so much of that sitting up there within easy reach.

He heard them scuttling about, the elves. Some were making their way down. No doubt, they could move far faster in that environment than Frem ever could. Frem had no interest in dying. His little daughter, Coriana, needed him. She was waiting for him back home. He'd been away too long already. He couldn't just never show up again. He couldn't. He started down the slope, sliding as much as stepping or climbing. He had to get down to the bottom. There was no way he could fight any group of elves on that slope. No way. One or two, he could take. But not a half dozen. Not a squadron. And that and more was what was coming. If he had to face so many, he needed to do it with his feet firmly planted on the ground, sword and shield in hand.

Frem caught up to the rearguard as he neared the bottom. He, Royce, Lex, Ward, and Ma-Grak held position at the bottom of the slope. The rest of the Pointmen had gone on ahead, down a tunnel decidedly smaller than those they'd been in.

Fint Lugron lay at the bottom of the slope, broken and bloody but not quite dead. One arm and both legs bent unnaturally, at least two compound fractures. He wasn't going anywhere.

"Can you see them?" said Royce looking back up the slope.

"I can hear them," said Ward.

"Two minutes up, I mark them," said Frem.

"I mark it as three," said Royce.

The men all looked to each other. The unspoken question, what to do about Fint? His breathing was labored, but his eyes were open. He was conscious, mumbling something. Probably a prayer. Unlike most Lugron, Fint had religion, and was always praying and such. Frem didn't know who he prayed to, but he hoped that they were listening.

"I'll carry him," said Ward.

"He's on Valhalla's doorstep," said Royce.

Frem pulled out his dagger and dropped to one knee beside Fint.

Fint's eyes were watery, blood spattered on his

face. "Do it, Captain," he said.

"No, let me carry him," said Ward.

"Don't let them elves get me, Captain," said Fint. "Beg you."

Frem knew that if they carried him, he'd slow them down such that the elves would catch them, and they'd all get dead. Even if they got lucky and got clear, Fint was a goner. Too many bad wounds. Out in the wild, no man could survive that. More likely than not, he'd be dead within minutes from blood loss. So they couldn't take him. And Frem wouldn't leave him behind. Not for the elves to make sport with. Never would he let that happen to one of his men.

So Frem cut his throat.

Then he plunged his dagger through Fint's chest. Into his heart.

He pulled the blade out and stood up. "Let's go."

Frem and his rearguard darted down the tunnel, hoping to put as much distance as they could between them and the elves before the elves got down the slope. So narrow was the tunnel that they had to go in single file. Frem couldn't stand straight up in it, though the others could, if barely.

As they ran down the tunnel, their way lit only by a small torch that Ward held, Frem wondered whether they'd lost the main group. Running as they were, he couldn't hear them, and with the twists and turns of the tunnel, he couldn't see them or their light.

What if he stumbled? And the others pulled ahead? In moments, they'd be out of sight and he'd be plunged into darkness. Would he even be able to get a torch lit before the elves were on him? He should've lit his own torch.

He looked over his shoulder time and again as they made their way. Each time, he expected to see the elf pack hounding his heels.

But each time there was nothing.

Nothing but the darkness. Those elves that followed them didn't have the speed or stealth of those they fought in the tunnels earlier. The elves' best warriors were dead. Frem figured, they were reserves, perhaps little trained. Frem reached into his pack and grabbed a small torch, not one of the ones hastily made at the monastery, but one that he carried with him always, for just such occasions. It was made to last many hours, and would stay lit in harsh conditions. He lit it from Ward's torch. Just that bit of extra light and heat made a big difference. Reduced his tension a bit, and he needed that. Traveling in such environs, enemies at your heels, the psychological battle was as tough as the physical.

The tunnel that they were in grew smaller and smaller the farther that they went, and continued down, sometimes dropping off such that they had to climb, but only for short distances, nothing like that great slope they passed. Frem had to turn sideways or duck his head, and sometimes even double over to get through certain areas. They past many side tunnels. Hundreds. All were small. Some were tiny, too small for a man. Who knows if they led anywhere. Frem had no interest in going down any rabbit holes. He prayed to Odin that the tunnel would open back up. They had to be heading somewhere, given that welcome sign that they passed at the Eye of Gladden. Perhaps they'd taken a wrong turn in the darkness. Maybe that's why the elf pursuit had lessened. Maybe they were headed toward a dead end or into a maze of tunnels that they'd not have time to get out of before they lost their light. And Frem couldn't even confer with Putnam. Hell, he didn't even know if everyone was still on the same path for despite their pace, they hadn't caught up to the others. All he could do was hope that the Pointmen were up ahead and that he'd soon catch up to them.

As the minutes wore on, and his fatigue grew, the air grew close and stale, yet it remained cold as winter, his breath rising before him.

He heard something behind him.

Elves!

A black dagger, curved and deadly, thrust at him in the dark.

42

SVARTLEHEIM, JUTENHEIM

OB

"What happened?" whispered Dolan a moment after the torchlight disappeared.

Before Ob answered, he heard the muted sound of Dolan pulling his sword from its sheath. The boy wasn't taking any chances.

"Went out by itself–" began Ob.

Then came a whistling. Not like the wind, but like a man whistling — a strange pitch to it, the tune unknown. It started out slow, a forlorn, haunting sound to it. A lament. But then its tempo sped up and grew louder. Its sound went manic and built to a frenzy. The acoustics of the tunnels were confounding; from which direction the whistling came was impossible to say. How far off the whistler was, unknown.

"Get it re-lit," hissed Dolan. "He's close; we need to see."

Ob's hand was already in his pouch, rummaging for his flint and steel and the jar of lamp oil that he kept stashed therein.

The whistling abruptly ended, but in its place came a voice — a whispering on the tunnel's breath, which grew louder and more ominous by the moment. A strange sound it was — a language clear enough, but one unknown to all but the learned few. Ob knew it at once.

Svartish, or Svartlespeak, as the gnomes called it. The language of the black elves. Some few men like Ob could understand it (if only in bits), but none could speak it, for a man's throat, be he Volsung, elf, gnome, dwarf, or small folk, could never form such sounds.

They were out there, the black elves, cursing them, taunting them, threatening them. No doubt, the little buggers were creeping up on them. And then Ob realized that it was a single voice that assailed them, and it was not just speaking, it was chanting – a discordant sound, oppressive to the ears. Oddly, even though it was not overly loud, it hurt Ob's ears and sent shooting pains through his head. He even began to feel nauseous. The hair atop his head (what little he had left) stood on end; his beard did the same.

Ob knew the signs; there was no mistaking them. Magic was in the air.

Dark magic.

Black elfin sorcery.

That told Ob that they were facing no ordinary Svart. Their foe was a Diresvart – one of the accursed dark sorcerers of Thoonbarrow.

"It's a stinking wizard," said Ob.

"I know," said Dolan. "We need that light."

Still fiddling with his firestarters, Ob heard a shifting of rocks. Not the stones that littered the tunnel floor being kicked by skulking elves, but heavy rock, moving, shifting, crunching. Scattered all along the tunnel's length, there were more than a few boulders that you'd have to step around or climb over, but that didn't account for what they were hearing. Ob couldn't make sense of it.

The rocky sounds came from behind them — from back towards the main party. But there was no glow from the others' torches, and the sounds were close; too close to be their friends.

Ob poured his oil flask over the torch's remnant. Then sparks flew as he hit his flint against the steel: once, twice, and a third time. The sparks washed over the oil-soaked torch, sizzling as they touched it, but the torch did not ignite. Ob tried again and then again.

"I can't get it. Makes no sense."

Then he heard the cackling. A strange high-pitched sound. The devil's own laughter. The Diresvart mocked him. And then Ob figured out why. Its magic was still at work on the torch; it would never light, no matter his efforts. He dropped it and pulled out his axe. The black elf was close; close enough to see Ob — it had to be. One strike was all Ob needed; he'd cleave the bugger in half if only the wizard had the guts or the stupids to get close enough.

Then Ob started when he heard glass break nearby his feet, and suddenly a large swath of the tunnel, centered on he and Dolan, was ablaze with blinding light – light as bright as the noonday sun. Half a heartbeat after the light appeared, Ob heard Dolan's bow firing. The arrow zipped over Ob's head, even as he realized that a shadow of something large loomed high on the tunnel's walls and moved toward him. Ob felt disoriented, his eyes stinging, unadjusted to the intense light. As he blinked and tried to get his bearings, squinting in attempt to make out the Diresvart, he thought he saw the very rock of the tunnel walls moving, shifting, as if they were alive. As if the mountain had come alive in answer to the Diresvart's evil call. Dolan fired again; the shaft passed close to Ob's left ear.

It wasn't the walls that moved. Something was coming out of the walls. Something large, massive. Something that looked like the stones of the tunnels, except that it was not lifeless rock, it was something else. Something that shouldn't exist. Something that wanted them dead.

43

SVARTLEHEIM, JUTENHEIM

CLARADON

Par Tanch gently tapped Claradon's shoulder as they walked along the shadowy tunnel side-by-side. "Lord Theta was quite rude to me," whispered the wizard, who uncharacteristically hadn't spoken a word of smalltalk since they started down the tunnels almost two hours earlier.

Claradon's face flushed; he looked to see if Theta had overheard. The tall knight walked three rows ahead of them and with the noise from so many armored men trudging along, he couldn't possibly have heard that whisper, or at least no normal man could have, but with Theta, you never knew.

Claradon wouldn't have been surprised to spy Theta gazing back at the them, those steel blue eyes boring through them, his brows pressed together and arched up the way they did whenever he grew displeased. Claradon had seldom had that look directed at him, though he'd seen it directed elsewhere all too often. He preferred to keep it at bay.

"Tanch," said Claradon, his voice so quiet that the wizard had to lean in to hear him, "he wasn't trying to insult you, or anybody. He just wanted to line up the troops in proper order."

"Proper order?" said Tanch, his voice growing slowly louder as he spoke. "Then why am I at the front? I'm not a warrior. Is he trying to get me killed? And you too?"

"Keep your voice down," said Claradon, his eyes wide, his hand gesturing for Tanch to close his mouth.

"Haven't you suffered enough on this quest?" said Tanch. "What do you think is going to happen when we catch up to the Leaguers? Do you think Theta and half a dozen men will keep them off us? We'll be right in the thick of it. I'll probably get dead in the first exchange and you might too. And for what? Why not put the knights ahead of us? Or even the archers? You should be at the center, where it's safest."

"It's madness. He acts like he's planning, like he has a strategy, but he doesn't. He's reckless. He's just trying to control everything. Everybody. It's all about him. Our lives mean nothing to him."

"Wanting you and Glimador near the front and close to him so that he can direct your magics isn't reckless," said Claradon. "It's smart."

"It's about control," said Tanch. "About getting his way. Usurping command from you. We shouldn't stand for this. You shouldn't. My back can't take much more of this stress; my head and my hands even less." Tanch held out one arm; even in the dark Claradon could see that the wizard's hand and much of his forearm were still red and blistered.

"The man knows things," whispered Claradon. "More than the rest of us. More even than Ob.

Maybe more than Sir Gabriel. I'd be a fool if I didn't make the most of that knowledge."

"That's what he thinks of you, you know? That you're a fool. That we all are. Use him all you want, but you need not turn over command to him. Your father would never have done that. He'd never approve of it. If you—"

"Enough," said Claradon, his brow now furrowed. He nearly bumped into Glimador's back; the men up front had halted. Claradon thought little of that, for they'd stopped a score of times since they started down into the tunnels. Each time, to navigate over or around some obstacle in the main tunnel or to send a scout to take a quick look-see down one of the side passages.

But then Claradon saw Theta's hand signal to go silent.

"What's that rumbling?" whispered Tanch. "An earthquake! Dead gods, the mountain is not about to erupt, is it? We're sitting ducks in these infernal tunnels. We'll be buried alive and—-"

And then there were shouts of alarm from behind. And screams of pain. The screams of dying men.

44

SVARTLEHEIM

FREM

Frem and his men moved quickly through the tunnels. Fast but not reckless. They watched their footing, for a twisted ankle was a death sentence in that place. They watched their flanks, wary of the occasional side tunnel. Frem kept his ears open for any sounds from behind, and he kept looking back whenever he had the chance. It was difficult, moving quickly like that in the dark, and still keeping alert. Frem was probably as good at it as most anyone, save for expert trackers like Moag. Yet the elves snuck right up on him.

Stealthy little buggers.

Frem heard something or else caught some glimpse of motion out of the corner of his eye — even he couldn't say which. He spun about, hand up defensively.

As a black dagger came at him out of the dark, seeking purchase in his flesh, he sidestepped and backpedaled.

Quick as that blade was, Frem was a hair quicker and evaded it. The elf came on again, but now Frem's dagger was in his hand. A thrust took the elf in the throat, the creature blinded by Frem's torch. It fell out of Frem's sight.

There were more elves behind. Frem dropped

the torch, pulled the shield from his back, and planted it before him. Due to the narrowness of the tunnel, that shield formed a wall. The elves would have to move Frem to breach it.

An elf came at him, slashing high, over the shield. A clumsy attempt. The fellow didn't know what he was doing. Frem put his dagger through the top of the elf's head. When it fell, he saw how wrinkled was its face, how shriveled its body. An elder. Ancient by any measure.

Frem didn't want to fight the black elves at all. He certainly didn't want to fight old folk. But they gave him no choice. Royce passed him a pike and moved up beside him as best he could in the narrow confines. The elves charged, five or six of them. "Go," said Frem to the men behind him. "Catch up to the others."

"I'm not leaving you," said Royce.

"I don't need help with these," said Frem as he skewered the first elf that came in. It practically ran itself onto the pike.

"Go before you lose the light," said Frem.

Royce stuck his pike in the next elf that came on, then turned and went after the others. Eight more elves came forward. Six fell to Frem's pike in a series of lightning thrusts. One fell to his dagger. The last leaped at him, spitting and biting. Frem's hand clamped down on its throat. His other hand grabbed its weapon arm and squeezed and twisted until it dropped its dagger. Frem couldn't see much in the general darkness, but he saw enough to know that the elf was female and young. When he saw her face, Coriana came to his mind. Why, he couldn't say, for that black elf resembled her not in the least. He had no interest in killing a female. Especially not one that was little more than a child.

"Why do you fight us?" said Frem. "Why?" he said, not expecting any answer, at least not one he could understand.

But the elf spoke. "Because evil you," said the elf in Lomerian, though with an accent harsh and strong. "Killers. Stop you we."

Frem stared down at her, keeping an eye to the tunnel behind her, checking for more of her kind. He heard them. The scurrying feet in the dark. More were coming. Maybe too many this time.

He was no murderer. He wasn't evil. Though he knew full well that some of the Leaguers were. Some of the leaders.

"How do I get out of here? Out of these tunnels, to the outside? Tell me and I will let you live?"

The black elf smiled, victory in her eyes. "You leave Starkbarrow not. You die here. You die here."

Frem slammed the ridge of his hand to the back of her neck — hard enough to stun her, perhaps knock her out, but not hard enough to break her neck or spine, which he could easily have done, if he so chose. He dropped her, grabbed his torch and gear, and ran.

Fifty yards down the tunnel, Frem had to double over, the ceiling down to four feet or so. That lasted for a hundred feet at least before it opened up again. Just beyond that the tunnel ended in a hole in the floor.

Frem looked down. Royce and Ward were just about to exit at the bottom, some fifty feet below. They saw him and he waved them away to keep going. He scrambled down the hole. The confines were so tight and the walls so pitted it was not that hard a climb. What made it challenging was the darkness, the need to hold the torch, and the fact that if the elves appeared before he got to the bottom, he'd likely get stones dropped on his head. Frem was sweating, his heart thumping in his chest; he could feel the pulse pounding at his neck. He had to make the bottom before the elves got to the top.

Just as he reached the bottom, he heard them. And he saw their light. The buggers carried torches too. So they couldn't see perfectly in the dark after all. Good to know.

The tunnel twisted and turned at the bottom of that shaft. Five feet high and narrow, barely wide enough for Frem to get through.

And then it wasn't.

Even sideways, Frem reached a spot that with his armor on he was too wide to squeeze through. He noticed that the uneven walls were a bit wider apart near the floor, so he dropped down and crawled. He got hung up for a moment and nearly panicked. Then he pushed through, but the elf pack was all the closer for it. Small as they were, they could run freely past such obstacles. Truth be told, most men could too. Usually Frem's size was a great advantage to him. Not so in Svartleheim.

Another few hundred yards in, the tunnel began sloping steeply down. Soon Frem spotted light up ahead. He'd caught up to the others. But why? Something had slowed them.

"Ahoy," Frem called before approaching the lit area.

"Come through," said a voice — Sir Carroll's.

Frem went forward, shield before him, pike at the ready, just in case.

The passage opened up into a small round chamber a couple of hundred square feet in size. Three men were there. Sir Carroll, one arm limp at his side, looking even more battered than he had when Frem had last seen him. And two men from 4th Squadron: Sir Grant, with a similar wound to Carroll's and some broken ribs; and Gilb Lugron, broken leg — he sat propped against the wall, a short spear in hand.

Frem quickly scanned the chamber. Only one exit. A hole in the wall that they'd have to belly crawl through.

"The others?" said Frem. "Royce, Lex, and Ward?"

"Through the hole they all went," said Carroll. "The whole squadron. We couldn't, so here we are."

"There must be another way," said Frem.

"There's no side tunnels bigger than this hole all the way back to that long drop," said Carroll. "And I'm not climbing back up that with one arm. Best you go through while you can, Captain."

Frem looked the men over. None of their wounds were fatal. Not nearly. They'd die here only because they couldn't crawl through the tunnel with their injuries and there was no time to try to pull them through.

"Putnam didn't want to leave us, Captain, but

he had to," said Carroll. "And so do you. There's plenty of fight left in us. We'll buy you a good bit of time before they pass us."

"We'll give them what for, Captain Frem," said Grant. "And see you again some time up Valhalla way."

"Get you gone, Captain," said Gilb. "You got more to do today. Them others need you. Mission still needs finishing."

Frem heard the elves coming. It sounded like a lot of them.

In every man's life there comes times when he has to make important choices. Choices that define him. Choices that make him the man that he is. Frem had a duty. He had a mission. An important one. He had to live to accomplish that. And he had to live to get back to his daughter. To see her again. But he also had a duty to these men. To not abandon them to die. What to do?

45

SVARTLEHEIM, JUTENHEIM

OB

Ob backpedaled, tripped over a boulder behind him, and landed on his rump. Dolan was beside him; he shot a third arrow. Ob watched it slam into the moving stone and bounce harmlessly off. And as Ob looked up, he was able to make out the thing's shape. Its form vaguely resembled that of a man, in that it had a head, two arms, a torso, and two legs — all made of dark gray basalt — the ancient, solidified lava of the tunnels — of Jutenheim's origin. The thing had a gaping maw from which smoke and wisps of flame spewed. It groaned, that monstrosity did; a moaning, deep and dark, as if it were a living creature and not some construct puppeted by the Diresvart's magic.

Ob felt icy tendrils moving up and down his spine, his throat constricted, and deep inside, his guts twisted into knots. It was fear assaulting him. The old enemy. It commanded him to freeze, ordered him to stop, demanded that he not resist — for a devil of the nether realms lumbered toward him, conjured up by the dark sorcery of Thoonbarrow — an evil beyond the ken of any goodly man. Another creature out of legend and nightmare.

If he gave up, if he surrendered, perhaps the fiend would let him live, or at least, agree to spare his immortal soul.

"We've got to get gone," said Dolan as he grabbed at Ob's shoulder. "We can't take that thing. Weapons no good against stone."

Ob hesitated a moment, just a moment, then pushed aside his fears, blasted those thoughts from his mind just as he had done a thousand times before. He scrambled to his feet, his heart racing. "Run," he said. "Just run!"

The bright light that flooded the tunnel dimmed by the moment. After they'd taken but a few strides, its intensity dropped to no more than that of a bright lantern. Shadows loomed all around them but they could see. The light emanated from a strange artifact that Dolan gripped in his hand. It was several inches long and flat, though it was too bright to focus on. And then Ob remembered that Dolan and Theta had used the same devices in the Vermion forest, in the old temple. Whether they were products of some olden magic that Theta had dug up, or the labors of alchemists and tinkers, Ob did not know. All that mattered, was that Dolan had one handy, or maybe it was the same one — who knew? Thank Odin for their bags of tricks.

They were running. Running. But every step they took Ob felt as if the tunnel were about to collapse upon them. The stone creature plodded after them. It picked up its pace with each stride. Moved faster than any massive thing should ever move. The Diresvart laughed its devilish laugh.

And the tunnel shuddered.

Stone shards fell from the ceiling and from the walls. Dust polluted the air. Choked their lungs. Clouded their vision. Ob nearly lost his footing several times as the tunnel's floor bucked beneath his feet when the creature took a step. It filled the tunnel, that thing did, even where the ceiling's height rose to nearly ten feet and its width to nearly eight.

Ob and Dolan leapt over rock and boulder, the passage sloping down, down, down; the grade growing steeper with every yard. But on they ran – directly away from their companions, from their friends, from the only help and hope that they had in the deep dark of Svartleheim.

After they'd run for a minute or more, the stench of death grew pungent and close. The smell was nauseating. But closer still came the creature. They had no choice but to continue on, for there was nowhere to go besides the main passage. And there was nowhere to hide.

The tunnel opened up into a good-sized chamber, high ceilinged and generally round. That's where the bodies were. Bodies of Svarts, monks, and soldiers – some men in red plate armor, others in chainmail. Dozens of corpses were there. And by the smell, all dead two days or more. The carnage was a frightful sight. The dead were variously stabbed and hacked, crushed and decapitated. A terrible battle. Which side had won, and even who fought who, was not at all clear, and Ob and Dolan had no time to study the scene. They rushed past the bodies, stepping between them where they could, on them where they had to. The only exit from the chamber was on the opposite side from the tunnel they entered through. The main passage continued on that way. But there was a problem. A big problem.

Just a few feet down the passage beyond the circular chamber, a tremendous rockfall had collapsed the tunnel. That cave-in had blocked all passage forward through the main tunnel. No side tunnel in sight; no door; no hidden passage; no hidey-hole in floor, wall, or ceiling that they could see. A dead end. Nowhere else to go, save back the way they came. And that's the way they went, and wasted no time about it. They had to find some side passage or some hole to hide in until the creature passed them by. Otherwise, they were trapped, good and proper. Trapped with a beast that they had no way to fight.

The thunderous beat of the creature's feet as they slammed the stone floor shook the tunnel. It was coming. It was near.

They ran for their lives.

They had barely entered the tunnel, back whence they came, when the stone creature emerged from the shadows, its great feet booming against the tunnel floor. Thump. Thump. Thump.

There was no side passage in sight. Nowhere to hide. Nowhere to run to. And no way past the creature, the monstrosity. A thing of magic, Ob marked it – a wizard's construct – but whether it be rightly called an elemental, a goblin, a homunculus, or some other, Ob could not say. Maybe Tanch could've named it. Maybe Theta. But it was beyond Ob and Dolan. All they knew for certain, was that no weapon at their command could damage, little less destroy, rock. Their weapons would break on it, and probably do it no harm at all.

And so they were trapped. Ob backpedaled, then turned and ran for the circular chamber.

"Douse the light," said Ob. "Get down in a corner and play dead."

Dolan closed his hand tightly around the glowing light stick, but that barely dimmed it; the light escaped between his fingers. He shoved it into an inner pocket, beneath his leather cuirass, but even then, he had to lie face down to stop the glow from escaping and giving away his position.

Before Dolan shuttered his light, Ob dashed to a spot along the chamber's wall where two red armored knights and a Lugron had fallen. Despite the cold, the bodies stunk. Ob lay down behind them, breathing through his mouth so he wouldn't gag, his back tight up against the wall, congealed blood beneath and beside him. Dolan was ten feet away, hiding along the wall; he doused the light. All the while, the tunnel and chamber rumbled and vibrated with the stone creature's thunderous footsteps. In the distance, Ob heard shouts. He imagined someone calling his name, though the voices were too far off, too indistinct to hope to make out, even for one with gnomish hearing. But there was no denying that voices were raised in alarm — the voices of many men. Ob tried to listen for the distinctive sounds of battle, of the clash of arms, but the stone creature's rumblings drowned any such sounds out.

Then he heard the explosions. Magical blasts

they were. Tanch's work? Or mayhap Glimador's? Or the Diresvart's?

Ob didn't know. And there was no way to tell. But he did know that the stone creature was much closer than those sounds. That meant that there were more enemies out there — not just the one that they faced. They were cut off from their comrades but good. Out on their lonesomes. And blind as bats.

46

SVARTLEHEIM

FREM

"**G**et you gone," said Gilb to Frem.

"We'll hold them back as long as we can," said Carroll, as he took position with his pike, Grant beside him. Gilb pulled himself to his feet, propped against the wall to hold his balance.

Frem turned toward the entry, raised his shield and readied his pike. "No," said Frem. "I will stand with you."

Grant smiled. "Then we will drink in Odin's hall together tonight, Captain."

"I hope the stinking Valkries can find us down here," said Carroll.

On came the elves in a mad rush, shouting, screaming, gibbering, black swords slashing and stabbing.

Most of them had no idea what they were doing. They didn't even know how to hold a sword, little less fight with one. Some, in their frenzy, stabbed their fellows with their blades, on accident. Old folk were some, the rest, females, untrained in combat. But they all had swords, daggers, axes. And every one of them was intent on killing Frem and his men. They rushed the room with no regard for themselves or their fellows. Ran right into the Sithian pikes and swords. For all their size, skill, and experience, Frem and the knights beside him couldn't hold them back. They came in too fast. Too many.

Frem didn't want to fight them. He didn't want to kill old people and women. He protected such people — any non-combatants whoever they were. That's what he'd always done. Protected people. Looked out for those smaller and weaker than he — which in truth was almost everyone. Only in his time traveling with Ginalli and his League of Shadows had he been involved with matters of questionable morality. And even then, it was not Frem that had done any black deeds. Never Frem.

What choice did he have with the elves? They were not non-combatants after all. They were the ones doing the attacking, wielding the weapons, out for blood. He shouted at them to stop. To go back. They didn't listen, if even they heard in the chaos of the battle. No doubt, few, if any amongst them understood a word he said, their language even more different, more alien, than their appearance. So it was kill or be killed.

Given that, the choice was clear.

So long as they came on, he'd kill them. If need be, he'd kill them all.

The small bodies piled up around the knights. The elves stood upon their fallen to get better reach. For all the knights' skills, they were hampered with Carroll and Grant having only one functional arm each. But they were well protected by their plate armor. A hundred times in that battle Frem heard the characteristic clank of the plate being hit by sword, dagger, or axe. More than a few times, but far less than his share, those impacts hit Frem.

His armor held. It was the heaviest type of plate armor made in Lomion. Constructed by a master smith in Dvyers to Frem's specifications. The elfin weapons could not hope to pierce it. But in their folly they tried and tried again. The elves paid little heed to the harder to reach but far more vulnerable areas. They should have gone for the joints at back of knee, at top of thigh, at the elbow, the underarm, the neck. They should have gone for the face. But they didn't; not many times, anyway. Because they didn't know any better. They were amateurs. Not trained in battle. Still, even Frem's more vulnerable spots were well protected with overlapping plates, stout chainmail, and layers of thick padded cloth. They might have got through if they tried hard enough, and distracted Frem's attention for long enough. But they didn't.

Frem's arms grew heavy as he swung his blade over and over and banged his shield into the elves, using it for offense as much as for defense. Slowly the elfin onslaught backed the knights up, a step here and then there, until they had their backs to the wall.

Frem didn't know what happened to Grant. At some point, he just wasn't there anymore. He and Carroll kept fighting and fighting. Frem found himself protecting Carroll more and more with his shield as the wounded man wearied to the point he could barely hold up his blade. The ranks of the elves thinned, but still they came on, howling and screaming, as if they didn't notice or didn't care about the slaughter around them.

They never stopped. They never gave up, the elves didn't. Even when there were only a handful left, still they came, howling, and cursing them in their strange language. And then it was over.

There were no more elves. All were down or dead.

Frem looked from side to side. Some of the elves were moaning, calling out, presumably for aid, but most of them were dead.

Carroll dropped to the floor beside Frem. He pulled out his dagger and stabbed every elf within reach to make certain that they were dead. Then he closed his eyes and lay back against the wall, his breathing labored, drenched in sweat.

Frem couldn't see Grant. He was buried somewhere under a heap of fallen elves. Gilb Lugron was slumped against the wall, in the very spot he'd started out at. He was dead. His pike was clear through the bodies of two elves. His dagger lay bloodied in his hand. Nearly a score of dead elves heaped around him. His throat sliced open. An elfin sword was stuck into his underarm. Another was embedded in his thigh.

Frem had a fleeting image flash through his mind of Gilb and Grant raising flagons and drinking their fill beside the honored dead in Valhalla. He hoped that they were.

Frem's strength was gone. He'd reached his limit. But he stood his ground there. Shield and dagger still in hand and at the ready. He listened. Were there more elves coming? He didn't hear any. He didn't think so. But there was enough moaning and groaning in that chamber of death that he couldn't tell for certain. The floor was awash with blood, inches deep. That's when Frem first realized that the elfin blood was cold. Cold to the touch. As cold as the caverns themselves. Not warm like the blood of a man or an animal. More akin to that of a fish or a reptile.

The smell in the place was horrific, owing to the disemboweled bodies. Frem slumped down atop one of the dead elves to avoid sitting in the pooled blood. He didn't like doing that, but he had to.

Frem had seen a lot in his time. A lot of horrors. Far beyond what most warriors ever saw. But this was something new. A horror that he would not soon forget. He closed his eyes and tried to steady his breathing. His clothes clung to him, dripping, sopping wet, his hair too. Blood covered his hands, his arms, his torso, tabard, everything. He was as red, head to toe, as was Carroll's Sithian plate armor. He couldn't move. He didn't want to. Two torches still lit the room, though it was heavily shadowed, and one torch sputtered, threatening to go out. Neither of them was Frem's special torch. He'd have to try to find that one and relight it. He figured he was going to need it, assuming that he didn't die outright from exhaustion, and that none of the fallen elves crept up on him and cut his throat.

He figured, he'd sit there a while. Try to catch his breath. Then he wondered whether he was wounded, bleeding. Whether if he closed his eyes, he'd ever open them again. Strange, he hadn't even thought of being wounded up until then. He hurt all over. He was covered in so much blood, and wrapped in his armor, how could he even tell if he was bleeding badly? His arms worked; his legs worked; he was breathing. He figured that that was good enough.

47

SVARTLEHEIM, JUTENHEIM

CLARADON

"To arms," shouted Claradon.

"What's happening?" said Tanch.

"The rear guard is getting hit," said Artol. "I'm heading back there."

Claradon turned back toward the front of the troop, expecting to see Theta wading through the men, making his way toward the rear. But he wasn't. He and the men around him were poised on the balls of their feet, weapons to hand, peering this way and that down the darkened tunnel. They'd seen or heard something up ahead. Something that riveted their attention more than whatever mayhem went on at the rear of the troop.

And then the very stone of the tunnel walls came alive around them.

All was cloaked in shadow, shouting, and chaos. Claradon saw something, something huge, like the wall of the tunnel itself, swat one of his men at the troop's vanguard. The thing was large and dark, and looked of stone. The man that it hit went flying across the tunnel to break against the far wall. A heartbeat later, another man suffered the same fate. Pikemen lunged at the thing — a huge, dark, stony shape that blocked the tunnel, a strange orange glow coming from up high on it. Claradon saw them drive their pikes into the thing's torso. Sparks erupted where the steel met stone, or whatever the thing was made of, but the weapons didn't sink in. Didn't do any damage.

And then Theta was at the thing, his midnight blue armor gleaming in the torchlight, his falchion in hand. Big as he was, Theta was dwarfed by that monstrosity, both in height and bulk. He charged straight up to it, fearless, sword swinging, shield held high. More sparks spouted when Theta's falchion hit the thing. Over and over he pounded it, his strikes so fast that the thing had little time to react, but that seemed to matter little, for the blows had no effect.

Claradon advanced. He'd help Theta as best he could with what magics he commanded. He needed to get closer. His first instinct was to pull his sword and wade into the action. He was a warrior first, a spell thrower second, if even that. His command of the Militus Mysterious was limited in depth and breadth, and focused on supplementing and supporting his martial attacks. But in that instance, seeing the ineffectiveness of Theta's weapons, Claradon knew that his sword and martial skills were useless. Only his sorcery might help. If even that.

Tanch grabbed Claradon's arm and sought to hold him back. The wizard shouted something at him. Told him to stop. To stay back. That he was going to get himself killed. Claradon pulled his arm free, blocked out the wizard's voice, and concentrated on the battle before him. There was fighting to be done, his men were in trouble, and by the gods, he'd do his part. Let Tanch go cower in a hole somewhere, but he'd not do that.

Claradon heard a loud crash, and then Theta rocketed through the air toward him. The creature had swatted him, just as it had the other men. Claradon dived down, but Theta's boot clipped him as he flew by. Claradon hit the tunnel floor hard. Stunned for only a moment, Claradon couldn't believe what had just happened. He turned and saw that Theta had crashed through several rows of men, bowling them over, before coming to a halt. Claradon couldn't tell whether Theta and the others were alive or dead. There was definitely more fighting going on farther back in the tunnel, but Claradon couldn't see it, though the sounds were clear enough. He quickly made his feet.

Most of the torches were down. He'd lost track of Tanch and hoped that Theta hadn't crushed him as he flew by. One moment the wizard was pulling him, the next he was gone. The whole thing happened in a handful of heartbeats.

Claradon looked to the front and found himself facing the stone creature who had continued to advance up the tunnel. It stood slightly stooped, too tall to stand fully upright in the ten foot high space. Its width nearly as wide as the tunnel.

No man stood between Claradon and that thing. And no one stood at Claradon's side. He saw that at least a few of the men that had been up ahead still lived, but they were off their feet, and in no condition to help him. It was all they could do to scramble back from the creature to avoid being crushed by it as it advanced.

For the moment at least, Claradon was on his own.

Despite the greater darkness within the tunnel, Claradon could see the creature better now, for its head glowed crimson and gold, orange and yellow, the fires of Helheim simmering in its toothless maw. The thing looked to be made of living stone. Eyes of black. Hairless. Unclothed. Nothing but cold stone.

The creature stepped toward him and as it did, Claradon heard an otherworldly cackling coming from who knows where. He didn't know what that sound was, and for the moment, he didn't care. He fixed his concentration on tapping the wellspring of power that was the Grand Weave of Magic. For all his training, Claradon was a novice to the world of magic. He knew so few of the words and gestures that called its power down to Midgaard. But those few mystical words that he knew — he knew well. He spoke them as an expert; he bent them to his will, so skillfully had the masters of the Karadonian Chapterhouse drilled them into him. He mumbled his words of power; those he thought best for the occasion. Ancient words of the Militus Mysterious were they. Words he'd seldom used in anger before that quest, but now which had become all too common. As he spoke them, he raised his sword arm toward the ceiling. A sound like a lightning bolt filled the tunnel, crackling and booming with such fury that stones fell from the roof of the tunnel. Then from out of the ether roared a blast of blueish flame from on-high that engulfed the stone creature, washing over it, head to toe. The flames appeared from nowhere, but did not disappear in an instant. They lingered for some moments, and poured over the creature like the fiery breath of a dragon from the *Age of Myth and Legend*. As the flames assailed it, the stone creature roared and thundered and pounded at the tunnel walls. Claradon's magic hit exactly where he'd aimed. He'd saved them all.

Moments later, the mystical flames fizzled out.

Nothing should have been left of the creature but a pile of ash or a bubbling soup of molten rock.

But it stood there still, the creature did, blocking the tunnel, as though nothing untoward had happened, though its entire body now glowed crimson hot. Fires burned here and there about the tunnel floor and Claradon heard the screaming of at least one man. A scream that lasted but a moment and died with its master. To his horror, Claradon saw that his conjuring had burned crispy two or three of his own men; one at least had been alive when his magic struck, the others, perhaps already dead from the creature's attacks. Unintentional though it was, Claradon had killed one of his own – an Eotrus man; a man who'd sworn an oath to fight and die for the great Lord of the Eotrus – for Claradon. And now he lay dead or dying by Claradon's own hand.

Claradon recalled Ob's words about the burdens of command; he remembered the lessons his father had taught him — about the hard choices Dor Lords faced; the burdens, the regrets. He buried those thoughts as quickly as he could; for loss of focus in battle was the swiftest path to Valhalla. Though he hoped to take that path one day, it was a journey he sought to put off for many years.

Within a few moments, the bright red glow of the stone creature turned to yellow, then orange, then brown, and then back to its original black. All except for its maw. That glowed orange and yellow, flames threatening to burst from it.

And then Claradon realized the folly of his flame attack, for he faced a creature born of flame as much as stone. The thing's mouth began to open and Claradon knew what was coming. He had nowhere to run or to hide.

There was no time.

48

SVARTLEHEIM

FREM

"Frem," said Carroll.

Frem's eyes popped open. Somehow, he'd fallen asleep. Fatigue or no, how that was possible after all the adrenalin that ran through his system, he didn't know. How long he was out for, he had no idea. Maybe only a few moments. Maybe much longer. Only one torch was left, and that gave him a clue. Half the room was dark, including most of the area directly around Frem and Carroll.

"We should move," said Carroll.

Frem nodded in exaggerated fashion to make certain that Carroll saw the movement. Then he listened for a few moments. Nothing but the scattered moaning of a few elf survivors. Frem hated those sounds — the sounds after a battle: the moaning, the crying, the wailing, the pleading, begging for help, the cursing — the terrible sounds of true pain, of true suffering. Of agony. He hated it. It was a thousand times worse to listen to those sounds than to fight the actual battle.

In battle, he knew exactly what to do. How to fight. How to win. How to stay alive.

But when it was over, what could he do? Help the wounded on his side? He was no leren. No healer. Help wounded enemies? That made little sense on the face of it, since they just did their best to kill each other. Yet somehow, it seemed the right thing to do. The human thing to do.

But if not help, then what? Kill them? That wasn't right. That wasn't honorable. How could it be? Yet Frem knew, on some occasions it had to be done: to ease the suffering of those fated to die that day anyway, to protect the survivors from enemies playing possum. But some men, they killed the wounded out of cruelty. Out of hatred. They enjoyed it. Frem had no stomach for that and no love or respect for any man that behaved that way. None at all.

Frem took up a pike and picked his way toward the fallen torch, worrying every step that one of the elves would strike out at him with dagger or knife, and find purchase with it.

He could've stabbed freely at the bodies, making certain that those he passed were dead, to protect himself. He'd be justified in doing so, wouldn't he? But he couldn't. He didn't have the heart.

Old folks. Women. That's who the dead elves were. Striking them when they were trying to kill him was one thing, stabbing them, even as they lay dead before him felt altogether different. He couldn't do it. It wasn't right.

So he made his way to the torch as best he could. He nudged the bodies he passed that were close enough to strike him, testing to see if any were wounded and lying in wait. But they weren't. They were all dead.

He retrieved the torch, but it wasn't the one

that he brought in with him. He needed that one — it would last several times as long as the common one he had just recovered. That extra light might mean the difference between getting out of the tunnels alive or not.

He stepped toward the entry, deciding to test his luck. He knew he dropped the torch just in front of where he, Carroll, and Grant had set their line. The entire floor in that area was piled high with corpses. He didn't want to touch them. He worried still of attacks. He didn't want to look at their faces.

Their dead faces.

Women, old and young.

Old men.

Unskilled.

People that had no business going to war. He had killed them. His throat constricted and his stomach churned. He could barely breathe. He focused on breathing. On staying calm. On keeping his breathing and heartbeat steady.

He picked each body up with one hand. It took him little effort, even tired, even drained. He'd moved a dozen before he found her. The girl he'd hit behind the head back in the other chamber. The one he'd let live — because he could.

She was alive.

She'd been trapped beneath the dead. A wonder that she could even take a breath beneath that gruesome heap. A big gash in the side of her skull. Enough to knock her out, but not to kill her. She tried to squirm away but there was nowhere to go, she was walled off, bodies of her fellows all around. She looked terrified.

Smoke rose from a few feet to her side — Frem's smoldering torch, buried beneath other bodies.

"Don't move," said Frem. Other than squirming, she didn't, maybe she couldn't. Maybe she understood him. Maybe she didn't. He tossed aside the other bodies and recovered the torch.

"On your right," said Carroll, his voice tense. "A live one."

"I see her," said Frem.

She looked so afraid. That strange alien face. The huge eyes, tiny mouth, bald pate. So unlike any Volsung girl, or a girl of any other race he knew. There was intelligence in those eyes. Emotion on that face. Feelings. Fear. Desperation. Hatred.

A girl.

Just a girl. A person with her whole life in front of her — if not for Frem and his fellows that came and destroyed her world.

She looked from side to side. He read disbelief on her face. And horror too. How had Frem and but three others killed so many of her folk?

But they had.

And now she was at his mercy once again.

"Lead us out of here," said Frem. "Out to the surface, and I'll let you live. We won't trouble you and yours any more. I—"

"You lie," said the elf girl. "You me kill as all and everyone. Evil. Evil," she said scrunching up her face and raising her voice.

"You people attacked us," said Frem.

"Invaders. Murderers. Evil."

"Do you want to live?" said Frem. "I'm giving

you a chance."

"I want kill invader, you."

"You can't kill me, but I can kill you," said Frem. "I can also let you live. Lead us out of here and I will."

Frem put the point of the pike up against the girl's throat to emphasize her peril, if she didn't understand it already. He wasn't going to stab her. He'd never do that. He just had to make her think he would. That would put the fear in her. Get her to cooperate.

The elf clenched her jaw. Then of a sudden she grabbed the pike's shaft and thrust herself up, stabbing the pike's tip through her own neck.

That blade was sharp. It sank deep, two or three inches, before Frem was able to pull it back. She was so small, her neck so slight, that was more than enough to do her in. Blood sprayed from the wound as Frem looked down in shock and horror. He stood there, frozen, until she stopped breathing. She had what looked like a smile on her face the whole time as she lay dying, blood pulsing from between her fingers. As if in killing herself, denying Frem his wish for a guide, she'd scored some victory against him. Her death at least had thwarted his wishes. A small victory indeed, but one that she was willing to die for.

Frem didn't understand it.

If he and his had been the aggressors, then maybe he could understand such hatred. But the elves had attacked them.

War often made no sense.

As a soldier, Frem knew, sometimes it was best not to think about it, and just to keep fighting.

That's what soldiers did. They just kept fighting. And if they were lucky, and the gods approved, they'd survive to fight another day.

Frem picked his way carefully back to Carroll who was now on his feet, checking his weapons and gear.

"Why do they hate us so?" said Carroll. "I mean, I understand them fearing us after what they've seen us do in battle. But the hatred. It seems like that came first. Why?"

"Maybe just because we're different," said Frem. "So different from them. Sometimes, that's all it takes. Or else, maybe, it's because of lies. Someone wanted them to hate us, so they made certain that they did, spreading stories about our evil deeds. Our atrocities. Stories that were naught but lies. Lies are the source of most hatred. And most misdeeds."

"Get Gilb's gear," said Frem. "All of it. I'll get Grant's."

"I can't go with you, Captain, same as I couldn't go with Putnam before. I can't crawl through that tunnel with one arm."

Frem pulled a rope from his pack. "You won't need to. I'm going to pull you along."

Carroll looked surprised. Perhaps a glimmer of hope shone in his eyes. "Even if you can, it'll slow you down too much."

"It may not matter any longer," said Frem. "It seems we've finished off all those that pursued us. It's been a while, and no more have come. With the gods' blessing, maybe we can move unmolested now, with only the tunnels as our enemy."

"Let's try it," said Carroll, "but I figure we haven't seen the last of the black elves."

Frem wrapped a rope through the arm loops of Carroll's shield and Carroll lay down upon it.

"Thank you, Captain," said Carroll. "I'd be dead now if not for you. I owe you."

"Yes, you do," said Frem with a smile.

49

SVARTLEHEIM, JUTENHEIM

OB

Ob went silent and still when he heard the stone creature lumber into the chamber; he feared to even breathe. He prayed that Dolan would stay hidden; the boy had too much guts for his own good, and was as likely as not to get up and take another useless shot at the thing.

Bones splintered when the creature stepped on one corpse, then another, and still more as it moved through the chamber, each corpse crushed to pulp in the monster's wake. Lying on the floor, Ob peeked above the shoulder of a dead man and he saw the creature. Saw it clearly. Orange and yellow flame danced in its maw and illumed the area around the creature. Wisps of smoke wafted from its mouth and hung heavy in the air. By all appearances, the thing was made of living stone, head to toe, save for the fiery mouth. Stone horns protruded from its forehead; great black eyes, lidless and menacing, sat above its maw, no nose, ears, or teeth to be seen. It turned its head from side to side, no doubt searching for Ob and Dolan, but it failed to spot them amid the darkness and the littered corpses. Then it lumbered toward the far tunnel that was blocked. Several bodies lay scattered within that collapsed passage, including one that was partly crushed beneath the rubble. The creature made a noise that sounded like a chuckle, as if it thought it had cornered its prey. It leaned back, its face upraised, its arms outstretched to the sides, and sucked in a great inhalation of air, the orange-yellow glow from its maw temporarily burning all the brighter, and its massive chest puffing out nearly half again its normal size. It leaned forward, and as it did, a continuous stream of flame roared from its mouth and raced down the tunnel. The flames slammed into the rockfall at the tunnel's end and billowed back over themselves, fully engulfing the whole of the short tunnel. That terrible flame blast continued for no less than ten heartbeats. The heat that came from it was terrible; Ob ducked down and shielded his face. Though he was more than thirty feet from the nearest flames, he felt as if he'd been dropped into a furnace. When the flames died, Ob popped his head up to look. The collapsed tunnel was empty — the corpses incinerated. The tunnel's rock walls were melted and deformed; molten rock, red-hot pooled about the tunnel's floor. But still, the passage remained blocked.

And then Dolan leapt upon the stone creature's back, dagger in hand.

"Oh shit," said Ob.

50

SVARTLEHEIM, JUTENHEIM

CLARADON

The stone creature's maw was opening. Claradon had nowhere to run, no cover to hide behind. And no magic that could counter a blast of fire. He'd soon join his father in Valhalla.

But then Tanch was there again, pulling him, shouting something. And Glimador. Good old cousin Glimador, with him at the end.

Glimador's hands weaved streaks through the air, magic manifesting around him, being drawn down through the ether by his will and his words — his mouth forming phrases from ancient high elvish — a language long dead but not forgotten. And when his words were done, he unleashed his sorcery. The magic coalesced into a shimmering wall of translucent blue energy, a bastion of mystical strength and protection, which appeared between the men and the stone creature. That wall hummed and vibrated and crackled, but stood firm from tunnel wall to tunnel wall, floor to ceiling; a supernatural shield to hold back the darkness.

And then came the creature's fiery breath. It exploded against Glimador's wall. Its flames thundered against it and blasted over it again and again.

Glimador strained against the force of those flames, his right arm outstretched, the source of his magic. His left arm braced the other, his knees bent, his legs firmly placed far apart. He would not yield. His face grew red and lined from the strain. Soon it was a mask of pain. Still he did not yield. The temperature rose within the tunnel; the magic wall could not keep all the thermal energy out. Smoke rose from the tunnel floor. The men picked themselves up and retreated from the heat; they backed away from the mystical wall. But Glimador stood firm. Claradon at his side. Tanch continued to try to pull Claradon away, but he would have none of it.

"He can't hold it," shouted Tanch. "We've got to retreat. We're—"

The stone creature's fire went out.

Glimador dropped to one knee, but his blue wall remained, though it fizzled and crackled and transient holes appeared in it. And still there was the inhuman cackling that came from all around.

And then the stone creature's fists began to beat upon the magic wall. A tentative touch at first, but when that did it no harm, the next blow was a crushing punch. Then another. And another. The wall bowed but did not break. At every strike Glimador groaned and shifted as if he himself were being punched.

"I can't hold it," said Glimador, even as his feet slid along the tunnel — the wall and he, together pushed backward by the might of the stone creature.

Claradon racked his mind and memory for

some spell, some sorcery that could save them. But he had nothing of such power to call forth. "Tanch—"

"I have nothing," said the wizard. "Fire will not avail us here, and I have nothing of great power that does not draw on that element."

"Then add your power to Glimador's," said Theta as he stepped up behind them, his breastplate badly dented and scarred. "I've seen you do it before."

Battle cries and screams continued from the rear of the troop, though all out of sight.

"Can you do it?" said Claradon.

"I will try." Tanch spoke some words — words of power like those of Claradon and Glimador, but as different from each of theirs as they were from each other. Words of the Magus Mysterious, the ancient tongue of wizards, held over from bygone days.

A terrible blow from the stone creature pushed Glimador a full step back, holes opened up on the wall, but it still stood, though it shimmered and shook.

Tanch's hand was on Glimador's shoulder and his eyes were closed. The Ring of Talidousen on Tanch's hand began to glow, and then a blue aura appeared about Tanch's arm and coursed onto Glimador's shoulder, down his arm, and onto his hand. That aura shot from Glimador's hand, in a continuous beam, at the magical wall. When the beam reached it, it spread out, covering all of the wall, bolstering it, deepening the blue shade of its energies. The wall now looked solid, barely still translucent. The stone creature's blows against it now sounded muffled, distant, and hollow; no longer did the wall shake or shudder.

"On your lives," said Theta before he turned and dashed toward the battle at the rear of their troop, "hold that thing here. Do not let that force wall drop."

51

SVARTLEHEIM

FREM

Frem ducked into the tunnel. He thought to go along on hands and knees, but the ceiling was too low for that. It might have worked for a smaller man, but not for Frem. He had to get down on his belly. He lay upon his shield. Then he pulled himself along with his arms, using his legs to help by pushing on the uneven side walls of the tunnel. Frem pulled Carroll along behind him, Carroll helping by pushing off with his legs against the walls. The shields were smooth and they slid along with less effort than if they lay directly against the tunnel floor. Carroll held a pike at the ready, in case any elves came up behind them.

There seemed no end to the tunnel. The minutes stretched to an hour, and still they crawled along. The tunnel never opened up. It never grew any larger — taller or wider. In fact, if anything, it seemed to grow shorter and narrower. But that might have been Frem's imagination; the walls closing in on him. Anyone would feel a bit of claustrophobia in a place like that. Frem never suffered from that ailment. But he'd never been in such tight quarters for so long. It was starting to get to him.

Every ten or twenty minutes Frem took a break. He had to. Not only was he hauling himself, he was hauling nearly three hundred pounds of man and gear behind him. There was a limit to a man's strength, to a man's endurance. Even a man like Frem.

Those few minutes, or however long it was, of rest that he had back in the battle chamber, laying amongst the heaped dead, were of help. But it wasn't enough. Not by a long way. He gritted his teeth and soldiered on. What else was there to do?

On their breaks, the two knights laid on their backs and stared at the tunnel's ceiling, light and shadow flickering against it, battling for supremacy. Most of the creepy crawlies fled from the light; some few stood defiant against it and kept the men from closing their eyes and finding any rest or relief. There were spiders aplenty in those tunnels. Small ones mostly; some were bigger, the furry kind. Frem hated them, but being in armor gave him some comfort — so long as the bugs didn't get down into the armor. That would put you in the deep stuff.

Silent crickets lurked in every crevice; they hopped about the tunnel and jarred the men's nerves with unexpected movement. Centipedes, millipedes, and whatever pedes there are what got a gazillion legs polluted the place. Most of them were squashed dead on the tunnel floor or walls, victims of their comrades' passage. Frem and Carroll squashed more whenever they got close. They figured, better safe than sorry; they had no interest in risking their bites. They couldn't afford to get poisoned down there.

At least there weren't any rats. Frem couldn't

suffer a tunnel like that with rats. And no bats either; that was a plus. He hadn't seen one in the entire tunnel system. Maybe the elves ate them. You never can tell with elves.

A second hour passed with no relief, no tunnel end in sight. Frem's nerves were frayed. He prayed that they'd find a way out soon. He didn't think he had the strength to make it back the way that they came, if it came to it. Their only chance was to keep moving forward and trust to fate.

Frem's stomach was twisted into knots. He needed to get up, to stretch, to see the light of day, to feel clean fresh air on his face. He needed to get out of there, and soon. He felt like he was going to puke. And that made him angry. That was a weakness. Frem had no time for weakness. He never did. He soldiered on.

And then a third hour of crawling along came and went.

And then a fourth.

Despite their fear of running out of light, they kept two torches lit during their long crawl, for they feared that light going out. They feared not being able to get another torch lit in the darkness.

The thought of being on their bellies or backs in that endless tunnel in the dark, in the pitch black, was horror.

Better to be dead. Better to be dead than that.

Frem thanked the gods that Carroll was with him. Being alone in that place would have been a hundred times worse. Urging each other along, helped a great deal. Having someone to talk to, helped even more.

For long stretches the tunnel seemed level,

but Frem could tell there was a gentle slope to it. Always downward. In some few spots, it grew steep, and that made it easier to move, gravity helping them on their way, reducing the friction between their shields and the tunnel floor, making it the easier to push themselves along.

"It's been getting steeper," said Carroll, "getting a lot easier to slide."

"If it gets much steeper," said Frem, "we'd best get off the shields and go forward on our backs. I'm not going to chance sliding freely down into who knows what. We might slam into a wall or else fall into a chasm."

"The tunnel is a lot narrower here," said Carroll. Do you have room enough to turn around and go down on your back? I think I can make it, but just barely. I may have to take off some armor to do it."

"Let me try it." Frem maneuvered around, scrunching himself up as best he could, and twisting in the narrow confines of the tunnel until he got his feet positioned out front. He barely did it. "The narrowing has been so gradual, I hadn't noticed it for a while. This could be a problem."

"It's more than a problem, Captain," said Carroll. "If we go down the wrong way, and can't turn around, it will be the death of us. If we get to a spot where the only way forward is face first and we're feet first, we'll get stuck and we'll have to climb all the way back to a point where we can turn around."

"But you're not going to be able to climb back," said Frem. "Not with that injured arm. And if it's so tight that we can't turn around, I'm not going to be able to climb past you to take the lead and pull you along."

"You're right," said Carroll. "We can turn back now, or else we're committed."

"So long as there is a chance of making it through," said Frem, "we can't go back. The others are still up ahead, plenty of signs of their passage."

"So what's our best chance?" said Carroll. "Face first? Or feet first? How do we know?"

"If we go face first," said Frem, and the tunnel turns up steeply, we can roll onto our backs and climb up, but if we're feet first, and the passage it tight enough, we might get stuck and then we'd be dead. If it turns down steeply, and we're feet first, we have a chance to climb down, if there are footholds. We've got rope, we can use it. But if we're head first, there might be no way to get a handhold or foothold. We'd be stuck at the edge or we'd fall into the shaft and get dead."

"I think there's a lot better chance of getting dead in here, than of getting out of here," said Carroll. "Not even considering the elves."

"I figure," said Frem, "it's more likely that we'll come to a steep decline or a shaft than we will a steep incline, since everything has been downhill so far."

"So it's feet first," said Carroll.

"Aye, and gods help us if we're wrong," said Frem.

"Quiet," said Carroll. "I hear something."

They both went silent and listened for some moments.

"Elves," said Frem with a deep sigh. "A lot of

them."

"How far back do you figure?" said Carroll.

"With the echoes in here," said Frem, "and the way sound carries, there is no way to tell."

"Then let's move," said Carroll.

Frem began moving faster down the tunnel, though it took much less effort than before, as the tunnel had grown steep indeed.

At one point they started sliding . But the elves were even closer. They needed to go faster to lose them.

"The way they're gaining on us," said Carroll, "they must be running through the tunnels. They're short enough that maybe stooped over a bit, they could run straight through here with little effort — even while it's killing us to move a hundred yards. We've no chance of outpacing them unless we let go and let the slope take us."

"Eventually we'll hit something," said Frem. "Or fall off into a chasm."

"We have to risk it," said Carroll. "We can't fight them in here. There's no room for us to maneuver. They'll carve us up."

"Aye," said Frem as he looked around at the close confines. "We can't fight them in here. Let's chance it." Frem pushed them along as fast as he could. He held nothing back. He used every ounce of energy he had in him to slide the two of them on their shields along that tunnel floor. And Carroll pushed with both his legs, his one good arm holding a torch, his injured, gripping the pike at his side.

Soon they slid along of their own accord, the tunnel slope steepening, and gravity taking over.

Now they had a chance to pull away from the elves, if only the slope stayed steep enough for a goodly while.

But they got more than they bargained for. For very soon they were going frighteningly fast.

Frem would've reached out with arms and legs to slow them, but he didn't.

The elves were still too close for that.

Faster and faster did they go.

A hundred yards they slid freely. Frem pushed his visor down to shield his eyes as sparks from his shield pecked at his exposed flesh. He gripped the torch like a vise, fearing to lose it.

The angle of the floor's slope passed twenty degrees.

Two hundred yards they'd traveled, sliding along. A wild, reckless ride.

Then the slope passed thirty degrees.

That's when they started to fly.

Their speed dizzying.

They held onto their shields for dear life.

Frem didn't wonder whether they'd crash. At that point, crashing was a foregone conclusion. The only questions were, how soon? And would they survive it?

52

SVARTLEHEIM, JUTENHEIM

THETA

Theta pushed his way through the men lined up in the tunnel. Most of them were braced; they gripped a triple coil of rope and strained from the effort. As he passed, the whole line jerked forward two or three feet — some few of the men pulled from their feet.

Then they held, sweat beading on their brows. They warned Theta of a demon — another stone monster immune to weapons. Some of the men were battered, apparently having tangled with the thing, however briefly, before they took position on the rope line. When Theta climbed over a short rise in the tunnel, he saw a sight unexpected. A stone creature, twin to the first he'd fought. It was down. On its back, the thing was, but still struggling, still fighting for all it was worth. The long rope line that Theta had passed was affixed about one of the thing's legs. Another rope was tied about its opposite arm; a third about its neck. Somehow, the soldiers had managed to pull the creature from its feet. Their efforts were keeping it down and off balance. More than a dozen men were on the leg rope, half a dozen on the arm rope, and two or three on the head. They struggled to hold the thing still. Artol, Little Tug, and the Bull stood on top of or around the creature, battle hammers working up and down with all their might. Bits of rock cracked, shattered, and flew off the thing. Such was the power behind those three men's strikes, that the dull thump of their hammers overshadowed (if only for a moment) all the noise within the place.

The bulk of the men could not aid them in their efforts, for they carried only bladed weapons, completely ineffective against the stone creature; they could do nothing save hold dear to one of the ropes.

Meanwhile, Sir Kelbor directed several pikemen who stabbed at the thing, probing for any vulnerable area that they could find at the thing's head, neck, or groin. They weren't having any luck.

"The mouth is firing up again," shouted Bull as the creature's maw began to glow golden, red, and orange. "We need more water, now!"

Two soldiers ran forward with water skins and dumped them on the creature's face, aiming for the mouth. The water sizzled, steamed, and bubbled at the mere touch of the creature's maw. But the water did its job. The infernal fires within the thing went out.

For the moment.

As he took in that scene, Theta smiled.

He stepped forward, sprang atop the creature (for there was no room to step around), and walked up its torso, toward its head. The thing writhed, but Theta kept his footing with seeming ease.

Little Tug was up by the creature's head. The monster was nearly flat on its back. Every time it lifted its head, Little Tug smashed Old Fogey into its stony face, now sorely battered: badly chipped and cracked.

Tug stood on the tunnel floor, just past the creature's head. When he spied Theta approaching, hammer in hand, he stepped back.

The creature lifted its head again and struggled against its bonds, trying to rise. Tug slammed Old Fogey into its head once more.

Standing atop the creature's chest, Theta hesitated not a moment. He raised his hammer high and slammed it down with all his might, directly onto the creature's forehead. When he did, it was as if a thunderclap hit the place — a deafening sound that shook the tunnel's very foundations and sent all the men reeling back. Upon that impact, the creature's head exploded into bits, pulverized from the unfathomable power of that blow.

Glowing red and orange ichor poured from the thing's neck. Its arms and legs thrashed this way and that for a few moments before they went forever still.

A great cheer rang out amongst the men. They raised their arms to celebrate their victory.

Theta looked around — the place was carnage. Several men were down: some wounded, some dead.

Bull bled from his forehead; Kelbor too. Neither was hurt badly.

"What was that bloody thing?" said Artol.

"A stone spirit from The Dawn Age," said

Theta, "awoken from its slumbers by the siren call of a dark wizard's magic."

"Well," said Tug as he leaned down to get a closer look at the pulverized head, "now it's just a dead rock."

"With orange and red blood," said Artol.

"Let's find that wizard and give him what for," said Tug as he turned back to Theta, but the big knight was already nearly out of sight, back down the tunnel.

53

SVARTLEHEIM

FREM

Frem's shield sparked and crackled every time an edge nudged the tunnel wall; he and Carroll battered with each impact.

Five hundred yards they'd gone. Sliding down into the black at breakneck speed.

The smell of hot metal and burning pitch from the torch filled Frem's nostrils. Burned his throat. Stung his eyes.

The tunnel nearly straight.

And ever downward.

The slope passed forty degrees.

Now they fell as much as slid.

He should have gone slower. Fought the elves if he had to. Now there was no way to stop.

They were going to crash. Going to get dead.

A thousand yards they went. No end to the tunnel in sight.

Faster and faster.

Sparks rained everywhere. The shrieking of metal was all he could hear. That and Carroll's curses.

On and on.

Two thousand yards.

More.

Farther.

Faster.

Frem could barely breathe. Waited for the impact. Knew it was coming.

The noise and sparks might scare off the elves. They could die in peace.

Frem shut off his brain. Grit his teeth. Endured.

Three thousand yards.

More.

Farther.

Faster still.

The ceiling grew closer by the moment. Less than a foot above him.

Ten inches.

Eight.

Six.

Closer.

Dead gods!

Sparks from both sides of the shield.

Shoulder plate scraped the walls. Sparked. Burned. Ceiling too close.

Shield ground against both walls. Edges burned. Curled. Melted.

Dead gods, it was on fire!

Slowing down.

Getting hotter.

Slower.

Slower.

Half their top speed now. Still too fast.

Burning!

And then the shield stopped.

Caught on the walls.

And Frem flew through the air. Armor afire.

He landed in water.

Ice cold water.
Momentum carried him deep.
Down into its icy depths.
Thirty feet. Maybe more.
Not dead.
Freezing water. Sapped his energy.
Which way was up?
Old Death shouted, Give up. Lay still. Rest.
The mission.
Coriana!
Damn him!
Swimming.
Gear weighed Frem down. Weapons too. Slowed him.
Need them. No time.
Just swim.
Keep everything.
Swim.
Up and up.
Just swim.
Up more still.
Keep going.
Swim.
Don't stop.
Where was the surface?
Was there a surface? Or did the water fill to the top?
Air! He broke the surface, gasping, coughing, and spitting. The ceiling far above him. Air aplenty.
And he could see. A torch sputtered — Carroll's — not far away. Mayhap ten feet from the pool's edge, which was twenty feet from him.
Frem swam toward that torch. He spied the

tunnel mouth they came from. Flames licked its edges — the shields still afire, still trapped in that shoot.

And then Carroll was there. Swimming and cursing beside him. Struggling. Barely keeping his head up. Spitting. Coughing.

Frem grabbed him under the arm. They swam together the last dozen feet to the side of the pool. It felt like a hundred miles.

Frem pulled himself out of the water, and then pulled Carroll out. Shivering head to toe, the both of them. Carroll's hair was scorched and his face had many small burn marks where sparks had found purchase. Carroll's pack lay on the cavern's floor, his helmet somewhere on the bottom of the pool. His pike was nowhere to be found; Frem was glad that it didn't end up in him. It could easily have skewered him.

They stripped off their armor and huddled near the burning shields, trying to warm up and dry off their clothes. Both had minor burns about their legs and shoulders where their armor had heated up from the friction.

"Look there," said Frem, pointing. "Sithian armor and gear, piled all neat. And no sign of battle in this place."

"There's no way out of this cavern," said Carroll, "save back up the tunnel or through the water. Putnam must have taken them through the pool. Must have figured there was a way through."

"Did you see any bodies in the water?" said Frem.

"I saw the light from my torch and the shields," said Carroll, "I saw the rocky walls down there. I even saw little fish in the water. But no bodies.

"Maybe they made it through," said Frem.

"Or drowned farther in," said Carroll. "It wasn't totally black down there. There was another light source, I'm sure of it."

"I'm not crawling back up that tunnell," said Frem, "and I'm surely not hauling your butt up there. I'd rather swim for it."

"Me too, one-armed or not," said Carroll. "At least that gives us a chance. If I have to die, drowning isn't the worst way."

"It's not one of the best either," said Frem. "But we have to chance it."

"Maybe take a bit of rest first?" said Carroll. "Warm ourselves up a bit. Get back a little strength. We've got food in the packs."

Then they heard the elves. They were far off. Far far off. But they were coming.

"There was never much chance we could lose them," said Frem. "There was no way out of the tunnel unless they turned back."

"I'm going to have myself a bite to eat, and drink a few swallows of wine," said Carroll. "Then I'm going to steal whatever few minutes of rest I can get. I figure that will give me my best chance to swim through that business down there. Right now I'm too tired to make it."

"If we do make it through," said Frem, "it doesn't mean it's over. The elves may well follow us through. We might have to face them on the other side. So we still need to stay ahead of them. We can't wait here until they're close."

"What about the packs, the supplies?" said Carroll.

"We take them. If nothing else it will help us sink down into the pool. It was deep and I suspect we'll need to go deep in order to find the other side. The weight of the packs may help us; the armor too."

"We can't swim in the armor," said Carroll.

"We'll wish we had it, if we get through," said Frem. "Let's lash it together, tight as can be, and sling it over our backs. It'll help pull us down. But we'll be able to drop it on the way up if we have to."

"That's smart Captain. Let's do it."

And so they did

Like all the Sithians, they carried a large oilskin bag in their packs. They stuffed their clothes in it; their torches and tinder already there. They sealed the bags up tight, making certain no air was trapped that would buoy them up. Then they wrapped a rope around each of their waists, tying themselves together. Each man had a dagger belted to his waist. They'd make it through together if they could, but they'd cut the rope if they had to. They hung a torch just over the edge of the pool to give them a reference point and some light as they swam down. They'd drop their bale of armor before them, to help pull them down all the faster.

"Are you ready?" said Frem.

"I'm scared," said Carroll. Frem had never heard Carroll admit to being scared before. He never seemed scared of anything. "Are you?" said Carroll.

"I'm more scared of staying here," said Frem. They both heard the elves, much closer now.

Maybe only a few minutes behind them. "Let's go," said Frem. On three.
And they jumped.

54

SVARTLEHEIM, JUTENHEIM

CLARADON

Claradon and Kayla knelt beside a soldier injured when Theta crashed into him. The man's leg was broken and crushed. He had broken ribs and was coughing up blood. Another man lay unconscious nearby; he'd been hit hard in the head. Claradon kept one eye on Glimador and Tanch, their wall holding steady despite the pounding it was taking. The stone creature's blows were powerful, but it paused for a few seconds between each punch. The mystical wall of energy shook and shimmered with each impact, but held fast.

"Claradon," shouted Tanch, his voice cracking with panic. "The dark wizard!" he said, pointing at the wall.

"Stay here; guard the wounded," said Claradon to Kayla. He dashed to Tanch's side. Several other soldiers were there, including Sir Trelman and Sir Paldor. The stone creature's glowing maw cast enough light to see a portion of the creature through the shimmering blue wall. Claradon had been watching it all the while. He saw it pivot each time it threw a punch. But now he saw something more. Something small, smaller than a man. It stood beside the creature, its silhouette illumed by the glowing tip of a staff that it held. The figure's hands weaved this way and that, tracing esoteric patterns in the air, and as Claradon drew closer, he heard it chanting. A strange sound, melodic at first, then discordant, and back again, at a pitch higher than any Volsung could reach, with strange pauses between the sounds, as if the pitch rose beyond the limits of human hearing before returning to more pedestrian levels.

"He's trying to dispel the wall," said Glimador, his voice strained, anxious, weak.

"We're not your enemies," shouted Claradon. "We're on the same side. We're trying to keep the portal closed."

The Diresvart continued his sorcery. Mayhap he couldn't hear Claradon's words. Mayhap he didn't understand. Or else didn't believe him.

"How do we stop him?" said Claradon.

"I'm putting all the power I can into it," said Tanch; his hands and arms shook; sweat covered his brow and rolled down his face. "I can do nothing more."

A blast of orange colored energy exploded against the far side of the wall, briefly turning the wall that color, before it returned to its natural blue, the Diresvart's counter-spell, ineffective.

Then came the Diresvart's voice again. Claradon didn't understand the words, but he knew cursing when he heard it. Again, the Diresvart weaved a spell: the orange attacked the blue and was repelled again.

The third time, just as the wall turned briefly orange, the Diresvart marched forward.

He stepped up to the wall, pressed against it.

The wall shimmered. A burst of orange light came from where the Diresvart lay hands on the wall.

And then a gap opened. A rift in the wall. Shimmering at its edges. Small it was.

Fleeting. But large enough.

The Diresvart pushed his way through before the rift closed. The stone creature remained trapped on the other side.

From the Diresvart came the wild, raucous laughter of a madman. A curious figure was he: short and flat, dark and wrinkled, spindly and long of limb and digit, overlarge of eye, hairless of head and body, with a very long staff of white bone in hand, topped with a great green gemstone that pulsed with magics unknown — the sigil of his trade.

Despite the unnatural chill within the place, no steam formed from the Svart's breath. It wore simple clothes of dark blue that blended into the shadowy surrounds. There was a foreign feel about that fellow, and a sense of vast age — as if he'd skulked about the nether regions of Midgaard for ages unknown. His generally manlike form notwithstanding, he was — alien; no more akin to a man, than is a scorpion or an adder.

"Stop," shouted Claradon. "We're not your enemies."

The Diresvart cursed at him in Svartlespeak, or so it sounded, and raised his hands to weave some foul sorcery.

Two pikemen rushed in. Thrust their polearms at the Svart.

The blades never touched his flesh. Never got close.

The Diresvart waved his arm and the weapons were wrenched from the soldiers' hands as if by the grip of an invisible giant.

The Svart pointed his palm at the men. A moment later, they flew backward through the air. They crashed to the ground several feet away, battered and winded.

Claradon spoke his words of the Militus Mysterious and he was immediately bathed in a mantle of white light from on-high. A light that would safeguard him from most dark magics, and even from the blows of his enemies, if only for a short time. Claradon stepped forward, sword at the ready, drawing the Diresvart's attention, several men backing him.

The Diresvart spoke its words, its arms aflutter, when an arrow pierced its shoulder. He stumbled back against the blue wall, blood spurting from his wound. When his back touched the wall, he screamed. A high pitched wail it was. So loud, so piercing, that it threatened the hearing of all around. Sparks flew. The Svart's tunic caught fire. He roared in anger. His voice loud and strong, though high in pitch. He was not done yet. He thrust both palms forward toward Claradon and the onrushing soldiers. Each was struck by an unseen force of terrible power.

Claradon felt the impact of that blow, but his protective magics spared him its bite. Nonetheless, it stunned him for a few moments. Knocked him backward. He fell to his backside. The other men went flying, crashed into the tunnel walls and floor.

A moment later, his head clearing, Claradon saw the Svart atop Glimador. It clawed and bit at his neck like a wild animal. Most of the Svart's back and legs were aflame, both clothing and flesh. It bellowed like a wild dog. Crazed. Out of its mind.

Tanch tried to pull the Svart off Glimador with one hand. His other worked to maintain the magic wall that still held the stone creature back.

Claradon stepped up and grabbed the Svart by the collar. Lifted him into the air. Ignored the flames coming off him. He thrust his Asgardian dagger through the center of the Svart's back. Claradon's gauntlets grew searing hot where the flames licked them. He had to drop the Svart and step back. No matter, the Svart was finished.

Glimador rolled over once and then again as he tried to put out the flames that had jumped to his clothes.

"The wall's down," shouted Tanch in alarm. "It's coming through."

Claradon turned toward the force wall. It was gone. The barest remnant of shimmering blue energy remained at its edges. And to Claradon's surprise, on came the stone creature.

The creature should have fallen. A magical construct died with its master. Or so Claradon had been taught. But the stone creature seemed unaffected by the wizard's demise. Then Claradon turned back to the wizard. Quick as he could he sank his dagger through the back of the Diresvart's head. That put an end to any spark of life that might yet have remained in it.

Claradon turned. The stone creature's giant foot was coming down atop him! Nowhere to move to. No time to try.

Theta crashed headlong into the stone creature. Overbalanced it. Pushed it back, one step, and then another. Claradon rolled clear. Theta had come in very fast — at a full sprint. He dived forward into the thing. Even so, how he developed enough momentum to move the creature was a mystery.

Theta's hammer was in his hand. He battered the stone creature over and again. Didn't give it time to maneuver or counterstrike. One blow caught the creature behind the knee; it lost its footing and went down on its back.

Theta leaped into the air, hammer overhead. His weapon came down full upon the creature's face with a thunderous impact. The stone of the creature's head chipped and cracked but still it fought on. It rolled over to its belly. Started to get up. Theta hit it again. Slammed his hammer to the back of its head, near the base of what would have been its skull.

That did it. The creature's head broke in two. Colorful ichor poured out the fissure. Within moments, the creature moved no more.

Claradon heard a groan at his feet. The Diresvart still lived. How, Claradon couldn't fathom. Claradon pinned the Svart's arms and turned him over. Part of its face was burned, the flesh charred and melted. It gasped for air. It spoke in the common tongue, its accent strong; its lips quivered and its teeth chattered, but its words were clear enough. "The master will stop you," it said. "You will not win this. The gateway will remain. . . closed."

55

SVARTLEHEIM, *JUTENHEIM*

OB

When Dolan attacked it, the stone creature roared. Its maw, aglow with yellow and orange flame; wisps of smoke drifted from its depths.

Dolan clung to its back like a spider. He plunged a dagger (the glowing one gifted him by Sir Gabriel months prior) into the nape of the creature's neck, where its brain stem should be. The ensorcelled blade sparked on impact but found no purchase. Dolan drove it down again and again; each time to no effect. The blade could not pierce the stone. Then he pried at the stones — as if they were scales that could be lifted up.

They were not.

The creature's torso twisted and turned. Its arm came up, fingers groping for the gnat upon its back. But Dolan was too swift. He dodged. Scurried from the center of the creature's back to the edge of its shoulder. Dagger plunging.

Again, it bounced off, sparks flying. Before the creature brought its other arm to bear, Dolan bounded up, quick like a rat, his feet upon the creature's shoulders. He leaped up. Spun. Twisted head over heels in midair. As he dropped in front of the thing, he stabbed at the creature's eye. His speed, too swift. His aim, uncanny. The blade's tip struck the creature's eye, dead center. With the power behind that blow, the blade should have sunk deep. The creature's eye should have been torn to shreds. It should have been blinded. Instead, the blade's tip snapped off with a skirling sound the moment that it hit. The thing's eyes were as stony and unyielding as its body.

Even as Dolan's feet landed on the chamber's floor, Ob struck. The gnome's axe blasted into the back of the creature's ankle, where its tendons should have been. The strength of that blow, coupled with the edge that that blade had, should've severed the thing's leg, thick as it was.

But it did not.

The axe rebounded off and shook and quivered in Ob's hands. The gnome staggered back, the jarring pain from that blow overwhelming. For a moment, his arms had no strength; his fingers had no feeling. He dropped the axe. Its ancient blade, unmarred for a thousand years, undamaged in countless battles, now lay notched and chipped from that single blow.

Ob looked up as the creature turned toward him. Its maw opened wide. Ob knew what was coming. His gnomish reflexes served him well. He dived and rolled to the side as the cone of flame roared from the creature's mouth and washed through the chamber.

Ob scrambled up. The creature's flame attack still poured out and trailed him, incinerating corpses as it went. Ob took two strides; he dived and rolled again. He came up running. This time, he ran directly toward the creature, quick as a rabbit. He ducked between its legs, too fast for it to grab him, and headed for the entry tunnel, back whence they first came. Dolan awaited him there, his attention on something farther up the tunnel. Ob prayed that the Diresvart didn't bar their path. Ob chanced a glance over his shoulder, hoping to spot his axe. Instead, he saw smoke and tendrils of flame near at hand. The back of his pants were afire. His boots too.

"Shit," shouted Ob as he dived yet again, rolled, and tried to smother the flame. He swatted at his pants with his gloves, but there was no time. The creature was too close. But he couldn't keep running, for in a moment, the flames would reach his flesh.

Then Dolan was there. A useful lad. Quite reliable.

Ob took the moments that Dolan gave him to slap down the flames that clung to him.

But then came a groan. And Dolan crashed into him. Knocked him to the floor. A moment later, Ob scrambled to his feet, but Dolan lay groggy before him, a gash and a terrible bruise forming on the side of his face. The thing had swatted him. And even now it bore down on them both. Just a few steps away.

Ob's eyes darted to the mouth of the tunnel, gauging whether they could make it. Getting there was their one chance of escape.

"Get up boy," said Ob. "We've got to run for the tunnel."

Dolan shook his head; he was dazed, groggy, glassy-eyed. No words escaped his lips. He mouthed something, but Ob didn't know what.

Then he saw motion in the tunnel.

Something lurked in the shadows. And it was moving closer. It could only be the Diresvart; the stinking black elf wizard coming to finish them off. Ob wouldn't let that bastard entrap them. He'd carve the thing up like a Wintersfest goose, and then they'd be off and running, back to their fellows.

Ob grabbed Dolan under the armpit and hoisted him to his feet. Just as Ob started for the tunnel, pulling Dolan along, he saw it.

Another stone creature.

A twin to the first, it was. It lumbered from the darkness; blocked the whole of the tunnel with its bulk. There was no carving that up. And no escape in that direction. They had no way to fight the creatures. And there was nowhere else to run to.

"When it steps in," said Ob, "we dodge by it. We run down that tunnel and we keep running until we find the others. Got it?"

Dolan didn't respond.

"Are you with me, boy?"

Dolan was out on his feet, battered but good, and coughing up a lung from the smoke caused by the creature's flame strikes. It was hard to breathe. Hard to see. Skinny as Dolan was, he was far too big for Ob to carry. The boy had to keep his feet.

Ob backpedaled. Pulled Dolan along with him. Stepped on and over more corpses strewn about the floor. Some of them were on fire. The place smelled of burnt and rotted flesh. The smoke stung Ob's eyes. Scratched his throat. Ob figured that if they moved far enough back from the tunnel entry, the second creature would come in after them. When it did, they'd make a mad dash for the tunnel. Dodge by the things as best they could. They'd make it or they wouldn't, as the Norns decreed.

But the second creature didn't oblige them no matter how far back they moved. It rooted itself at the tunnel's mouth. Rock or not, it was no fool. It wasn't going to give them a chance to get by. The first creature moved toward them, though its flames were now silent, its maw closed.

"There's no way out, boy," said Ob.

"Then we'll go down fighting," blurted Dolan as blood streamed from between his lips.

"And me without my axe," said Ob.

"Keep moving," said Dolan. "You might be able to squeeze by it. Do it if you can."

"I'll not leave you, laddie," said Ob. "That's not the gnome way. We're in this together, do or die. Shit, it's gonna flame us again," he said as the first creature's maw began to glow again.

A booming thunderclap rocked the chamber. The creature that blocked the tunnel shot forward, hit by something massive from behind. Bits of stone broke from its back. Several feet did the creature fly through the air before it crashed to the chamber floor, landing on its knees, squashing the dead beneath it. It roared. Groaned. Pulled itself to its feet.

Another dark figure now stood at the tunnel's entry.

Theta.

Ancient battle hammer in one hand. Massive battle shield in the other.

56

SVARTLEHEIM, JUTENHEIM

OB

Ob had seen Theta do many things. Things no man should be able to do. Things that should be impossible. Things that were impossible. And yet, still Ob was shocked when he saw Theta standing there at the mouth of the tunnel, hammer in hand. That stone creature, it must have weighed five tons or more. How could a hammer blow knock its bulk across the cavern? It made no sense. It defied all logic and reason. No man could be that strong. Odin himself couldn't be that strong. And no hammer could survive such a blow.

But there was Theta, with his steely eyes and grim expression, poised to strike again, hammer at the ready. Saved were they?

Saved by the devil himself?

The first stone creature was as distracted by the attack on its fellow as were Ob and Dolan. It turned its back on them and lumbered toward Theta.

Ob and Dolan rushed forward, headlong. Every ounce of strength and speed that they had left, propelled their legs towards that tunnel mouth. Toward Theta. Toward escape. If they could outdistance the first creature. If they could make it to the tunnel mouth just a few strides ahead of it. Maybe they'd have a chance. Maybe they'd get away. Maybe Theta would get another good strike in and they'd all get clear.

But that's not what happened.

Theta yelled a war cry at the creature. Bold words about coming forth and meeting its doom. And then he charged straight at the first rock monster, hammer held high.

A madman.

Suicide. Even for him.

The creature's maw went wide, flames erupting from within.

Dolan and Ob dived to the side, covered up as best they could.

The flames roared unerringly at Theta.

The sound was deafening, the heat, scorching. Ob and Dolan were out of its range yet they felt roasted, their clothes threatening to spontaneously combust.

The roaring flames went on and on as the moments ticked by.

Theta never even had a chance to scream.

Ob couldn't look. He didn't want to see the great man die. He kept his eyes averted, waiting until the flames died away. Then he'd see the ashes, if even that much remained of Theta.

He didn't want to look. But he couldn't wait.

He had to know.

He had to see for himself.

He chanced a glance, the flames still spouting from the creature's maw.

Ob couldn't believe what he saw.

There crouched Theta, his shield braced before

him — its metal burning white hot and all aglow. The flames blasted upon and around it, but Theta stood firm, unyielding, his hammer still poised to strike, the shield deflecting the flames around him, leaving him all but unscathed. And no sooner did the monster's flame die out then did Theta launch himself at it in a single bound.

He rose up into the air with a great leap.

His hammer swung in a mighty arc.

Came down with godly might upon the stone creature's head.

When that blow hit home, Ob heard another thunderclap and saw stone explode in all directions — including at him. Some of that stone hit him. Hit him hard. His head! And then his world went dark and Ob knew no more.

57

SVARTLEHEIM

FREM

Frem's heart thumped in his chest at the very thought of making that swim: fear and exhilaration fighting for supremacy. Deep breath after deep breath got his adrenaline pumping. He was as ready for it as he could be. Yet one second after diving into that frigid water, he was a hundred years old and on his deathbed. The gelid water instantly sapped his energy. His chest tightened up. His arms went numb and limp. So did his legs and his back. His head felt muddied, lost in a fog. He needed to let out a breath and scream from the pain and shock of it. He scrunched up his face and somehow held in all his air.

He let the armor's dead weight carry him down. For a few seconds, that's all he could do. Then his body began to adjust. Life returned to his limbs. His eyes darted this way and that, searching for any light other than that from their torch above. If it was there, he had to find it. And fast.

And he saw it, quick as that and plain as day. Some fifty feet away but well up above him. At first he feared that he'd gotten turned around. That he was just looking back into the same cavern they'd jumped from. But he wasn't. He saw the light from both.

Frem swam toward the new light with all the speed he could muster. Carroll behind him, a silhouette in the darkness. Carroll struggled along, only able to use one arm. But he soldiered on. At first, he moved nearly as quickly as Frem, but the farther they swam, the more Frem felt Carroll's weight on the rope as he began to lag behind.

Frem didn't panic when he felt that weight. He kept his head. He pulled them both along, just as he suspected that he'd need to. It was okay, for now he knew that salvation was within reach. He could reach that light before he ran out of breath. He was certain of it. And where there was light, there was air, and a way forward. The darned tunnels hadn't beat him. So long as a gang of elves weren't waiting for them there, reaching that light meant life. And Frem was going to get there one way or another.

He swam and he swam and he swam.

Until his calf snagged on something.

His leg was stuck fast, so he reached down to try and pull it free of whatever snagged it. Then at once, it squeezed his leg in a pythonic grip and jerked him downward. Startled, Frem nearly lost his air. The water rushed past him and he saw the light from up ahead grow farther away by the moment. He tried to wrench his leg free, but it felt stuck in a vise.

Frem couldn't see it, the thing that had him. All black below him.

Then he felt another tug, this time at his waist

— the tether between him and Carroll. Carroll was above him now. Frem felt him pulling, trying to hold him back.

The thing that had his leg was far stronger.

Frem's dagger was in his hand. A long thin silhouette rose up out of the depths before him. What little light trickled down gave him the impression of a grayish colored tentacle, thick but tapering toward its end, landscaped with round suckers up and down its length. As luck would have it, he raised the dagger just as the tentacle flicked toward his face.

Impaled on his blade, the thing went wild. Frem held fast to the dagger and was thrashed about until the weapon pulled free and the tentacle retreated.

The tentacle on his leg squeezed so hard that he thought his leg would sever. He had to get free fast or he'd be dead. Frem stabbed and sawed at it, all his power behind those cuts. For all its strength, the creature's flesh was no match for good Lomerian steel. A few strokes and he cut the tentacle in two.

Free and swimming upward again was Frem. He chanced a glance downward. So dark, so black it was. He couldn't clearly see the creature, but he had a sense of shape and shadow — a round area, a bit lighter than the surrounds. And large.

A monster.

Some weird squid or octopus it had to be.

Frem swam like a madman and prayed to the gods that the thing wouldn't chase him.

His lungs were afire. Weighed down by the armor and gear, he knew he'd never make it. The light was too far away now. He had too little air left.

He dropped his gear and armor pack, but held on to its tether — prepared for such an occasion was he. The Sithians were always prepared, owing to their training. He had a hundred feet of thin but strong cordage attached to that gear bundle. All he had to do was keep the cord wrapped about his wrist as he swam. So long as the slack didn't run out before he surfaced, he'd be able to haul the gear up when he was safely out of the water.

A gamble. A dozen ways that that could go wrong, not even considering the creature that had tried to eat him. But what could he do?

He swam.

Thirty seconds later, he passed Carroll who still struggled along, bubbles trickling from his mouth.

Closer to the light Frem swam.

Forward and upward.

Closer still.

No tentacle on him. No jaws clamped down on him.

The last twenty feet of that swim, Carroll felt like dead weight. Frem looked over his shoulder. Carroll was still swimming as best he could, more bubbles trickling from his mouth. His eyes still determined. He wasn't going to give up any more than Frem was.

Up and forward, one stroke after another. To Helheim with his burning lungs. To Helheim with the cold. With everything. He swam for that light, and all the demons of the Nether Realms couldn't stop him from getting there.

And then his head popped through the surface

and he took the deepest breath of his life.
It felt good.
Another cavern much like the last lay before him, and no elves were in sight. Five seconds later, Carroll burst through the surface, gasping.
"Out of the water," said Frem as he pulled himself over the lip. The cavern was half again larger than the last and had two torches waiting for them, stuck into the ground, burning bright. Sithian torches – Frem knew them at once. His men had left them to light their way.
Like the last, that chamber had but one exit. This time, it was a tunnel of respectable height, right down at floor level, where it should be — instead of a rabbit hole that dropped you down from near the ceiling. From somewhere down that exit passage, filtered in more light.
A small campfire sputtered before them, built in a depression some feet from the water's edge. Another gift from Putnam, no doubt. They'd need it. Both were shivering worse than before. Carroll rolled and crawled toward the fire.
Frem felt a tug on his wrist — the tether to his gear. Carroll's arm was outstretched toward the pool, his own tether tugging, though he closed his eyes and ignored it.
Frem reeled in the rope, praying it wouldn't snag on anything, alive or not. He pulled it in, hand over hand, until his gear bundle appeared at the pool's surface. Frem hauled it up. It felt ten times the weight it had before — waterlogged and arm weary.
"Pull your gear up," said Frem. Carroll didn't respond. He lay shivering by the fire's edge.

Frem stood, checked his sword and dagger, and then started hauling up Carroll's gear.

"Just let me rest a minute," said Carroll, "and then I'll pull it up. It's my job."

"I've got it," said Frem. The bundle appeared some moments later, intact, the same as Carroll had packed it. Just as Frem pulled it from the pool, he noticed a disturbance in the water.

He backpedaled from the edge even as a monster out of nightmare burst from the pool's surface.

An octopus of giant size. Tentacles flailing. A foul, fishy scent filled Frem's nostrils. The thing filled the entire surface of the pool. Water poured over the edge and doused their fire, which steamed and crackled.

Frem tripped over something and fell to his rump as tentacles lashed out at him. Those tentacles were long. Long enough to reach anywhere in the chamber. Though an octopus it appeared, the creature had far more than eight legs. A single great eye did it have, as big as a saucer. Below it, a maw like a bird's beak. It clicked, clattered, and clamped together with frightening force.

Then Carroll was there. Sword swinging. A blur of motion.

He cut one tentacle in two with a mighty stroke. Pinkish ichor spewed from the wound. He severed a second tentacle before Frem could even make his feet.

Both knights stepped farther back. Another tentacle came at them. Carroll lopped off its tip. It came in again, and he cut another foot from it, his strokes like lightning, all signs of fatigue gone. Still the thing didn't give up. Both men ducked its next swipe. Then Frem stepped forward and cleaved the tentacle in two. Ten feet of tentacle fell to the cavern floor and flopped about, refusing to die. The creature screamed, a strange piercing cry, at once high and then low of pitch. It sent more tentacles at them as the men backed away. How many it had was impossible to say.

"Grab the gear," said Frem as they backpedaled toward the exit corridor. The thing coiled a tentacle about Carroll's gear bag. After all the trouble they had hauling that gear through the water, they weren't about to abandon it. As one, both men stepped forward. Carroll chopped at the tentacle and Frem guarded against the others that swooped toward them. He severed one and then another.

Then they were running. All their gear with them.

They didn't stop until they reached the end of the corridor, some fifty feet from the cavern. The creature didn't follow, if even it could. They stepped out of the tunnel into another cavern. And when they did, their eyes gazed upon a sight the like of which they had never imagined before.

58

SVARTLEHEIM

OB

"The main tunnel is blocked up good and proper," said Artol. "A month of sweat, picks, and shovels to get us through. We best find another way."

"There are only two choices left to us," said Claradon. "Back whence we came, out through the monastery and down the cliffs, Rikenguard to guide us. Or else we try a side tunnel and hope to bypass the blocked passage."

"There be a hundred side tunnels," said Artol. "Most, little more than rabbit holes. We've no business delving there."

Ob sat against the tunnel wall, red-stained bandages wrapped about his head. "What say you, Mister Fancy Pants?"

Theta held his ankh in his hands and mumbled something under his breath. "Follow me," he said as he walked to one of the side passages. He bent low and entered.

Surprised looks on their faces, the men hesitated a moment, then scrambled after Theta.

Two steps into the side tunnel, Theta had to get down on his knees to fit and to continue moving through. He did so.

Artol stopped at the mouth of the passage. "It's a rabbit hole. We can't go in here. Theta, there must be another way."

Theta said nothing and kept moving down the tunnel. Dolan pushed past Artol and entered the tunnel. The others followed. Ob was able to walk straight in. Artol was last. No doubt he figured that if he got stuck, and couldn't go in farther, at least he'd be able to back out, and the others could continue on without him.

The passage was damp and echoey. Crawling along on hands and knees for even a short distance was tiring, painful, and slow going, but that tunnel seemed to go on forever. Crawling made the place seem so much the colder, and it was darned cold enough already. The stone leeched the body heat right out of a man. Pulled it from their legs, from their hands and forearms. And the creepy crawlies were a constant nuisance, dropping from the ceiling onto the men, crawling on their backs, slithering up their legs. Maybe there were more of them in the smaller tunnels, or mayhap it just seemed so because the space was so constricted and you couldn't steer well clear of them. Spiders, crickets, centipedes, millipedes, and lots of other types that the men couldn't name, ruled that place. The Lomerians didn't know which ones, if any, were poisonous. So they had to assume they all were, or pretend that none of them were, each to his own. Some men took to fits every time a bug got on them. Others paid the insects little heed, trusting to fate that a bug bite wouldn't end them.

The tunnels were the insects' world. Their Midgaard. The Lomerians were the strangers in that place. The intruders.

As they went on, three times did the tunnel open up into a small cavern with several exits. In two of those caverns did the ceiling rise high enough for the men to stand, though they were crowded in the space, some still backed up in the tunnel. Theta's ankh guided their way, or so he let on, selecting which passage for them to take whenever a choice presented itself. Ten minutes into the third side tunnel, the passage narrowed down — so much so that the men had to crawl through on their bellies. Luckily, there still was enough width to the tunnel for broad shoulders capped with armor.

"We need to turn back," said one man in the troop.

"Aye, we should turn around," said another.

"Aye, aye," said a bunch more.

"Stow that chatter," shouted Ob.

"We'll get stuck," said one man.

"No we won't," said Ob. "We'll get through this, just keep your traps shut and keep moving."

"If the tunnel narrows any more and just one man goes down," said someone, "we won't be able to back out. We'll be trapped."

"Nobody is backing out," shouted Artol from the rear of the troop. "Unless you think that you can get by me."

And that was the end of the debate.

And soon they were through it. Theta stood up, raised his torch, but it did not find the ceiling. The cavern they were in was at least forty or fifty feet across. They explored it.

"A watch post," said Ob as he sifted through the remnants of a fire pit near the center of the room. "This place has been used regularly for many years," he said. "By the elves, I imagine."

"Over here," said Artol no louder than he needed to, to get the men's attention. He stood on the far side of the cavern, beside the entry to another tunnel, his torch upraised. The walls around that tunnel's entry were framed in bones.

Bones.

Bones nailed to the walls. And a pile of bones three feet tall stood at the mouth of the tunnel.

59

SVARTLEHEIM

FREM

Frem and Carroll stood before the ancient Svart city of Starkbarrow. It was built in a cavern as high as the sky and as broad as the world. Or so it seemed as they stood there, nearly naked and shivering, in the twilight. The place was lit by glowing lichen that clung here and there about the cavern floor and walls, and blanketed its ceiling, hundreds of feet above the city and its surrounds.

Starkbarrow was a rare work of stone-craft. No mortar polluted the stones' joints. Every piece fit, formed, and cut with precision and care. The city's light gray and white stonework stood out against the backdrop of black basalt that comprised the cavern walls.

Much like the black elves themselves, the city's towers were thin and delicate, but they were tall. They rose to heights unimaginable for such slender structures. Taller even than the grand towers of Lomion. Higher than the spires of the Tower of the Arcane in Lomion city. Much of Starkbarrow was built into the great cavern's rock walls, upon terraces that reached for the ceiling. At its base, the city's outer walls rose some forty feet above the surrounds, constructed of white marble with triangular crenelations along its top.

The architecture of that city was not mere utilitarian, it was art. Beautiful. Magnificent. Built by an army of master craftsmen the like of which Lomion could boast of only a few.

The city gates waited half a mile from where Frem and Carroll stood. Pathways, pounded smooth and cleared of rocks, bisected the intervening space, going this way and that across the rocky landscape, barren yet beautiful in its way. Perhaps it was a trick of the light, or a clever coating, but from where they stood, the gates appeared to be made of gold.

So far underground, in the bowels of Midgaard were they, and yet, it was as if they stood before the city of the gods. More like Asgard was that place than a realm of mortal beings. And for a moment, Frem wondered whether it truly was a city of the black elves. Or were they merely the guardians of that place? Its caretakers? Their duty to keep away all who might venture too close?

The knights were shirtless. Wet undergarments covered their privates. Their hair dripping wet from their recent swim. Weapon belts about their waists. Swords still in their hands. Shivering from the cold. They pulled dry clothes from their oilskins, donned them, and their armor.

"Your plan worked perfectly," said Carroll as they put on their gear. "Getting through the water, I mean, all our stuff intact."

"We got lucky," said Frem. "If the cavern had been a hundred feet farther on, we probably would be dead. If it had been two hundred feet farther, we'd definitely be dead. Luck."

Frem stared off into the distance for a moment, thinking. And then he said. "Luck is often enough to see a man through, if his courage holds."

Carroll pointed to a spot in the distance. "Bodies."

With the majestic city capturing their attention, they hadn't noticed it before, but there were bodies aplenty on the field of stone far off in front of them. A battleground. But whose bodies and how many it was hard to say. They were too far away."

Newfound energy coursed through them, strengthening them, as they walked toward the battlefield. The thought of combat brought up their energies, instead of bringing them down, for they were warriors. Men who lived to fight and fought to live. It was all Frem could do not to run toward that battlefield. He kept himself at a walk, albeit a fast one, and banished his fatigue to the back of his mind. Carroll did the same. They needed to conserve their energies. There was more work to do that day. And surviving to the morrow was still far from certain.

"I see elves," said Carroll as they drew closer. "Two score bodies at the least. It must've been the Pointmen what killed them. Must've been Putnam."

"I see none of ours," said Frem.

And when they reached the spot, they saw that the battle had been larger than they thought. Much of it hidden over a low rise in the cavern floor. One hundred black elves lay dead there. Maybe more. All about a tiny high point in the terrain. The spot in which Putnam had made his stand. In amongst all that killing they found but five Sithian bodies. All men from 2nd and 4th squadrons. Frem knew their faces but only one or two of their names.

"You think they captured the rest of our boys?" said Carroll.

"Putnam wouldn't have let them take him alive," said Frem. "He would've died here rather than that. As would Royce, Lex, Moag, and most of the others. None of them are here. I think they won. I think these elves sallied forth through the city gates and Putnam took them apart."

"Then on to the gates," said Carroll. "But what if they have archers on those walls?"

"Then we run away," said Frem.

There were no archers. There were no guards along the wall. Not a single black elf greeted them. None alive, anyway. There were plenty that were dead. Nearly a score by the gate.

"The ones out on the battlefield looked like sturdy warriors," said Carroll. "These gatemen are mostly old. Far past their time."

"Some few are very young," said Frem. "Little more than children. It seems the elves sent their last troop of reserves out to stop Putnam's advance, and he killed them all. Only the old, the sickly, and the very young were left to guard the gates and the city beyond."

The gates were wide open.

"Not broken in," said Carroll. "It looks like someone opened the doors for them."

"Not on purpose," said Frem pointing to two ropes that hung from the crenel atop the wall not far away. The ropes dangled all the way to the ground.

"He had our boys scale the walls," said Carroll. "Probably Moag and Wikkle. Then they skulked about, maybe dropped a guard or two, and opened the gate from the inside. Smart."

"The elves had to know they were coming," said Frem. "They must have but a sparse defense left. Maybe these gatemen are the last of their fighters."

Frem and Carroll walked through the gates and into a deserted city of wonder. Starkbarrow had streets of stone slabs and cobbles polished to a shine — its colors marvelous and diverse. Each street with a different vein of marble or a different grain of granite. Its buildings, some of marble, some of granite, or other polished stones — each one more beautiful than the last. The walls were adorned with carvings of scenes rich in beauty and complexity, the artisans as skilled as any craftsman Frem had ever seen. The art depicted events and figures unknown to Frem. All the figures, even those carved into original walls, and weathered by time, were black elves. Proof enough for Frem that Starkbarrow was their city. The elves had built it, not usurped it. A place the elves had wrought from the raw stone of Midgaard back in ages past, beyond human memory. How many hundreds of years had the elves lived here? How many thousands? Tens of thousands? More?

Perhaps they'd never know.

Perhaps no one would know.

The streets were empty. It was not a large city for all its wonder and beauty. Not large at all despite the great height of the buildings, despite their grandeur and presence. Even the individual buildings were small structures in breath and depth, regardless of their height. Spindly, alike the elves.

Perhaps a few thousand elves lived there in Starkbarrow. Not many more than that.

The doors to the buildings were not barred. The windows were not shuttered. But much was in disarray. Things dropped, overturned, left open. There'd been an exodus from that place. The people had left in a great hurry. And Frem knew where they went.

They went to war.

The whole city had been unleashed against them. Was anyone left?

Perhaps only those few that guarded the gate.

From within a small pocket of an oilskin pouch, Frem produced a whistle. A signaling device carried by each officer in the company. He put it to his lips. Fear of discovery ebbing after what he'd seen. He sounded the whistle and waited for a count of five, and then five more.

And then he blew it again.

Not two breaths later he heard the response. Three long pips from a whistle. It was Putnam. The Pointmen were alive.

Every ten breaths, came Putnam's signal. They followed it. The whistles led them true to course toward the others. After a time, deep in the heart of the city, at last, they came upon their fellows at the entry to one of the largest buildings. Sir Royce was there, whistle in hand. With him was Ma-Grak Stowron, Sergeant Grainer of 2nd

Squadron, and Lieutenant Bradik and Stanik Lugron of 4th Squadron.

Pleasantries concluded.

"The palace," said Royce referencing the building behind him. "We assume the elf king and whatever other nobles that remain are hidden within. What looks like the inner chambers, mayhap a throne room, is locked up tight as Tammanian Hall's vaults. Putnam and Sevare are up there with our boys trying to get in."

60

SVARTLEHEIM

OB

"Defensive positions," said Ob after they spied the bones. The men complied, all going quiet. Ob jogged over to where Artol stood. Some of the bones were clearly human. Some others were not, though of what origin they were was not easy to say.

"How far down does the passage go?" said Ob in a quiet voice.

Artol angled his torch in. "Farther than I can see, the ceiling high. There's that at least."

Ob motioned Dolan over. "Dolan, me boy," he said, "send us an arrow down thataway, afire if you please."

Dolan's arrow hit a wall a hundred or so feet down the passage and fell to the tunnel floor, its flames still burning.

"The passage turns to the left," said Artol.

Theta stepped up next to them, ankh in hand. "This is the way."

"The way to what?" said Ob. "This doesn't look like a way out to me. In fact, this looks like a warning. Don't go past here. Danger and such. If you do, you'll end up dead — like these bones."

"It's the way that I must go," said Theta.

"That thingamabob don't know shit," said Ob,

pointing to the ankh. Why are you leading us down this way? What's down there? Come clean, Theta. What do you know?"

"I think this way leads back to the monastery, but first I have to deal with something dangerous that's down there."

"We've had our share of danger already, don't you think?" said Ob. "Perhaps we can take a less dangerous route? Can your whatchamacallit find us that way?"

"I must go this way," said Theta. "And I've no means to map an alternate route for you."

"Of course you don't," said Ob. "Clearly, there's no other option than to do exactly what you demand. Same as always."

"You can go whichever way you want," said Theta.

"Going back is not an option," said Ob. "We could be crawling around in here for days. We could run out of light."

"So stop complaining and follow me," said Theta as he turned and stepped into the passage.

"What's down there?" said Ob. "If we're about to go calling on it, we need to know."

"Something of Nifleheim," said Theta. "The ankh can sense it but little more."

"Could it be that temple that the Leaguers are after?" said Ob.

"Korrgonn would have headed straight there if it were," said Theta. "But there's no evidence that the Leaguers came this way. I think it's a creature born of Nifleheim. Mayhap more than one. Something held over from the Dawn Age.

"Stinking Nifleheimers are everywhere these

days," said Ob. "Common as cockroaches. How do you figure something from the Nether Realms could get way down here in the bowels of Midgaard?"

"The same way that we did," said Theta. "Except that it's been here a long time."

"You aim to kill it?" said Ob.

"I do."

"Well, then, we're in," said Ob. "Killing monsters is what gnomes do best."

"It's the gnome way, you know," said Artol.

Ob gave Artol a dirty look and kicked him in the shin.

The passage was wide enough that the men could comfortably walk three abreast. Theta, Artol, and Ob took the point. Claradon, Dolan, and Tanch just behind. The others followed.

"When they'd gone about halfway to where Dolan's arrow lay smoldering, Artol raised his hand in signal to stop the group. "I sense something. Felt it since we stepped past the bones. Thought it was my imagination. But it's not. Do you know what I mean?"

"My hair has been all prickly since we stepped over them bones," said Ob. "There's something down here, for certain. Something evil. Something magic. Seems Theta's thingamabob is square on, this time."

At Theta's signal, Dolan moved ahead of the group, slowly, cautiously. The others stood silent and still — only the crackling of the torches and the men's breathing marred the silence of the place. Dolan made his way down the tunnel and up to the burning arrow. His passage made not the slightest sound.

"How does he do that?" whispered Ob.

Dolan inched forward and peeked around the corner from the far side of the tunnel. He looked down that way for several moments, then waved the others forward.

"The tunnel goes on as far as I can see, which ain't far," whispered Dolan when the others reached him.

"Retrieve your arrow," said Theta, "and send it on."

Dolan did. It hit the ground about 150 feet away, its light revealing bones.

Stark white bones laying about the floor.

The tunnel opened up into a large cavern down that way. How large, they couldn't say, for the light from that single arrow couldn't hope to reveal it all.

"Perhaps we should turn about while we still have the chance," said Tanch. "The bones back there were a warning. Now we've got a bunch more bones. Something down there is deadly dangerous. The elves were afraid of it and this is their domain. We should be too. We should—"

"Stop your blabbering, Magic Boy," said Ob. "Theta, you still say that the way out of these tunnels lies thisaway?"

"I believe so," said Theta.

"Then through here we're going," said Ob. "If anybody else don't like it, keep your mouths shut about it. And that's it."

They moved slowly forward down the corridor, Theta holding his ankh and his shield in his right hand, his falchion in his left.

"You see any movement?" whispered Theta to Dolan as they neared the end of the tunnel, where it opened up.

"I smell something rotten," said Dolan.

"Something dead," said Ob. "Been tickling my nose for a while now."

"Put another arrow in that corner," said Theta. "I want to see more of this place before we step in."

Dolan doused another arrow with oil and set it aflame. A few moments later it hit the far wall of the cavern, nearly three hundred feet away, then fell to the ground. The light revealed little more than more bones, scattered all about the cavern. The bones were too large to be Svart. They were human sized, if not larger. They'd have to get closer to tell more.

"Empty, save for the dead," said Ob. "Let's see if there's a way through on the other side."

Theta put his arm out and stopped Ob as the gnome sought to move by. "Wait," he said, sheathing his sword in favor of his battle hammer. "Put another arrow up high. Shoot for the ceiling."

Dolan lit another arrow and shot it up at a high angle.

Something up high moved.

A flutter.

The arrow's flame went out.

"Back up!" said Theta as he raised his shield.

"Did you see that?" said one man.

"What was that?" said another.

A mild breeze sprang up from nowhere. A thin veil of smoke or mist washed through the group, emanating from within the cavern. The mist moved too fast for them to escape it. A vile stench it had. When that cloud went past them, all their torches went out, one after another, all the way down the line.

Claradon doubled over, gagging.

Men coughed and retched all around.

Ob felt as if something evil clutched as his insides. It groped, grasped, and hunted for his heart, or mayhap his soul. It sought to tear it from his breast. His mind spun, heart raced, his strength ebbed, and his stomach fled reckless toward his throat.

"Back down the tunnel," said Theta, coughing, the putrid, barrow stench of death and decay even affecting him. Few, if any, of the men heard him or could comply.

Theta spoke an odd word and his falchion began to glow — lit up with some mystical light, its origin and nature unknown. As much light came off it as from a good torch. He glanced around. Every man in the company was down, all the way back down to the end of the line, all retching and gagging, rolling on the ground, some unconscious, maybe dead. It had happened in an instant.

Theta stood alone.

There was a rattling of bones from one side of the cavern, and then from the other. More rattling from the center. The nearest bones that littered the floor were just within the circle of light provided by Theta's sword.

The bones began to move.

"Oh shit," said Theta.

61

CITY OF STARKBARROW, SVARTLEHEIM

FREM

Frem made his way through the Svart palace, Royce at his side, torches in hand. Carroll remained at the entry to take a rest and have his injured arm properly seen to. The facade of marbled splendor about the Svart city was far more than skin deep. The inside of the king's palace was no less ornate than the outside. Marble tiles, thick and weighty, covered the floor and walls — smooth and polished. The ceiling was comprised of great granite slabs. How the spindly elves constructed the place, Frem couldn't imagine. But it was black elf design for certain — their art was everywhere: statuary at each stair landing, friezes along the walls, crown molding carved and fluted.

But for all its beauty, the place was stark. Barren. So uncluttered as to look unlived in. There were no carpets, no curtains and draperies, no tapestries and sundries. Perhaps the stuff to create such items was scarce or non-existent in their subterranean world.

Every sound and step echoed, much more so even than in the tunnels. The place was as bitter cold as the caverns. There were no hearths about the building. As if the Svarts embraced the cold.

Were it not for the cleanliness of the place, Frem would have thought it long abandoned.

As Frem climbed the stairs, the smell of death came at him. At the top of the stairs on the third level was a grand mezzanine that overlooked the levels below, a delicate rail of sparkly stone making safe the edge. Two great stone doors, inlaid with gold and jewels, stood open on the interior side of the grand balcony. Putnam and the Pointmen sat on the floor outside the doors. Par Sevare was there, his hands and arms heavily bandaged, his face pale and drawn, his jaw clenched. He managed a nod, but that was all. Moag Lugron was there beside the wizard, twirling a black dagger in one hand. Nearby were Lex, Ward, Wikkle, Torak, Borel, Maddix, and Drift. Those were all that remained of Frem's famed platoon, the best of the Sithian Mercenary Company. Putnam looked up at Frem's approach, but no smile crossed his face, which was red and wet. "They killed them, Captain," he said. "They killed them all. Blades and poison."

"Who killed who?" said Frem as he approached the open doors. It was from there that the stench came.

Frem's eyes went wide at the terrible sight.

Hundreds upon hundreds of black elf bodies lay about a huge hall. Most were children, tiny and frail. Many were young women — their mothers. Some few were the very old. Those were all those amongst the elves that could not or would not fight. Their noncombatants. All dead. Every one. And by their own hands. Pitchers and drinking mugs lay about, some partly full, others toppled and empty. Frem picked one up and sniffed. An acrid odor that he didn't recognize, but it was surely poison. They coughed up black blood in their death throes. So too did they bleed from nose and ears.

More than a few had their throats cut — no doubt, those that refused to drink. Some lay huddled about the exits to the room, positioned such that it was clear they sought to escape, to push or claw their way out of the place. But the doors held. Their throats were cut. A scene of horror. True horror.

"They feared us so much?" mumbled Frem.

Putnam appeared beside him. Royce too.

"There is one door we haven't yet breached, straight to the back. All gold and glittery. Perhaps the chambers of their king or chieftain. Would you have us breach it?"

"We've come this far," said Frem. "Open it. After, gather what supplies we can: food, water, torches, and a map if we can find it. But we must not linger here overlong.

Soon the Pointmen breached the final door. The space within, a grand audience hall of a king. Empty and stark as the rest of the city, it was. Two figures lingered within. A female lay unmoving on the floor, fallen from a high seat, a poison cup beside her, glass shards all around.

A male Svart sat upon a grand throne. Small and dark was he. His face lined and solemn. His body thick and strong, limbs and chest robust compared to his fellows.

His eyes were open. He yet lived.

Frem strode through the hall, confident but wary.

The black elf spoke. "I not depart Midgaard life before evil faces I see," he said in the common tongue, heavily accented. "Faces of death."

"Then look into a mirror, not at us," spat Putnam. "We don't murder children."

Frem had the sense that the elf did not follow Putnam's words, they were too fast for him, his grasp of the language lacking.

"You are chieftain here?" said Frem.

"Throonbilg biln Mac-Murth, first and last of name mine. King last of Starkbarrow the ancient. Lord of dead race named Svartalfar. What call you they?"

"Frem Sorlons."

"Name of evil. Face of evil. Destroyed us you have. Not win will you. Not win."

"You've destroyed yourselves," said Frem. "Why did you attack us? Why murder your own?"

"Not allow brood mine enslaved by you evils. Tortured by you evils. Females abused by you evils. People proud we be good. Better death we have."

"You've destroyed yourselves for nothing," said Frem. "We only sought passage through your tunnels to get to the lands beyond. Had you not attacked us, we'd have done you no harm."

"Lies, face of evil, spew you," said the elf. "Lies why now? Over it is. Dead we be. Dead all. Coming of you we knew. Prophesies. Omens. Portents. Warnings old and new. Waiting for you, old one is. Stop you will he. Not win. Not win."

"Who is waiting for us? And where?" said

Frem.

"Fear tell you not I," said the elf king, "knowledge no good you. Uriel. Waits he, temple long. Ready long, Uriel be. Stop you, face of evil. Nifleheim door, closed will stay. Midgaard destroy, not you. Open never it you will, no matter evil what do you. You not. . ."

A cup fell from the king's hand. He coughed once and then again, and black blood dribbled from his mouth over his chin and chest. Then he let out a piercing, anguished scream — as if to announce his coming to whatever afterlife the black elves go to. He slumped forward, chin to chest, and moved no more.

62

SVARTLEHEIM

THETA

"**G**et up," shouted Theta as the bones strewn about the cavern floor began to move of their own accord. He tried to rouse Artol and Ob, who were closest to him, but they were down. Incapacitated.

All the men were.

All save for Theta.

"Dolan! Claradon! Glimador! Up!" said Theta. But none of them could rise, if even they heard his words, coughing and gagging as they were.

At the edge of the light, the bones slid across the floor, coming together in heaps, as if moved by unseen hands. Were it not for the mystical light from Theta's blade, the entire cavern would have been utterly dark. Only the rattling of the bones would have warned of what was coming.

The bones came together. And when they did, they took on the general shape that they held in life. A grayish black smoke swirled at every joint and juncture, somehow gluing the bones together and animating them.

And then the skeletons stood up, though they were yet but half formed. More bones slid toward each figure: a rib here, a finger bone there, a tooth, a toe. They slithered up the skeletons, from foot to femur, around and around, and on up, searching out their rightful places.

But they were not the bones of men.

The skulls each had two horns of bone that protruded from their foreheads. The rib cages were too large. They all approached seven feet in height.

Theta stepped boldly forward, his jaw set, shield held close before him. His falchion crashed through the nearest skeleton. Broke it into several pieces before the thing had fully formed. A moment later, those bones came together again, the breaks merely another joint to be stitched together by the swirling black smoke.

Theta cut through it again. And through its neighbor, but the bones came together again nearly as quickly as he blasted them apart.

He stepped back, pulled some small device from his belt pouch and threw it against the tunnel wall behind him, back by the downed men. When it hit, it burst with light, basking the tunnel in bright light that quickly ebbed and dwindled, though still it had the brightness of a clutch of new torches.

Vomit covered the tunnel and the men. Most coughed and gagged, dry heaved or retched. Some lay still. Others shook in convulsions.

Theta shouldered his shield, shifted his falchion to his right hand, and pulled forth his great battle hammer. He stood at the edge of the tunnel, not venturing more than a few steps into the eerie cavern.

He heard them walking, the skeletons. The bones of an olden race of demons. Creatures that once polluted several parts of Midgaard but were long since dead and all but forgotten. The Throan Gron Sek Nifleheem they were called in the Old Tongue, which meant, the thrice horned demons of Nifleheim.

The Throan Gron Sek were creatures of flesh and blood, despite their otherworldly origins. Dark magic it was that animated them in death. Necromancy on a grand scale. Theta saw more than a score of them approaching him. And who knows how many more were still hidden by the darkness. Perhaps twenty times that number.

Theta positioned himself between the undead and his fallen comrades. He could have run. He could have fled back the way they'd come, leaving the others to their fate, perhaps dragging one or even two to safety, and been marked a hero for doing so. He could perhaps even have fled forward, running to the other side of the cavern, finding whatever other exit might exist, and be out of there. Who could have blamed him for such a decision? No man could stand alone against a horde of undead demons. What could he do, but die beside his fellows? His mission failed. Korrgonn and the League left to freely open their gateway to Nifleheim and destroy the world. Stopping that from happening was Theta's priority. His companions held value so long as they aided him in that goal. No aid could they now provide. He should have run. The mission was more important than anything. All Midgaard depended on it. He could not fail. He had to flee. He had to survive that place to stop Korrgonn. He had no choice. And who could question his decision?

No man.

No man that understood the way things were. The choice was simple once emotions were cast aside.

But Theta didn't do that. He didn't run. He didn't abandon his men.

His companions.

His friends.

He could do that no more than could the sun choose not to rise in the morn. For leaving them was against his nature. Against everything he stood for; everything he had ever stood for. A brave hero could do no less.

Or else, perhaps there was another reason that Theta held that ground. A selfish reason? Some dark purpose? All part of his grand evil plan? In the end, who could say?

The creatures came at him. Theta's hammer thundered. His sword a blur as he cut this way and that, blocking bony talons and razored teeth. Theta smashed one demon skeleton atop the head. Shattered its skull into a hundred bits. Bits that soon slunk together again. The skull reformed. The pieces held together by undulating black smoke.

Theta staved in another skeleton's skull. He crushed the sternum of another. Every moment that went by, the skeletons moved faster. Their movements more coordinated. More fluid. Their attacks faster. Stronger. More precise. Theta sidestepped one way and then the other. He spun. Jumped. Weapons swinging.

But the tunnel was too wide. Fifteen feet was

too broad a passage for one man to block, however skilled, against the press of enemies. And press him they did. The demons closed in from front and forward flanks, massing before him. Hellbent on tearing him to pieces.

Theta was a whirlwind of destruction. Despite all his speed, all his skill, talons scraped against his arms. They screeched against his breastplate, his back. There were too many of them. And everywhere they touched him, smoke rose. Putrid smoke. Decayed. Much like the deadly breeze.

And then Claradon was at Theta's side, coughing and pale, but fighting, his eyes wide with shock and fear. The two each blocked half the corridor.

"Let none pass you," shouted Theta. "Not one."

It seemed like they fought for hours, no hope of victory, Claradon's armor took a terrible beating. His arms grew so weary he could barely swing his sword. Barely held up his shield.

And then Dolan and Artol joined them, weapons working. Now the tunnel was crowded. Claradon dropped back. He readied a sorcery.

A blue bolt of numinous energy shot past Claradon and blasted into and through one of the creatures, blowing it apart. That bolt of energy continued and blasted apart the skeleton just behind, and the one behind that, and so on, until it struck the rear wall of the cavern, far in the distance. It was Glimador's magic. He was up and fighting. So were others. Ganton the Bull charged forward. So did Sir Kelbor, Sergeant Vid, Captain Slaayde, and Captain Graybeard.

Claradon said his mystic words. He pulled fire

down from on-high. A blast that erupted amongst the massed skeletons. It charred their bones to ash. Each one touched by that holy fire was utterly consumed. But still, the demons came forward. No end to them in sight.

63

CITY OF STARKBARROW, *SVARTLEHEIM*

FREM

"How do you know this is the right way?" said Putnam as he started up a narrow flight of steep stairs carved out of the rock, all the Pointmen following, fully laden with what supplies and spoils Starkbarrow offered.

Moag Lugron stopped and turned toward the sergeant. "A great stair, well hidden, and what goes forever up. If it don't lead to the surface, where goes it?"

The stair was well built and situated within a narrow fissure that ran up the rock face at the very back of Starkbarrow. It was too small and too far away to see from anywhere outside the city and nearly everywhere within. To find it, you almost had to know it was there, and then, look in just the right place.

None of the Pointmen knew anything about the Svart city. The only living Svart they'd encountered beyond the front gates was the king, and he didn't say much before he died, poisoned by his own hand. But Moag could sniff out a trail anywhere, if you gave him the chance, and a bit of motivation. And getting out of the tunnels of Svartleheim was a powerful motivation for any sane man. So find the stair he did. And up they went, the whole squadron, what remained of it.

"You didn't take much," said Putnam to Frem.

"A few baubles," said Frem, tapping the side of his pack, which wasn't as full as it could have been.

"This is the biggest score the company has ever had by a hundredfold," said Putnam. "Gold, silver, emerald, diamond, dulcite, graban, and ruby everywhere. Even the common elves had enough coin or jewels squirreled away to make a princess swoon. And you didn't even fill your pack? Sometimes, you confuse me, Captain."

Frem shrugged.

"The art is what impressed me," said Sevare. "Paintings, drawings, etchings, and sculptures everywhere. In every room. In every home. Most expertly crafted."

"I thought it odd," said Putnam, "that besides that art, they had almost no stuff. Coins and jewels they had, but almost no furniture. Maybe two or three changes of clothes. A few pieces of cookware, a musical instrument or two, and that's about it. They lived with next to nothing. Yet had riches. I don't get it."

"What would they buy and where?" said Frem. "Not a lot of shops hereabouts."

"True enough," said Putnam. "In any case, I hope to enjoy their coin and jewels a good deal more than they did. In fact, I'm thinking about early retirement."

"You say that after every mission," said Frem.

"This time I mean it. Now I've got the money."

"We have to get home alive first," said Frem.

"We will, Captain," said Putnam. "Don't lose faith now. We're almost done with this business."

"Not so quick," said Frem. "There will be more knife-work before it's over. And maybe worse than what we've seen so far."

"I figure I'll get me a nice big manor house overlooking the river, maybe down Dor Malvegil way," said Putnam. "Hire some servants to take care of things, keep everything up. Live a life of ease. Count Putnam they'll call me. How does that sound?"

"Why not Earl or Duke while you're at it?" said Frem.

"Them titles might call a bit too much attention to me," said Putnam. "A low profile suits me best."

"How are you going to limit yourself to one woman?" said Frem.

"I wouldn't dream of it," said Putnam. "That'd be cruel to the Lomerian ladies."

"They don't have books," said Sevare. "Not in the palace. Not in the Diresvarts' tower. No library. Not a single scroll."

"There are runes all about," said Putnam. "Carved all over the walls."

"Carvings, yes," said Sevare. "But no parchment. Not a single sheet. And what's on the walls are just simple sayings, no real history or stories; no detail."

"They must keep an oral history," said Putnam. "Passing stories down from person to person. I've heard some Southron Islanders do that, and some folk way out east past Churthick, over the mountains out that way."

"Then it's all lost," said Sevare. "Their whole history. Everything they ever were, ever did. Gone. Because of us."

"There are some left," said Frem. "Me and Carroll had a bunch coming up behind us in the tunnel, other side of the water. Mayhap only a few; mayhap a lot. Don't forget that they attacked us when they could have let us pass by. They fought to the last man when they could've run or given up. They set their old folk and young women against us, knowing that they'd be slaughtered, but hoping that they'd overwhelm us with numbers. They killed their own noncombatants when there was no need to. We just defended ourselves, same as anybody would've done in the same spot."

"We did what we had to do," said Sevare. "And I suppose that they thought that they did the same. We'll never know what was in their minds. But that doesn't change the fact that their culture is destroyed."

"So go write a book about them, to keep their memory alive," said Putnam. "I'll not cry a drop for them. Like Frem said, they brought this on themselves. Stinking little imps."

"Can you imagine what secrets they had?" said Sevare. "Some of their magic was unlike any I've seen. I went through that tower, top to bottom. No journals, spell books, or scrolls. No records of any kind."

"Your pack looks full enough," said Putnam.

"I found some trifles of interest," said Sevare. "More than I could carry — killed me to leave most of it behind. But the knowledge. The secrets. Lost.

Lost forever."

"Show us what you picked up," said Frem.

"Later," said Sevare.

"You found some magical whatchamacallits, didn't you?" said Frem.

"Only things of interest to a wizard," said Sevare.

"Magicked up?" said Putnam.

"Ensorcelled," said Sevare. "And dangerous. It'll take a good deal of study to handle them safely."

"I'm interested in seeing it all, anyway," said Frem.

Sevare nodded.

"The boys wanted to take some of them musical instruments we found," said Putnam. "Had them in every house. Sounded like pipes and flutes. Beautiful sounds, but the things are so darned delicate. Just wrapping up a couple of them damaged them. So we left them, except for a little flute or two, but I don't think even they will make it back in one piece."

"Some of the men took paintings and drawings," said Frem. "Cut them from their frames and rolled them up."

"What do you figure them artsy things be worth?" said Putnam.

"Masterpieces from a dead civilization?" said Sevare. "Maybe more than the jewels you picked up."

"Enough talk," said Frem as they neared the ceiling of the great cavern, having trudged up two or three hundred feet of steep stairs. "We need to keep sharp and keep our ears open; if we get sloppy and all day-dreamy in here, we're liable to end up dead. This job isn't over yet. Not by a goodly ways."

The stair switched back and forth several times as it made its way up the cavern's wall to its ceiling where it continued up through a circular hole in the rock. That hole led to vertical shaft, generally smooth of sides, but with circular lines and shallow grooves around it. The stair itself became a spiral that wound up and up inside that shaft, and continued far beyond their sight.

The Svarts didn't believe in handrails, which made the climb all the more stressful, dizzying, and dangerous.

The shaft went up hundreds of feet and then hundreds more. There seemed no end to it.

When at last they neared the top, they heard faint sounds: rumblings, thumping, and what might have been shouts. But the sounds were so faint, so indistinct, that they couldn't be certain whether the sounds were real or imaginary. The men went silent. Nobody had to tell them to; they just knew.

The stair ended at a small stone door of irregular shape. It was well concealed, that door, as its edges followed the grain of the surrounding stone. Its hinges and pull gave it away, as did the fact that without its presence, the stair would have dead ended.

Moag Lugron crept up on that door as if it were a sleeping cat. He put his ear to it.

After some time, he looked back at the others. He flashed a sign to stay silent. Another sign warned that someone was on the other side of the door.

Frem, Putnam, Royce, and Lex crowded together behind Moag, though far enough back that he could pull the door open, if it opened inward. They drew their weapons carefully, quietly.

Moag held a long dagger between his teeth, his hands free to work the door.

He pushed and pulled to no effect. Moments later, he spied a lever not far from the door pull. It had been right under his nose, but blended so well into the background that he hadn't seen it at first, nor had any of the others.

He pulled the lever. There was an audible click and the door moved inward an inch or so.

Moag thrust the door open. Looked in. And sprang forward, knife in hand. The others followed.

64

SVARTLEHEIM

CLARADON

"**W**ho dares disturb my slumbers?" boomed a voice from somewhere in the cavern. A voice that drowned out the cacophony of the battle between the Lomerians and the demon skeletons. It spoke in an olden tongue of man, a language long dead and forgotten. No man amongst the expedition understood its words, except for Theta. He remembered that tongue, though the creature spoke it with an accent and it stumbled over the words, as if it hadn't spoken them in an age. "Who dares use petty sorceries in my presence?" said the voice.

Claradon sought the source of the voice. It came from above them, up high in the cavern.

There was a great fluttering and flapping, as if by vast wings — then another foul breeze washed over the men, now somehow immune to its debilitating effects. Claradon saw something drop down far behind the demon skeletons, on the other side of the cavern. Something large. Huge. A creature more of shadow than substance. A large toothy maw, enormous wings, long talons, and large body. With that came a sense of age. And decay. It was a thing of death. Something that crawled from the pits of Helheim.

"Back down the tunnel," shouted Theta, though the battle with the demon skeletons had turned in their favor. "Turn and run! Now!"

Most of the men did. Still coughing, staggering. Theta made no move to retreat. Nor did Dolan.

"Are you coming?" said Artol and Claradon at the same time.

"No," said Theta. "Get you gone. This creature is beyond you all. Run for your lives."

"What is it?" said Artol.

"A shadow demon," said Theta. "An ancient evil that endures from the First Age of Midgaard. You have no craft or skill that can harm it. Flee now or I cannot save you."

"What will you do?" said Claradon. "You cannot face this beast alone."

"I can and I will," said Theta. "Go, now, while you still can."

65

SVARTLEHEIM

THETA

"Let's go lads," shouted Ob as Theta prepared to confront the shadow demon. "Let's go while we can."

Claradon, Ob, Artol, and their knights and allies backed down the corridor, slowly at first, then more quickly.

A deep, throaty chuckle came from the creature before next it spoke. "Puny man-creature," said the shadow demon as it drew closer to Theta, "why do you not flee with your fellows? Tired of your petty mortal life, are you? A hero's death do you desire? Fall now into my embrace and I shall gift it to you."

"What be thy name, creature?" shouted Theta as he bashed in the skull of another skeleton.

A monstrous, shadowy hand waved, black talons as long as swords reflected in the limited light, and the skeletons broke off their attack. As one, they moved aside. Went still as statues.

The cavern fell silent, save for the echoing footfalls and chatter of the fleeing Lomerians.

"Know not my name, do you?" said the creature, most of the energy gone from his voice. "Disappointing that is to me. Pains me in ways a little thing like you would never understand."

"In the days of yore all Midgaard knew my name," said the shadow demon. "The masses trembled when they heard it spoke. Great kings and emperors wept when I came calling. By the thousands the people cowered before me, offered me their sacrifices and supplications. They begged. They pleaded. They did my bidding. Served my every whim and pleasure. But most of all, they worshiped me as their lord and master."

"Who am I, you ask, petty little man-creature. You stand before Borkoth Garaktok, the Lord of the Shadows, Arch-Duke of the Nether Marches — or at least I once was, long ago, though the knowing of my name and titles will profit you nothing. The power of names is beyond your ken. Beyond any of your kind. Fodder, food, and slaves — that's all that your kind has ever been good for."

"Once Arch-duke of the Nether Marches of Nifleheim," said Theta, "but now, naught but king of the cave crickets. Baron of bones. Sovereign of spiders. The lord of long forgotten."

"Ha, ha," spat Borkoth. "Seek you my wrath? You will not have it. I'll give you no power over me, manling. Bow down before me. Beg mercy, forgiveness. Beg it well and proper, and we may yet speak more."

Theta didn't respond.

"Dare not defy me, puny man-thing. I have not eaten in many an age. Before I devour you, I'd have your name too, so that I might remember you in future days when I gaze upon your sorry bones.

Theta stood with his shield held before him. His battle hammer in his left hand. He mouthed some words. Sparks erupted from his hammer, and then a white light that came from who knows where bathed him head to toe, illuming him for the shadow lord to see.

"You know my name," said Theta. "I am the reason you've hidden here for years beyond count, cowering in the darkness, hoping that I'd never find you."

"What!" said the shadow lord as he shifted and twisted, his outline more visible with every movement. His body was enormous — a hundred feet across or more, but ghostly in appearance, winged and clawed with a great spiked head that called to mind a dragon, though it seemed more smoke than solid, more spectre than serpent, more of the world of the dead than of the living.

"This be no place for you," said Theta. "This is the world of man. For you, there is only the void. There I'll send you to be with all your brethren."

"You cannot be he," said Borkoth. "You bluff me, manling. But I will not be bluffed. I will eat you all the same. I ask you for the last time, what name or title do you claim?"

"They call me the Harbinger of Doom," said Theta.

"Aargh!" went Borkoth, his voice booming. "You lie," he shouted so loudly that the cavern shook. He drew back and lifted himself up. "You cannot be. Not here. Not now."

"I am THETAN," shouted Theta as he flung his hammer toward the shadow lord.

66

SVARTLEHEIM

BORKOTH

As the manling's hammer flew at him, Borkoth saw that the olden runes inscribed upon it, glowed with energies and powers unknown.

An ensorcelled weapon! And no common one, if any such things could be called common. It oozed of magic like the famed weapons of old — those that carried their own names, had their own reputations. It shown so brightly to Borkoth's eyes, he could barely look upon it. The Weave was strong in it. Truly, a thing of uncommon make.

That meant one of two things.

Either it was a manling of consequence that stood so boldly before him. A hero like those of old, looking to slay his dragon.

Or else, the manling was an agent of the Svartalfar. A hired killer. Perhaps the greedy little worms had decided to be rid of Borkoth at long last and had magicked up a shiny bauble to do the trick. Gifted it to a trumped up hedge knight to whom they promised fame and fortune, if he but rid them of a strange squatter in their tunnels. Once dead, the Svarts would take his territory for their own. As if the endless tunnels were not enough for them.

Borkoth never once considered that the

manling may have spoken the truth. That he was the one and true Harbinger of Doom. Such a possibility was too unlikely. Too disastrous. Too terrible to face. That fiend could never have found him. Not down there, so deep, so quiet, the caverns. He had been safe there down through the ages. Quiet and safe. Only the Svarts delved that deep. And even they, only once in an age.

Besides, the Harbinger must be long dead. A son of man was he at best report. An ephemeral thing like all of them. Long since gone to dust and memory, if even that.

The manling hurled the hammer at his core. Borkoth had no time to dodge. No room to maneuver.

He'd take the blow.

He'd weather its sting — and that's all it would be, even if the hammer were of Svartish make. Borkoth was beyond the power of mortal weapons, whatever their pedigree. He'd withstand it.

And then he'd crush the manling.

He'd make him pay for his bluff and his bite. Or so he planned.

But when that hammer hit, the very heavens thundered and Midgaard shook to its core. A wave of invisible energy that came from that hammer passed through every being in those caverns and who knows how far beyond, and took them all from their feet, threatening to stop their beating hearts in their chests. The hammer carried Borkoth through the air and smashed him against the cavern's far wall, all his bulk notwithstanding.

Stunned he was by the blow. A blow harder

than he had ever felt. A blow that would have instantly killed any mortal creature, even one as large as he. But Borkoth Garaktok was no ephemeral thing like the children of Midgaard. He was a scion of Nifleheim, born in those Nether Realms before time itself. Long now trapped on Midgaard after a conquest that failed. A folly for which he long regretted. Only by hiding there in the depths of lightless caverns, enduring the passage of years beyond count, biding his time, had he survived. He lurked there, hoping for salvation. For escape. For freedom. For a chance to return whence he came, or better still, to conquer Midgaard, to bring all the manlings and their kind under his yoke.

He always believed that that day would come. If he but endured long enough.

Eventually, by some craft of man or demon, twist of fate, grand celestial alignment, or happenstance, the portals betwixt the worlds would open again. And when they did, the hordes of Helheim would spring forth and claim their due. That day, Borkoth would emerge from the caverns triumphant. He'd resume his rightful place. He need only hold out until that time came.

As he grunted, cursed, and tried to rise, tried to pull himself up, he knew that he'd been undone. He knew that that day would never come.

The manling before him had spoken true. He was the Harbinger of Doom. The bane of all Borkoth's kind. The one the Midgaardians called Thetan. Only he had the physical and mystic power to wield such a hammer. To strike such a blow.

Borkoth had endured all his trials and pains for naught.

He'd only postponed the inevitable reckoning.

Death beckoned.

But Borkoth would not take that last road alone.

He'd drag the Harbinger down with him.

67

JUTENHEIM

FREM

The stone door at the top of the Svart stair opened into a cave. Moag Lugron rushed through, dagger to hand. Fresh air flooded the stairwell — signaling nearness to the surface. Frem and the Pointmen rushed through the door moments behind Moag. There were figures in the cave. Fighting.

Moag had jumped them.

Two men — big, broad of shoulder. One was already down, clubbed by the butt of Moag's dagger. The other turned and Frem saw his face.

A Lugron, Frem marked him, but of a tribe unknown to Frem — his skin, grayer; his height, taller; his frame, heavier; his clothes well crafted of animal skin, but of a primitive style.

Moag jabbed him in the face — once and then again.

The Lugron lunged, but Moag sidestepped him and ridgehanded him to the back of the neck. A vicious chop that should have stunned him. Dropped him to his knees.

It didn't.

It barely slowed him. The man was a brute.

He grabbed hold of Moag. Lifted him into the air as if he were a child. Began to squeeze the life out of him.

Frem stepped forward. He punched the big Lugron in the jaw, holding little back. Instead of crashing to the floor dazed or knocked out, the Lugron merely grunted and stepped back. His grip on Moag never loosened.

Frem was shocked. That punch would've dropped a horse.

Frem hit him again. Even harder. As hard as he could. Caught him cleanly on the side of the jaw.

That did it.

The Lugron dropped Moag and Moag rolled out of the way. He'd had enough of that brute and had no interest in getting between him and Frem.

Frem stepped forward. Kicked the Lugron in the gut. Blasted him with punches to the face. Five, six strikes to his head before the brute went down. Solid punches they were. Thrown by an expert: Frem whose arms were as big around as most men's legs. No one should have withstood five punches like that from Frem. But that Lugron did.

The moment the Lugron hit the floor, the Pointmen pounced. They pinned his arms behind his back. And that was that.

"Tie them up, boys," said Putnam. "And gag them too."

"There's a hidden exit at the far end of the cave," said Torak.

"Guard it close," said Putnam.

"Them two we trussed," said Putnam to Frem, "is

the lot of them, but we've got three dead elves." The dead elves lay about the small cave's floor. Each bore terrible wounds. "This one died quick," said Putnam, pointing to one of the elves, the one farthest from the rear of the cave. "A dagger to the kidney. See the marks on his jaw and throat? Grabbed from behind and stabbed but good. One thrust and it was over. These other two had it worse. They got tortured. See the shallow cuts? The bent fingers? The bruises? The Lugron went at them slow and vicious. Searching for secrets were they."

"The elves didn't give up their secret door," said Frem. "Brave."

"If they had, the Lugron would've opened it," said Putnam, "or at least been wary of it. We'd not have gotten the drop on them. These elves must be the door guards. I figure that the Lugron jumped them, probably when the elves were listening for us coming up, all distracted and such, probably ready to pee themselves. No doubt, we've picked up a reputation hereabouts of late."

"Maybe the elves didn't understand their questions," said Sevare. "Maybe there be no common language between them. Mayhap the Lugron tortured them for fun."

"We only do that to wizards," said Moag, an evil leer fixed on Sevare.

The wizard rolled his eyes and turned away.

"Why did the Lugron just happen upon this place now?" said Frem. "A strange coincidence." Just then, a booming sound came from somewhere in the distance. From outside the cave.

Frem, Moag, Putnam, and Royce crept around the bend in the cave and they saw daylight filtering past the edges of boulders that blocked the mouth of the cave. One big stone was pushed aside — the Lugron's entry point. Closer now to the cave's entry, they heard the outside sounds more clearly. Someone was moving around outside. A lot of someones.

The Pointmen moved forward and skulked up to the boulders at the entry, silent as mice. The entry was wide, but uneven, and very low to the ground. They'd have to go on their bellies to crawl out. The Lugron must have pushed in the boulder as they crept inside.

There were bushes and brambles aplenty outside the cave entrance obscuring their vision, but a brief glance told them they were on high ground, up a rocky slope, and that many figures were gathered farther down the slope. Figures arrayed for war.

Something leapt down from above and outside the cave mouth, only several feet from where the Pointmen lay.

Two thick hairy legs. Facing away from them.

Much larger than a man's were they.

With a whooping, deep growl, the figure bounded down the hill toward the others already gathered there — its fellows. Another of its kind landed before the cave entry, same as the first. Then came another. And another. A wave of them. Luckily for the Pointmen, all their attention was focused downslope. Not a one seemed to notice the cave, which was behind them and well concealed. They ran down the slope, howling.

Manlike, but hairy like a bear were these people. Thick and broad. Very tall. How big, Frem couldn't guess from the limited view he had, crouching down in the darkness. But far bigger than a normal man. Far bigger even than he. More and more of them passed over the cave entry. Hundreds of them. Jumping down from the rocks above.

The Pointmen kept quiet and still. They barely dared to breathe. More than one wondered whether they should head back down the stair. Close that secret door behind them and take their chances in the tunnels. More than one of them wanted to do just that.

Then Torak sniffed out a watch spot, high up on the cave wall. The irregular stone was such that you could walk right up the wall, like a disjointed and uneven stair, and find a perch some eight feet up. Torak had seen light shining through around the edges of a stone up there. The stone was loose, easily removable. It was clear enough that that was no random loose rock. It was pried and dug out, and the steps up the wall had been manipulated. It was a spy hole. A watch post that gave the black elves a clear view of the valley below.

Frem made his way over to the watch post as quietly as he could; he needed to see for himself. The view from the cave mouth was just too obscured. He couldn't size up what went on out there, other than seeing it was a large gathering of folk geared for war. He needed more information. Who was fighting who? And why? What were their positions and numbers?

And then, he needed to come up with a plan. Hiding in that little cave, hoping to not be discovered, wasn't a sound plan, as the elf guards recently learned.

"That's a sight," said Torak as he moved aside.

Frem slowly stepped up to the watch spot, moving tentatively, testing each stone, making certain that it could carry him and not shift, prior to putting his full weight on it. He made it safely up to the watch spot and what he saw was a wonder.

Just downslope from their cave, the hairy giants were gathered in their hundreds. They wore no clothes, but carried primitive weapons of wood, stone, and bone: spears, clubs, and makeshift blades of this design and that. Frem guessed that they were half again the height of a tall man, and probably three or four times the weight.

On the opposite rise, on the other side of the valley floor, was assembled their opponents: a Lugron army, or at least, what looked like Lugron — hard to be certain given the distance. Frem saw several companies of them, all footmen aligned in formation, shoulder to shoulder, decked out in full battle gear. Officers sat atop tall, hairless, humpbacked animals and paced back and forth between their squadrons.

Then from farther south, above the rise, came Lugron cavalry. Two or three squadrons strong — set atop, not horses, but great lizards, the like of which Frem had not seen before. From farther north, another contingent of Lugron pulled a force of siege equipment into view: ballistae and catapults aplenty. Dozens of them.

It would be a battle the like of which had not been seen in an age — at least not by civilized men. A Lugron horde against an army of primitive giant men.

Then began the drums. Frem knew that sound. Lugron war drums. Where the drummers stood, Frem could not see. In response, the giant men began to grunt and chant in their guttural tongue, if even they were words at all. Both forces began to move toward each other. Slowly. There was a good deal of ground between them, much of it rough terrain. They took their time, their drums, drumming, their voices chanting and howling — their forces moving inexorably closer, destined to meet somewhere on the valley floor. The Pointmen practically piled atop each other, on their bellies, at the cave entry, trying to see whatever they could.

The more the giant men moved down the slope the less they blocked Frem's view of the valley floor below. Soon Frem spied a clutch of figures gathered at the very center of the valley, halfway between the two opposing armies.

"Oh, shit!" went Frem.

"What is it?" said Putnam. "What do you see?"

"The Company is down there," said Frem. "On the valley floor. With` the Leaguers."

"What?" said the men, gasping.

"They're set up in a circle facing outward. I can see Big Red and Mason. The wizards too, I think."

"How many?" said Putnam.

"Maybe fifty," said Frem. "Maybe more. There's Lugron dead on one side of them and giants on the other."

"Those armies aren't gathered to fight each other," said Frem. "They've gathered to fight us."

"Oh shit," said Putnam.

"Oh shit," said the Pointmen.

Wikkle Lugron appeared below Frem's position. "Captain," he spat. "They're coming up the stairs. The elves. More of them."

Frem and all the others close enough to hear turned to face Wikkle.

"How many?" said Frem.

"All of them, I expect," said Wikkle. "Hundreds."

"Oh shit," said Frem.

"And they got more rock giants," said Wikkle. "A bunch of them."

"Oh shit," said the Pointmen.

68

SVARTLEHEIM

THETA

Theta charged the shadow lord. Already halfway across the cavern was he. Despite his bulk and heavy armor, even a champion sprinter could not have matched his pace. His falchion was out. He leapt through the air — a higher jump than any mortal could dream to make, sword pointed at shadow. A burst of blue numinous energy erupted from the sword's tip. It crackled and sparked like a lightning bolt and blasted into Borkoth's head. Seared his eyes. Burned his cheeks. And then Theta's sword opened a great gash in the beast, shoulder to chest. That cut released a stream of icy black ichor and acrid fumes.

The cavern shook as the monster screamed.

It reeled back. Whatever sorcery cloaked it in shadow, ebbed. Perhaps from pain. Perhaps Theta's magic sapped its energies. Whatever the reason, Borkoth's body coalesced. It solidified and grew more visible by the moment. And when it did, Theta saw its frightful form.

Its shape was like that of a winged lizard — though a giant one, as large as a manor house, but its aspect was decayed and putrid as if a month dead — gaping holes in wing and limb, cheek and tail, all blackened and shriveled of skin and scale. A dessicated husk of whatever it once was. Or mayhap, it was ever thus. An undead demon of the pit.

Its great arm lashed out. Too large, too quick even for a hero of yore to avoid. It crashed into Theta with a terrible thump and clang of metal. Sent him flying across the cavern.

Theta smashed to the floor. Slid a dozen yards before friction stopped him.

Borkoth lunged in for the kill. Its jaws were open — jaws big enough to swallow a man. Teeth large enough to cut him in two in a single bite. Theta sidestepped and leapt, sword swinging. That blade flashed across Borkoth's open maw, all Theta's speed and power behind it. It connected with one of Borkoth's great fangs, pitch black and razor sharp. Sliced it cleanly in two. When the tooth struck the cavern floor it shattered into untold pieces like a thing of glass.

Borkoth reared back again. He lifted his head on high with a great intake of air. He lunged down once more opening his maw. From that pit came a spray of black fire that burned with all the heat of Helheim.

Even as Borkoth unleashed his attack, about Theta there appeared a sparkling blue dome — a mystical shield he called up by means known only to him. The magic's energies emanated from the center of Theta's battle shield. The sorcerous mantle wrapped around him, helmet to boot, front to rear.

Black hellfire washed over that dome-like shield. It battered it. Charred it. On and on did it burn. It peeled back layer after layer of blue energy. Blackening it. Devouring it. Theta's force shield flickered. Its energy failing. Threatening to go out. Sweat beaded on Theta's face as the temperature soared within his sanctuary.

As Theta crouched behind his shield, his hand rummaged in his belt pouch. He extracted something. Put it to his mouth and bit down. What it was, who could say?

The cavern floor all about Theta, save for the small area protected by his magical shield, melted and bubbled from Borkoth's fiery spray. The very stone dissolved away. Pits and divots formed all about. The demon's ichor that pooled there was akin to black tar in appearance. Fumes rose from it. Noxious. Toxic. Foul.

Luckily, Theta's mystic shield kept those fumes out.

Theta's left arm stretched out, palm forward, fingers cupped as if reaching out to grasp something, and held there, waiting, even as Borkoth's attack fizzled out.

The last of the black fire dripped from its maw. It sizzled and sparked when it hit the cavern floor.

The moment Borkoth's fire quieted, Theta's hammer roared. It flew of its own accord from where it lay on the cavern floor. Rocketed back into Theta's outstretched hand.

Borkoth spied the hammer. The dark red pits of his eyes grew wide, and he drew back again, pulling away, and tried to flee.

Theta leapt into the air, defying gravity, buoyed by some esoteric magic he employed. He flew at the shadow lord with frightful speed, hammer raised.

Borkoth swatted at him.

This time, the creature was too slow. Theta's hammer came down with unimaginable force. It struck between the monster's eyes. When it hit, a great thunderclap sounded. That impact crushed Borkoth to the cavern floor as if a weight ten times his own fell upon him.

Borkoth thrashed on his back. Groaned. Cursed. Smoking black ichor dribbled from his mouth, nose, and ears.

Theta stood upon the beast's chest. His boots sizzled and sparked where they touched the demon's flesh.

Borkoth tried to grab the knight, to crush him within his fist, but Theta's blue domed shield came up again and thwarted its efforts, fending off the mammoth hand.

Theta pounded the hammer to Borkoth's chest — once and then again. That sapped the demon's strength and prevented it from rising. Borkoth tried to fling Theta off. As its arm swatted him, somehow, Theta's force shield diverted or absorbed its momentum, and took the blow without being thrown back.

Then Theta's falchion went to work again. He raised it high. Plunged it into the center of the demon's chest. Sank it to the hilt.

Borkoth screamed — a piercing, deafening wail.

Theta pulled the sword out. Moved it over a bit, and plunged it in again. Then again. And again. And again, carving its chest like a slab of meat. All the while, Borkoth screamed and pounded on Theta's mystical shield, which still flickered and sparked but deflected every blow.

And then the mystical shield collapsed.

When Borkorth's claws came in anew, Theta's falchion sliced them off with a sharp-pitched whine. They flew across the cavern and shattered. Borkoth's eyes were wide with disbelief as he screamed and screamed.

Theta reached down and with a great heave and strain pulled out a huge mass of flesh that he'd sawn from the demon's chest. That exposed the black, beating heart of the monster. Without a moment's pause, and in single motion, Theta dropped to his knees and plunged his sword deep into the demon's flesh. Through its still beating heart.

The monster thrashed and convulsed for some moments, spewing garbled curses for as long as its strength allowed. Then it went still.

Its great body melted away in mere moments. Dissolved into black vapors that dispersed in the air, and left nothing of it behind. Not claw, bone, or blood. Utterly gone, as if it had never been there at all.

The horned demon skeletons collapsed in heaps where they stood, for the evil magic that powered them died with Borkoth.

Theta staggered, his boots, hands, and arms smoking, his armor and shield dented and scarred. He paused, drew his round, metallic flask from his belt pouch, carefully unstoppered it, his every movement precise and measured as if he held a newborn babe in his arms. He chanced the tiniest of swallows, perhaps only a single drop, then carefully stowed the flask away.

He made his way back to the tunnel from which he'd entered the shadow demon's cavern. Dolan lounged against the cavern wall, grinning. Claradon was there. So too was Ob, Artol, Tanch, Glimador, and the Eotrus knights. They stood awestruck at what they'd seen, mouths open, disbelief on their faces.

Artol dropped down on one knee. The others did the same, save for Par Tanch who looked horrified at the gesture, and Ob, who just wouldn't.

"My lord—" said Artol.

"Get up you fools," said Theta.

"Only a god could do what we just witnessed," said Artol. "Tell us true, are you the thunder god, the son of Odin All-father?"

Theta walked the rest of the way up to them, studying their faces before he spoke again.

"One need not be a god to do great or wondrous deeds," said Theta. "One need only have courage, conviction, skills, and the right tools for the job," he said, displaying his hammer. "As you have no doubt guessed, this is Mjollnir, the famed hammer of Donar, eldest son of Wotan, Lord of the Aesir. Donar has need of it no longer, so I carry it now and have for many years."

"No man can wield Mjollnir," said Artol. "Only a god can lift it. Or even move it."

"Some stories grow taller in the telling," said Theta as he held out the hammer to Artol. "Take it. Feel its weight."

"I dare not."

"Take it," said Theta in a voice the brooked no

argument.

Artol reached out and grasped Mjollnir's handle. Theta let go and Artol was nearly pulled down, the hammer's head hitting the tunnel floor.

"Lift it," said Theta.

Artol's face took on a determined look. He grimaced, and lifted the hammer from the floor; held it in hand, his muscles bulging. He tried to bring it up to his chest, but he could not until he used both hands, and then stood tall, the hammer looking large even against his seven foot tall frame.

"See now, you've lifted it," said Theta. "Are you a god?"

"I am but a man," said Artol.

"Then I have answered your question."

"No you haven't," spat Ob. "All you did is show us that Artol can pick up a stinking heavy hammer. That's not news to nobody. Are you or are you not a god? One of the Aesir? And which one?"

"Loki," said Tanch. "He is Loki." All eyes turned to the wizard. "The trickster."

Theta shook his head in annoyance. "I should have known better than to open my mouth," he said, though whether he was talking to the men or himself wasn't clear. "Do you intend to aid me in stopping Korrgonn and the wizards that follow him? Will you or not?"

"That's why we're here," said Artol as he handed back the hammer.

"That and rescuing my brother," said Claradon.

"If thinking that I'm a god makes you happy, or makes you more willing to follow me, or just helps to keep your teeth together — then consider me a god and ask me no more foolish questions.

"Goodly men may not follow the trickster," said Tanch. Or else be led to ruin."

"I am not the Loki of legend," said Theta. "And I am no trickster."

"Which is exactly what Loki would say," said Tanch.

"Enough," said Theta. "I've given you my answers and spoken true. I will indulge your superstitions no longer. Dolan — search the cavern. The demon likely had a cache of riches that may be of use to us. Rout it out. But do not dare touch it, not one bauble, until I give you leave — it may harbor great danger. And for Odin's sake, someone go after the others. Hopefully, they aren't still running. We've no more time to waste.

69

MONASTERY OF IVALD, ISLAND OF JUTENHEIM

OB

"This mission of yours is cursed," said Captain Slaayde as the bedraggled group made their way through the lower levels of the Monastery of Ivald. "Every step we take we're dogged by demons and devils, wizards and whatnot. There's no chance of us getting through this quest alive. You know that, don't you?"

"We're out of the tunnels," said Ob, "and I say, that means things are looking up. So quit your complaining."

"Looking up?" said Slaayde. "We left five men down there, two of them mine. Now we have to climb down a sheer cliff just to get to Jutenheim's interior. What is it, four hundred feet down? Five hundred? More? And then cross a swamp with a worse reputation than those blasted tunnels. Days of slogging through shit no man was meant to pass through. And then what? We don't even know where we're going. If that's looking up, that just shows how bad off we are."

"Nobody said this mission was going to be easy," said Ob.

"I was just a ferryman," said Slaayde. "For me it was no mission at all. Ferry you down river, maybe down to Dover, or on to Tragoss Mor, maybe farther; drop you off, maybe wait a time for you to do your business, then haul you straight back to Lomion City; drop you on Duke Harringgold's doorstep, and be on my merry way. That's it. That's all it was supposed to be. A long voyage, mayhap, but that's nothing new for me and mine, but it wasn't supposed to be this."

"The Duke's people told you this would be a dangerous thing," said Ob.

"Danger is part of my business," said Slaadye. "It goes without saying. But I wasn't supposed to lose half my crew. I wasn't supposed to fight monsters out of myth and story. I've had enough. Too much. It's all too much."

"Aye, it is, lad," said Ob. "And you've suffered through it, bravely despite your bellyaching. You and your men have made a darn good account of yourselves through it all. But however tough it's been, and however tough it still will get, we've got to see this quest through. All Midgaard depends on it, and you know it. Our best chance is to work together. To keep watching each other's backs. We'll accomplish the mission because we have to. There's no other choice. Know they it or not, all the world is depending on us."

"I only half believe it," said Slaayde. "I believe the Leaguers want to open their gateway to wherever, but I don't believe that they can. I don't believe such things are possible. Yet I can't deny I've seen things on this voyage that don't belong on Midgaard. Maybe they are from the Nether Realms. Or maybe they're just relics from the Dawn Age. I don't know. I was just supposed to ferry you around. That's all."

The line of men stopped and went quiet. They were halfway through the monastery, nearly at the top of the basement stair. Ob pushed his way through the ranks as quietly as he could.

"What goes on?" whispered Ob when he got up to the front by Theta, Claradon, and Dolan.

"Dolan smells the sea," said Claradon.

"So?" said Ob.

"That's it," said Claradon. "So we're watching and listening."

"We're on an island, you morons," said Ob. "Of course he smells the sea. The breeze comes straight through. Let's get moving. At this rate, I'll be an old fart of four hundred before this mission is done."

Theta put up his hand to stop the gnome. "Dolan, do you think someone lies in wait for us?" said Theta. "In the monastery?"

"A bunch of someones, Lord Angle," said Dolan. "Men off a ship, if my nose tells me true."

"Did he say that his nose is talking to him?" said Ob. "The boy's gone daft. His brains are scrambled. Hit one too many times. He hasn't been the same since the fight with that bloodsucker in the alley."

"Form the men up," said Theta. "Shield wall at the front. Pikes behind. Archers at the ready."

"Might there be enough men out there to threaten our group?" said Claradon. "Who could they be?"

"There's more than enough warriors amongst the locals to give us what for if they rose up on us," said Ob. "We'd have us another run for our lives like back in Evermere Bay and Tragoss Mor. We got lucky twice, I'd not care to tempt fate again."

"Hopefully, it's just a few wayward monks back from fishing," said Theta. "Or else some small contingent that the Leaguers left behind for some reason."

"You don't really believe it'll be that easy do you?" said Ob.

"No," said Theta. "It's probably an ancient red dragon that commands the Weave, or else a gang of mountain giants. That's why we're sending you in first, gnome — to scout about and see what's what."

Everyone looked toward Theta. His face wore not the hint of a grin.

70

MONASTERY OF IVALD, *ISLAND OF JUTENHEIM*

OB

"**W**hat ho, lads," said Ob as he marched across the monastery's great hall toward several men that lounged about on couches and chairs in the sitting area in the far corner. Dolan and several of the expedition's soldiers walked behind him.

The men popped up from their seats. They were not monks. Their clothes casual and of Lomerian style, not Juten. Their hands went immediately to their weapons, swords and daggers, though they didn't pull them.

"Who goes there?" said one man.

"Don't you mind us, lads," said Ob with a toothy smile. "We're the sewer guildsmen. We've been working on that plumbing backup that's stinking up the place."

The men looked back and forth to each other uncertainly.

"You don't look like sewermen," said the speaker, his accent, distinctly Lomerian. His hand moved to and rested on his sword hilt. "Best you hold where you are."

"And you don't look like the monks what hired us," said Ob as he continued to walk toward him, half a smile still on his face. "We've been up to our elbows in monk crap since yesterday, trying to get that clog cleared for the holy men and we expect to get paid. Now go and rouse those slackers from their meditations for us or we'll have both our guildmaster and the constable on you."

Seconds later, Ob had his sword tip against the man's throat. Dolan and the others had the drop on his fellows. Not a one was quick enough to even pull a weapon.

"Now laddie," said Ob, "tell me who you are and what you be doing in this old monastery."

"We're merchants down from Dover, up Lomion way," said the man. "We come to trade with the monks every year, and sell them whatnots they can't get or make in these parts. Who are you?"

Theta, Claradon, and the rest of the expedition emerged from the corridor in which they were hiding and proceeded across the great hall toward Ob and the merchants.

"Dead gods," said the man, "who are you people? Please tell me you didn't do away with the monks."

"Somebody has, laddie," said Ob, "but it weren't us. We're the good guys."

When Theta and the men were about halfway across the main hall, a large man stepped out of the shadows toward the back of the hall. The moment he showed himself, scores of men emerged from hiding all about the perimeter of the room, their positions well concealed. Almost all of them held crossbows, loaded and lowered, aimed at Theta and company.

"Hold right there, Thetan," said Milton

DeBoors, known as the Duelist of Dyvers, a famed bounty hunter hired by House Alder to capture or kill Claradon and Theta. DeBoors moved forward and closed the distance between them. His crossbowmen did the same, keeping aim with their weapons as they moved.

"Best we shoot them while we can," said Edwin of Alder, his father, Blain, and uncle, Bartol, by his side.

"You have three seconds to order your men to stand down and drop their weapons," said DeBoors. "If not, my men will shoot them. Your armor may well be bolt proof, but I'd wager that theirs are not."

"One.

Two.

Three!"

END

GLOSSARY

PLACES

The Realms
Asgard: legendary home of the gods
—**Bifrost**: mystical bridge between Asgard and Midgaard
—**Valhalla**: a realm of the gods where great warriors go after death
Helheim: one of the nine worlds; the realm of the dead
Midgaard: the world of man
—**Lomion**: a great kingdom of Midgaard
Nether Realms: realms of demons and devils
Nine Worlds, The: the nine worlds of creation
Nifleheim: the realm of the Lords of Nifleheim / Chaos Lords
Vaeden: paradise, lost
Yggdrasill: sacred tree that supports and/or connects the Nine Worlds

Places Within The Kingdom Of Lomion
Dallassian Hills: large area of rocky hills; home to a large enclave of dwarves
Dor Caladrill:
Dor Eotrus: see Eotrus Demesne below
Dor Linden: fortress and lands ruled by House Mirtise, in the Linden Forest, southeast of Lomion City
Dor Lomion: fortress within Lomion City ruled by House Harringgold
Dor Malvegil: fortress and lands ruled by House Malvegil, southeast of Lomion City on the west bank of the Grand Hudsar River

Dor Valadon: fortress outside the City of Dover
Doriath Forest: woodland north of Lomion City
Dover, City of: large city situated at Lomion's southeastern border
Dyvers, City of: Lomerian city known for its quality metalworking
Farthing Heights: town ruled by House Farthing.
Grommel: a town known for southern gnomes
Hollow, The: a town;
— **Ancestor Hill:** cemetary
— **Azrael's Manor, known as Virent Hall**
— **The Constabulary:** sheriff's office
— **House Falstad Manor**
— **The Odinhome**
Kern, City of: Lomerian city to the northeast of Lomion City.
Kronar Mountains: a vast mountain range that marks the northern border of the Kingdom of **Lomion**
Lindenwood: a forest to the south of Lomion City, within which live the Lindonaire Elves
Lomion City: see below
Portland Vale: a town known for southern gnomes that are particularly skilled bridge building masons
Tarrows Hold: known for dwarves

Eotrus Demesne

Dor Eotrus: fortress and lands ruled by House Eotrus, north of Lomion City
— **Citadel, The**: a generic name for the main part of Dor Eotrus — the castle itself. It is also often used to specifically refer to the castle's

central tower.
— **Courtyard, The**: open area between the main citadel walls and the central tower and other buildings.
— **Keep, The**: synonymous with Citadel
— **Odinhome, The**: temple to Odin located in Dor Eotrus; also used as a generic terms for temple/church of Odin.
—**Outer Dor, The**: the town surrounding the fortress of Dor Eotrus. Also used generically as the name for any town surrounding a fortress.
— **Underhalls, The**: the extensive basement levels beneath the citadel.
Berrill's Bridge: a large bridge over the Ottowhile River, northeast of Dor Eotrus, on the West Road
Eastern Hills: in the northeast section of Eotrus demesne
Hollow, The: town where Azrael lives
Markett: a village east of Dor Eotrus, within Eotrus demesne
Mindletown: a town of 400 hundred folk, a few days northeast of Dor Eotrus, in Eotrus demesne. Recently wiped out by trolls.
Ottowhile River: a large river northeast of Dor Eotrus, passable only via bridges for much of the year.
Rhentford: small village on the road between Dor Eotrus and Mindletown. Recently sacked by trolls.
Riker's Crossroads: village at the southern border of Eotrus lands, at the crossroads that leads to Lomion City and Kern.
Roosa: a town

Stebin Pass: a pass through the foothills of the Kronar Mountains, northwest of Dor Eotrus.
Trikan Point Village: village east-northeast of Mindletown, in Eotrus demesne
Vermion Forest: foreboding wood west of Dor Eotrus
Temple of Guymaog: where the gateway was opened in the Vermion Forest
West Rock: at the northwest edge of Eotrus demesne, at the foothills of the Kronar Mountains.
Wortsford: a northern town within Eotrus demesne

<u>Lomion City</u> (aka Lomion): capital city of the Kingdom of Lomion
  — **Baylock's Rest**: an inn.
  — **Dor Lomion**: fortress within Lomion City ruled by House Harringgold
  — **Channel, The**: moat around Lomion City, 150 ft. wide by 30 ft. deep; connected to Grand Hudsar Bay
  —**Fister Mansion**: a fancy old hotel in Lomion City
  —**Grand Hudsar Bay**: the portion of the Grand Hudsar River that meets Lomion City's south and east borders.
  —**Great Meadow, The**: picturesque swath of grassland outside the city gates
  —**Tammanian Hall:** high seat of government in Lomion; home of the High Council and the Council of Lords
  —**Tower of the Arcane**: high seat of wizardom in all Midgaard; in Lomion City

—**The Heights**: seedy section of Lomion City
—**Southeast**: dangerous section of Lomion City

Parts Foreign

Azure Sea: vast ocean to the south of the Lomerian continent
Black Rock Tower: Glus Thorn's stronghold
Bourntown:
Churthick: a land well east of Lomion
Darendor: dwarven realm of Clan Darendon
Dwarkendeep: a renowned dwarven stronghold
Dead Fens, The: mix of fen, bog, and swampland on the east bank of the Hudsar River, south of Dor Malvegil
Evermere, The Isle of: an island in the Azure Sea, far to the south of the Lomerian continent.
— **The Dancing Turtle**: Evermere's finest inn
Grand Hudsar River: south of Lomion City, it marks the eastern border of the kingdom
Emerald River: large river that branches off from the Hudsar at Dover
Ferd: Far-off city known for its fine goods
Jutenheim: island far to the south of the Lomerian continent (see below for more details).
Karthune Gorge: site of a famed battle involving the Eotrus
Kirth: Par Keld is from there
Kronar Mountains: foreboding mountain range that marks the northern border of the Kingdom of Lomion.
Lent
Minoc-by-the-Sea: coastal city
R'lyeh: a bastion for evil creatures; Sir Gabriel

and Theta fought a great battle there in times past.
Saridden, City of:
Shandelon: famed gnomish city
Southron Isles: islands in the Azure Sea
—Hargone Bay:
Starkbarrow: underground Svart city on Isle of Jutenheim.
Thoonbarrow: capital city of the Svarts; underground
Trachen Marches: Theta and Dolan fought the Vhen there.
Tragoss Krell: city ruled by Thothian Monks, on the coast of the Azure Sea.
Tragoss Mor: large city far to the south of Lomion, at the mouth of the Hudsar River where it meets the Azure Sea. Ruled by Thothian Monks.

Jutenheim

It's an island continent in the far south of Midgaard's southern hemisphere. It's also the name of the primary human settlement (a large town with a significant port) on the continent.

Anglotor: Svart name for the temple of power where Korrgonn seeks to open a gateway to Nifleheim.
Eye of Gladden, The: stone arch within the tunnels of Svartleheim (Starkbarrow)
Grasping Grond, The: an inn
Monastery of Ivald: populated by the monks of Ivald.
Starkbarrow: underground city of the Black

Elves;
Svartleheim: tunnels within and below the cliffs separating Jutenheim Town from the interior of the Isle of Jutenheim.

PEOPLE

Peoples of Midgaard
Emerald elves
Lindonaire elves (from Linden Forest)
Doriath elves ('dor-i`-ath') (from Doriath Forest)
Dallassian dwarves (doll-ass`-ian) (from the Dallassian Hills). Typically four feet tall, plus or minus one foot.
Gnomes (northern and southern), typically three feet tall, plus or minus one foot.
Humans/Men: generic term for people. (In usage, usually includes gnomes, dwarves, and elves)
Lugron (usually pronounced 'lou-gron'; sometimes, 'lug`-ron'): a barbaric people from the northern mountains, on average, shorter and stockier than Volsungs, and with higher voices.
Mistkelstrans: an extinct race
Picts: a barbarian people
Stowron (usually pronounced 'stow`-ron'): pale, stooped people of feeble vision who've dwell in lightless caverns beneath the Kronar Mountains
Svarts (black elves), gray skin, large eyes, spindly limbs, three feet tall or so.
Vanyar Elves: legendary elven people

Vhen, The: cousins of the Lugron; dwell in northernmost mountains; sometimes eat people.
Volsungs: a generic term for the primary people/tribes populating the Kingdom of Lomion
Zorns: an extinct race.

High Council of Lomion
Selrach Rothtonn Tenzivel III: His Royal Majesty: King of Lomion
Aldros, Lord: Councilor
Aramere, Lady: Councilor representing the City of Dyvers
Balfor, Field Marshal: Councilor representing the Lomerian armed forces; Commander of the Lomerian army
Barusa of Alder, Lord: Chancellor of Lomion; eldest son of Mother Alder
Cartagian Tenzivel, Prince: Selrach's son, insane; Councilor representing the Royal House.
Dahlia, Lady: Councilor representing the City of Kern
Glenfinnen, Lord: Councilor representing the City of Dover
Harper Harringgold, Lord: Councilor representing Lomion City; Arch-Duke of Lomion City
Jhensezil, Lord Garet: Councilor representing the Churchmen; Preceptor of the Odion Knights
Morfin, Baron: Councilor
Slyman, Guildmaster: Councilor representing the guilds; Master of Guilds
Tobin Carthigast, Bishop: Councilor representing the Churchmen
Vizier, The (Grandmaster Rabrack Philistine):

The Royal Wizard; Grandmaster and Councilor representing the Tower of the Arcane

House Alder (Pronounced All-der)
A leading, noble family of Lomion City. Their principal manor house is within the city's borders
Batholomew Alder: youngest son of Mother Alder
Bartol Alder: younger brother of Barusa, Myrdonian Knight
Barusa Alder, Lord: Chancellor of Lomion, eldest son of Mother Alder.
Blain Alder: younger brother of Barusa
Brock Alder: 6th son of Mother Alder (deceased)
Dirk Alder: eldest son of Bartol Alder
Edith Alder: daughter of Blain; a child
Edwin Alder: son of Blain
Mother Alder: matriarch of the House; an Archseer of the Orchallian Order
Rom Alder: brother of Mother Alder

House Eotrus (pronounced Eee-oh-tro`-sss)
The Eotrus rule the fortress of Dor Eotrus, the Outer Dor (a town outside the fortress walls) and the surrounding lands for many leagues.
Aradon Eotrus, Lord: Patriarch of the House (presumed dead)
Adolphus: a servant
Claradon Eotrus, Brother: (Clara-don) eldest son of Aradon, Caradonian Knight; Patriarch of the House; Lord of Dor Eotrus
Donnelin, Brother: House Cleric for the Eotrus (presumed dead)

Ector Eotrus, Sir: Third son of Aradon
Eleanor Malvegil Eotrus: (deceased) Wife of Aradon Eotrus; sister of Torbin Malvegil.
Gabriel Garn, Sir: House Weapons Master (presumed dead, body possessed by Korrgonn)
Humphrey (Humph): Claradon's manservant
Jude Eotrus, Sir: Second son of Aradon (prisoner of the Shadow League)
Pontly, Castellan: House Castellan prior to Ob.

Knights & Soldiers of the House:
— **Sergeant Artol**: 7 foot tall veteran warrior.
— **Sir Paldor Cragsmere**: a young knight; formerly, Sir Gabriel's squire
— **Sir Glimador Malvegil**: son of Lord Torbin Malvegil; can throw spells
— **Sir Indigo Eldswroth**: handsome, heavily muscled, and exceptionally tall knight
— **Sir Kelbor**
— **Sir Ganton**: called "the bull" or "bull"
— **Sir Trelman**
— **Sir Marzdan** (captain of the gate, deceased)
— **Sir Sarbek du Martegran** (acting Castellan of Dor Eotrus), a knight captain of the Odion Knights
— **Sir Wyndham the Bold of Weeping Hollow**: knight captain (deceased)
— **Lieutenant, The**: veteran cavalry officer (deceased)
— **Sergeant Vid**
— **Sergeant Lant**
— **Sergeant Baret**
— **Trooper Graham**
— Trooper Harsnip (deceased), Sergeant Balfin (deceased), Sir Miden (deceased), Sergeant

Jerem (deceased), Sir Conrad (deceased), Sir Martin (deceased), Sir Bilson (deceased), Sir Glimron (deceased), Sir Talbot (deceased), Sir Dalken (deceased)
Malcolm Eotrus: Fourth son of Aradon
Nardon, Eotrus, Lord: Aradon's father
Ob A. Faz III: (Ahb A. Fahzz) Castellan and Master Scout of Dor Eotrus; a gnome
Pellan, Captain (aka, the beardless dwarf)
Pontly: former Castellan of the House prior to Ob being appointed to that position
Sirear Eotrus, Lady: daughter of August Eotrus (deceased)
Stern of Doriath: Master Ranger for the Eotrus (presumed dead)
Talbon of Montrose, Par: Former House Wizard for the Eotrus (presumed dead), son of Grandmaster (Par) Mardack
Tanch Trinagal, Par: (Trin-ah-ghaal) of the Blue Tower; Son of Sinch; House Wizard for the Eotrus. Aliases: Par Sinch; Par Sinch Malaban.
Sverdes, Leren: House physician and alchemist

House Harringgold
Harper Harringgold, Lord: Archduke of Lomion City; Lord of Dor Lomion, Patriarch of the House. He has a brother in Kern.
Grim Fischer: agent of Harper, a gnome
Marissa Harringgold: daughter of Harper, former love interest of Claradon Eotrus.
Seran Harringgold, Sir: nephew of Harper

House Malvegil
Words: *"Honor and vigilance always"*
Torbin Malvegil, Lord: Patriarch of the House; Lord of Dor Malvegil, Lord of the Eastern Marches.
Landolyn, Lady: of House Adonael; Torbin's consort. Of part elven blood.
Clan MacRondal: ruled the Eastern Marches prior to the Malvegils. MacRondal warcry: *"You've no idea what we're made of"*
Eleanor Malvegil Eotrus: (deceased) Wife of Aradon Eotrus; sister of Torbin Malvegil.
Gedrun, Captain: a knight commander in service to Lord Malvegil
Glimador Malvegil, Sir: son of Torbin and Landolyn; working in the service of House Eotrus.
Gorlick the Bold, Master: House Weapons Master – 29th Weapons Master to the Malvegils; son of Thraydin and Bernda
Gravemare, Hubert: Castellan of Dor Malvegil
Hogart: harbormaster of Dor Malvegil's port.
Karktan of Rivenwood, Master: Weapons Master for the Malvegils
Leren Tage: House Physician, circa 1242.
Mordel: Castellan of Dor Malvegil circa year 1,212 - 1,24x.
Ronald, Brother: House Cleric
Rorbit, Par: House Wizard to the Malvegils
Stoub of Rivenwood: Lord Malvegil's chief bodyguard; brother of Karktan (deceased)
Tage, Leren: House physician
Torgrist, Brother: Dor Malvegil's high cleric.
Troopers Bern, Brant, Conger: Malvegillian

soldiers
Tybor, Red: House Master Scout; a Pict

House Morfin
Baron Morfin: Patriarch of the House; a member of the High Council
Gallick Morfin: eldest son of the Baron.

House Tenzivel (the Royal House)
King Selrach Rothtonn Tenzivel III: (deceased) His Royal Majesty: King of Lomion
Cartagian Tenzivel, Prince: Selrach's son; insane.
Dramadeens: royal bodyguards for House Tenzivel
— **Korvalan of Courwood, Captain**: (deceased) Commander of the Dramadeens.
— **Mavron**: second in command of the Dramadeens; a hulking brute

Other Noble Houses of Lomion
House Tavermain
House Grondeer
House Dantrel

House Forndin
A minor House loyal to and located within Eotrus lands. Their major holding is known as Forndin Manor.
Alana Forndin, Lady: matriarch of the House
Sir Erendin of Forndin Manor: eldest son of the House (deceased)
Sir Miden of Forndin Manor: younger brother of Erendin (deceased)

Sir Talbot of Forndin Manor: younger brother of Erendin (deceased)

House Hanok
A minor House loyal to and located within Eotrus lands. Their major holding is known as Hanok Keep.
Sir Bareddal of Hanok Keep: in service to the Eotrus (deceased)

House Mirtise
The Mirtises rule over the area surrounding the fortress of Dor Linden, which lies south of Malvegil lands on the west side of the Grand Hudsar River.
Lady Mirtise: matriarch of the House
Leren Jrack: House Physician

OTHER HOUSES AND GROUPS

Clan Darendon of Darendor
Royal clan from the dwarven kingdom
Bornyth Trollsbane, High King of Clan Darendon.
Galibar the Great: the prince of Darendor, first son to Bornyth and heir to Clan Darendon
Jarn Yarspitter: councilor to Bornyth

The Black Hand
A brotherhood of Assassins
Brethren, The: term the assassins use for fellow members of The Hand.
Grandmistress, The: the leader of The Hand
Mallick Fern: an assassin; The Hand's second ranking agent (deceased)
Weater the Mouse: a Hand leader

Brood tet Montu of Svartleheim

The royal house of the svarts
Diresvarts: svart wizard-priests
Guyphoon Garumptuss tet Montu: high king of Thoonbarrow, Patriarch of Brood tet Montu, Master of the Seven Stratems, and Lord of all Svartleheim, offspring of Guyphoon Pintalia of the Windy Ways, Traymoor Garumptuss the Bold, and Trantmain lin Backus tet Montu, great king of the undermountains
Cardakeen rack Mortha: a svart seer
Orator, The: the spokesman for the svart king

Black Elves (Svarts) of Starkbarrow

Diresvarts: Svart wizard-priests
Karaka Bertel: The Seer of Starkbarrow
Ramluk the Diresvart: High Magus of Starkbarrow
Rock Elementals: giant, fire-breathing minions of the Starkbarrow Svarts.
Throonbilg biln Mac-Murth: high king of Starkbarrow

The Lords of Nifleheim and Their Minions
Azathoth: god worshipped by the Lords of Nifleheim and The Shadow League/The League of Light; his followers call him the "one true god".
Arioch: a Lord of Nifleheim
Bhaal: a Lord of Nifleheim; came through the gateway in the Vermion but was banished back by Angle Theta
Hecate: a Lord of Nifleheim.
Korrgonn, Lord Gallis: son of Azathoth
Mortach: (aka Mikel): a Lord of Nifleheim; killed by Angle Theta
— **Reskalan**: demonic foot soldiers in service to the Lords of Nifleheim
— **Zymog**: a reskalan
— **Brigandir**: supernatural warrior(s) of Nifleheim
— **Einheriar**: supernatural warriors of Nifleheim

The Asgardian Gods

Odin (the All-father) (aka Wotan): king of the gods
Thor (aka Donar): son of Odin
Tyr (aka Cyo):
Heimdall (aka Vindler):
Loki:
Baldr:
—**Valkyries**: sword maidens of the gods. They choose worthy heroes slain in battle and conduct them to Valhalla.

Other Gods
Dagon of the Deep: appears as a giant lizard; lives in caverns beneath an uncharted island deep in the Azure Sea.
— **Dwellers of the Deep**: very large, bipedal sea creatures that worship Dagon.
Thoth:
Donar: worshipped by the Jutens; akin to Thor; son of Wotan.
Wotan: worshipped by the Jutens; akin to Odin

Great Beasts, Monsters, Creatures, Animals

Barrow Wight
Borkoth Garaktok, the Lord of Shadows; Duke of the Nether Marches:
Blood Lord: legendary fiends that drink blood and eat humans.
Dire Wolves: extremely large breed of wolves
Duergar: mythical undead creatures
Draugar: undead creatures that feast on the living
Dwellers of the Deep: worshippers of Dagon; huge, bipedal fishlike creatures
Fire Wyrm or "**Wyrms**": dragons
Giant (aka Jotun, pl. Jotnar):
Grond: a type of large monkey or ape native to Jutenheim
Gronsel: they smell bad
Holyphant: a mammoth
Jotnar: giants (plural of Jotun)
Jotun: a giant
Ogres:
Leviathan: a huge sea creature

Red Demons of Fozramgar: Mort Zag is one.
Saber-cat: saber toothed tiger
Shadow Demon: a monstrous dragon of the Nether Realms, perhaps, undead, or else immortal.
Shamblers: undead; zombies.
Throan Gron Sek Nifleheem: Thrice Horned Demons of the Nether Realms
Tranteers: the lithe, speedy horses bred in Dover
Trolls, Mountain: mythical creatures of the high mountains
Wendigo: monster of legend that eats people.

The Crew of *The Black Falcon*
Slaayde, Dylan: Captain of *The Black Falcon*
Bertha Smallbutt: ship's quartermaster
Bire Cabinboy: ship's cabin boy — was in league with Darg Tran
Chert: a young seaman
Darg Tran, son of Karn, of old House Elowine: ship's navigator; secret wizard & traitor (deceased)
Eolge: a crewman (deceased)
Fizdar Firstbar "the corsair": former first mate (presumed dead)
Gurt, Seaman: (aka Gurt the Knife) a crewman; known for knife fighting skills
Guj: boatswain. A half-Lugron. (deceased)
N'Paag: First Mate
Old Mock: a crewman (deceased)
Ravel: ship's trader and medic (deceased)
Tug, Little: Near 7 foot tall part-Lugron seaman; Old Fogey — Tug's battle hammer

The Passengers of *The Black Falcon*

Sergeant Artol: 7 foot tall veteran warrior.
Claradon Eotrus, Brother: (Clara-don) eldest son of Aradon, Caradonian Knight; Patriarch of the House; Lord of Dor Eotrus
Dolan Silk: Theta's manservant
Ganton, Sir (the Bull): a knight of House Eotrus
Kayla Kazeran: part Lindonaire elf, rescued from slavery in Tragoss Mor
Kelbor, Sir: a knight of House Eotrus
Lant, Sergeant: a soldier of House Eotrus
Lomerian Soldiers: a squadron of soldiers of House Harringgold, assigned to assist House Eotrus. Under the command of Seran Harringgold.
Malvegil, Sir Glimador: first cousin to Claradon; son of Lord Torbin Malvegil and Lady Landolyn
Malvegillian Archers: a squad of soldiers assigned to assist House Eotrus by Lord Malvegil
Ob A. Faz III: (Ahb A. Fahzz) Castellan and Master Scout of Dor Eotrus; a gnome
Paldor Cragsmere, Sir: a young knight of House Eotrus, formerly, Sir Gabriel's squire
Seran Harringgold, Sir: nephew of Arch-Duke Harper Harringgold — assigned to assist House Eotrus
Tanch Trinagal, Par: (Trin-ah-ghaal) of the Blue Tower; Son of Sinch; House Wizard for the Eotrus. Aliases: Par Sinch; Par Sinch Malaban.
Theta, Lord Angle (aka Thetan): a knight-errant from a far-off land across the sea. Sometimes called the Harbinger of Doom

Thothian Monk, a: an elderly fellow; taken prisoner during the incident with Prior Finch at Tragoss Mor
Trelman, Sir: a knight of House Eotrus
Vid, Sergeant: a soldier of House Eotrus

The Crew/Passengers of *The Gray Talon*
Alder Marines: squadrons of soldiers from House Alder
Azura du Marnian, the Seer: Seer based in Tragoss Mor.
Bartol Alder: younger brother of Barusa; a Myrdonian Knight
Blain Alder: younger brother of Barusa
DeBoors, Milton: (The Duelist of Dyvers). A mercenary
Edwin Alder: son of Blain
Kaledon of the Gray Waste: a Pict mercenary
Kleig: Captain of *The Grey Talon*
Knights of Kalathen: elite mercenaries that work for DeBoors
Myrdonian Knights: squadron of knights assigned to House Alder

The Crew/Passengers of *The White Rose*
Brackta Finbal, Par: female archmage of The League of Light
du Mace, Varak: Captain of *The White Rose*
Ezerhauten, Lord: Commander of Sithian Mercenary Company
Frem Sorlons: captain of the Sithians Pointmen Squadron
Ginalli, Father: High Priest of Azathoth, Arkon of The League of Light.

Hablock, Par: an archmage of the League of Light (deceased)
Keld, Par of Kerth: a middle-aged wizard of the League of Light, short, stocky, balding, and nervous.
Landru, Par: a wizard (deceased); has several brothers
Lugron: a barbaric people from the northern mountains, on average, shorter and stockier than Volsungs.
Mason: a stone golem created by The Keeper of Tragoss Mor; companion to Stev Keevis.
Miles de Gant: a sithian soldier (deceased). Son of **Count de Gant**
Morsmun, Par: an archmage of the League of Light (deceased)
Mort Zag: a red-hued giant
Oris, Par: an elderly wizard of the League of Light; former mentor of Par Keld.
Ot, Par: an archmage of the League of Light (deceased)
Pointmen, The: an elite squadron of the Sithian Mercenary Company
Rascelon, Captain Rastinfan: former captain of *The White Rose* (deceased)
Rhund, Par: a wizard of the League of Light
Sevare Zendrack, Par: Squadron wizard for the Pointmen
Sithians: mercenaries under the command of Ezerhauten; some are soldiers, some are knights
Stev Keevis Arkguardt: an elven archwizard from the Emerald Forest allied with The League of Light; former apprentice of The Keeper
Teek: Lugron guard/jailor

Tremont of Wyndum: a sithian knight (deceased)
Weldin, Par: a wizard of the League of Light
Thorn, Par (Master) Glus: an archwizard of the League of Light; a sorcerer
—**Lasifer, Par**: Glus Thorn's gnome assistant/apprentice.
—**Nord**: a stowron in Thorn's employ
Tribik: Lugron guard/jailor (deceased)

Sithian Mercenary Company

Ezerhauten, Lord: Commander
Frem Sorlons: Captain, Pointmen Squadron
Bradik, Leutenant: 4th Squadron
Cotter the Dandy: company wizard (deceased)
Grainer, Sergeant: 2nd Squadron
Landru, Par: a squadron wizard (deceased)
Markus, Captain: 2nd Squadron's captain
Miles de Gant: a knight; son of Count de Gant (deceased)
Rewes of Ravenhollow, Sir: a knight (deceased)
Stanik Lugron: 4th Squadron
Tremont of Wyndum: a knight captain (deceased)

The Pointmen (an elite squadron of the Sithian Mercenary Company)

Frem Sorlons: captain, Pointmen Squadron
Sevare Zendrack, Par: squadron wizard for the Pointmen
Putnam, Sergeant: Pointmen, 1st Squad

Boatman: Pointmen (deceased)
Borrel Lugron: Pointmen
Bryton: Pointmen (deceased)
Carroll, Sir: Pointmen; a knight
Clard: Pointmen; a Lugron
Drift, Trooper: Pointmen
Dirnel: Pointmen; a Lugron (deceased)
Held: Pointmen (deceased)
Jorna: Pointmen (deceased)
Lex, Sir: Pointmen
Little Storrl: Pointmen,1st Squad; a young Lugron
Maddix, Trooper: Pointmen
Ma-Grak Stowron
Maldin, Sergeant: Pointmen,2nd Squad, (Badly wounded, spear through chest)
Moag Lugron: Pointmen,1st squad; Master Scout
Roard, Sir: Pointmen,1st Squad; a knight (deceased)
Royce, Sir: Pointmen; a knight
Torak Lugron: Pointmen
Ward, Sir: Pointmen
Wikkle Lugron: Pointmen

The Regent's Expeditionary Force

Alder, Brock (aka The Regent): 6th son of Mother Alder (deceased)
Alder, Dirk: eldest son of Bartol Alder
Alder, Rom: brother of Mother Alder
Bald Boddrick: (aka 'The Backbreaker')
Bithel the Piper:
Black Grint:

Gar Pullman:
Kralan, Captain: a Myrdonian Knight in command of the Myrdonian cavalry squadron (deceased)
Martrin, Captain: the Lomerian guard captain in command of the regulars (deceased)
Sentry of Allendale

Militant and Mystic Orders

Caradonian Knights: priestly order; patron—Odin
Churchmen: a generic term for the diverse group of priests and knights of various orders.
Freedom Guardsmen: soldiery of Tragoss Mor
Grontor's Bonebreakers: a mercenary company. The Lugron, Teek and Tribik belonged to it.
Halsbad's Freeswords: a mercenary company that Pellan once worked for.
Kalathen, Knights of: mercenary knights that work for Milton DeBoors
Myrdonians: Royal Lomerian Knights
Odions, The: patron—Odin; Preceptor—Lord Jhensezil; Chapterhouse: in Lomion City
Orchallian Order, The: an Order of Seers; Mother Alder is one of them.
Order of the Arcane: the wizard members of the Tower of the Arcane
Rangers Guild, The: Chapterhouse — Doriath Hall in Lomion City; Preceptor: Sir Samwise Sluug; loyal to House Harringgold.
— **Drydan, Captain**: a guard captain
Sithian Knights, The: Preceptor—Lord

Ezerhauten
Sundarian Knights: patron: Thor; Preceptor: Sir Hithron du Maris; Chapterhouse: hidden in Tragoss Mor
Tyr, Knights of (aka Tyrians): patron—Tyr

People of Jutenheim

Angel of Death, The: a seer / "woman of the bones" / the crone of Jutenheim. Travels with a large boy and wolf.
Darmod Rikenguard: a guide. Works with his two sons.
Helda: Rothmar's wife; Ragnar's mother.
Kordan: a guide
Juten: generic word for a resident of Jutenheim
Old Fortis: proprietor of The Grasping Grond
Red Demon of Fozramgar, The: its coming was foretold by the Angel of Death.
Ragnar: Rothmar and Helda's son
Rothmar: owns Jutenheim's leading smithery; husband of Helda; father of Ragnar
Seer's Boy: the grandson of the crone of Jutenheim.

Monastery of Ivald, The

Brother Abraxon: chief monk of the Ivald Monastery
Brother Bertold: the monastery's keeper of maps
Brother Rennis: he's a guard post in the seventh underhall
Old Brother Hordin: former keeper of maps

(deceased)

Others of Note

Azura du Marnian, the Seer: Seer based in Tragoss Mor. Now travels with the Alders on *The Gray Talon*.
Gorb: Azura's bodyguard (deceased)
Rimel Stark: Azura's bodyguard and famed Freesword
Dirkben: Azura's bodyguard (deceased)
Balthazar: battled with Azrael the Wise in ancient times
Brondel Cragsmere, Sire: father of Sir Paldor of Dor Eotrus
Coriana Sorlons: daughter of Frem Sorlons
Dark Sendarth: famed assassin in league with House Harringgold and House Tenzivel
Du Maris, Sir Hithron: Preceptor of the Sundarian Chapterhouse in Tragoss Mor; from Dor Caladrill
Graybeard, Captain: the captain of the schooner docked at Evermere
Halsbad: a mercenary leader
Harbinger of Doom, The: legendary, perhaps mythical, being that led a rebellion against Azathoth
Jaros, the Blood Lord: foe of Sir Gabriel Garn
Keeper, The: elven "keeper" of the Orb of Wizard beneath Tragoss Mor
Krisona, Demon-Queen: foe of Sir Gabriel Garn
Kroth, Garon: newly appointed High Magister
Mardack, Grandmaster (Par) of Montrose:

famed wizard; father of Par Talbon of Montrose
McDuff the Mighty: (aka "Red Beard"); a dwarf of many talents
Pipkorn, Grandmaster: (aka Rascatlan) former Grand Master of the Tower of the Arcane. A wizard.
Prior Finch: a prior of Thoth in Tragoss Mor (deceased)
Sarq: a Thothian Monk. Known as the Champion of Tragoss Mor
Shadow League, The (aka The League of Shadows; aka The League of Light): alliance of individuals and groups collectively seeking to bring about the return of Azathoth to Midgaard
Sluug, Sir (Lord) Samwise: Preceptor of the Rangers Guild; Master of Doriath Hall
Snor Slipnet: Patriarch of Clan Rumbottle; a gnome
Spanzileers, The: attacked the Eotrus by way of the eastern hills.
Sons of Ivaldi: Beckir and Birkir; Svarts; makers of magical wonders
Talidousen: Former Grand Master of the Tower of the Arcane; created the fabled Rings of the Magi.
Thothian monks: monks that rule Tragoss Mor and worship Thoth
Throng-Baz : an ancient people that used runic script
Valas Tearn: an assassin said to have slain a thousand men; foe of Sir Gabriel Garn
Valkyries: sword maidens of the gods. They choose worthy heroes slain in battle and conduct them to Valhalla.

Vanyar Elves: legendary elven people

Titles

Archmage / Archwizard: honorific title for a highly skilled wizard
Archseer: honorific title for a highly skilled seer
Arkon: a leader/general in service to certain gods and religious organizations
Battle Mage: a wizard whose skills are combat oriented.
Castellan: the commander of a fortress/Dor; in service to the Dor Lord.
Constable: chief law enforcement officer of a village or town.
Dor Lord: the leader of a fortress; usually a noble, and often the Patriarch/Matriach of a noble House.
Freesword: an independent soldier or mercenary
Grandmaster: honorific title for a senior wizard of the Tower of the Arcane.
Hedge Wizard: a wizard specializing in potions and herbalism, and/or minor magics.
High Cleric: the senior priest of a church/temple, or of a religious order.
High Magister: a member of Lomion's Tribunal.
High Priest: the senior priest of a church/temple, or of a religious order.
House Cleric: the senior priest in service to a noble House
House Wizard: a senior wizard in service to a noble House
Leren: (pronounced Lee-rhen) generic title for a

physician
Mage: a practioner of magic; a wizard.
Magling: a young or inexperienced wizard; also, a derogatory term for a wizard.
Marshal: a law enforcement officer; typically reports to a Constable of village or town.
Master Oracle: a highly skilled seer.
Master Scout: the chief scout/hunter/tracker of a fortress or noble House.
Par: honorific title for a wizard
Seer (sometimes, "Seeress"): women with supernatural powers to see past/present/future events.
Sorcerer: a practitioner of magic; a wizard.
Tower Mage: a wizard that his a member of the Order of the Arcane.
Weapons Master: the senior weapon's instructor/trainer/officer at a fortress.
Wizard: practitioners of magic

Wizards of the Arcane Order

Arcane Order: formal organization of wizards. Their home base is the Tower of the Arcane, also known as, the High Seat of Wizardom in Lomion City.
Gatwind, Par: a wizard originally from the Southron Isles; a member of the Freedom Council.
Pentarkian Order: an order of war wizards within the Arcane Order
Pipkorn, Grandmaster (aka Rascatlan): former Grand Master of the Tower of the Arcane. Aka, "Old Pointy Hat"

Spugnoir, Grandmaster: a grandmaster of the Tower of the Arcane
Trask, Par: a member of the Freedom Council (deceased)
Triman, Par: a member of the Freedom Council
Vizier, The (Rabrack Philistine): aka The Royal Wizard; High Councilor representing the Tower of the Arcane

The Freedom Council

Grandmaster Pipkorn; Grandmaster Mardack; Sir Samwise Sluug; Lord Mirtise; Lord (Duke) Harringgold; Par Trask (deceased); King Tenzivel (deceased); Baron Morfin; Gallick Morfin; Grandmaster Spugnoir; Captain Korvalan (deceased); Par Triman; Par Gatwind; Lord Smirdoon of Lockely Bay; et.al

Arkons of Azathoth
Arioch; Azrael the Wise; Bhaal; Gabriel; Mikel; Mithron; Thetan; Uriel the Bold

THINGS

Miscellany
Alder Stone, The: a Seer Stone held by House Alder
Amulet of Escandell: a magical device that detects the presence of danger; gifted to Claradon by Pipkorn
Articles of the Republic: the Lomerian constitution

Asgardian Daggers: legendary weapons created in the first age of Midgaard. They can harm creatures of Nifleheim.
Axe of Bigby the Bold: made of Mithril; gifted to Ob by Pipkorn
Bellowing Banshee, The: one of the ships lost in the Fens
Book of the Nobility: treatise containing the traditional Lomerian laws with respect to the nobility.
Bloodlust, The: name for the affliction affecting people in The Hollow
Chapterhouse: base/manor/fortress of a knightly order
Dargus Dal: Asgardian dagger, previously Gabriel's, now Theta's
Dor: a generic Lomerian word meaning "fortress"
Dulcite: a precious gemstone
du Marnian Stone, The: a Seer Stone held by Azura du Marnian
Dyvers Blades: finely crafted steel swords
Dyvers Thraysk: a short wide sword.
Ether, The: invisible medium that exists everywhere and within which the weave of magic travels/exists.
Ghost Ship Box: calls forth an illusory ship; created by Pipkorn and gifted to Claradon.
Graban: a precious gemstone.
Granite Throne, The: the name of the king's throne in Lomion City. To "sit the granite throne" means to be the king.
Mages and Monsters: a popular, tactical war game that uses miniatures

Mithril: precious metal of great strength and relative lightness
Mjollnir: the legendary hammer of the god Thor / Donar.
Orb of Wisdom (aka Portalis Nifleleir): mystical crystal spheres that can be used to open portals between worlds.
Ragnarok: prophesied battle between the Aesir and the Nifleites.
Ranal: a black metal, hard as steel and half as heavy, weapons made of it can affect creatures of chaos
Raspen Brandy:
Rings of the Magi: amplify a wizard's power; twenty created by Talidousen
Seer Stones: magical "crystal balls" that can see far-off events.
Shards of Darkness: the remnants of the destroyed Orb of Wisdom from the Temple of Guymaog.
Spottle: a dice game that uses a live frog
Sventeran Stone, The: a Seer Stone loaned to the Malvegils by the Svarts.
Tribunal: the highest-ranking judiciary body in the Kingdom of Lomion; members of the tribunal are called "High Magisters."
Valusian steel: famed for its quality
Weave of Magic; aka the Magical Weave: the source of magic
Wintersfest: a winter holiday celebrated in Lomion.
Worfin Dal: "Lord's Dagger," Claradon's Asgardian dagger
Wotan Dal: "Odin's Dagger"; gifted to Theta by

Pipkorn.
Yggdrasill: sacred tree that supports and/or connects the Nine Worlds

Miscellany: Herbs, Medicines, Poisons, Food and Drinks
Arrowroot Leaf: chewable painkiller
Barsen's Reserve: a high quality brandy
Brombottle:
Cavindish Wine: a sweet white wine made in Lomion
Cottonrounds: chewable painkiller
Dwarven Rum:
Essence of Elmwood: can be used to preserve parchment
Essence of Nightshade: a lethal, fast-acting poison; carried by Black Hand agents as suicide pills to thwart capture.
Essence of Tarrow Root: powerful pain killer.
Gnome Mead:
Gnome Whiskey:
Mearn: comes in a jar
Oil of Adarisk: topical burn remedy; smells bad
Raspen Brandy:
Tinger Leaf:
Treant Leaf Resin: has curative properties, dulls odors when smeared on face.

Sigils and Standards
Standard of the Lomerian Guard: a white tower on a field of green. Soldiers wear red helmets and red and gray tabards with the standard embossed on at the center of their chests

Lomion Colors: red and gray
Myrdonian Knight Colors: emerald greed armor and weapons

Languages of Midgaard

Lomerian: the common tongue of Lomion and much of the known world
Cleritus Mysterious: ancient mystic language of the priests of the Aesir
Magus Mysterious: olden language of sorcery
Militus Mysterious: olden language of sorcery used by certain orders of knights
Old High Lomerian: an olden dialect of Lomerian
Old Tongue, The: a long-dead language from a previous Age.
Throng Baz: a dead language
Svartish (aka Svartlespeak in gnome): language of the svarts
Trollspeak: language of the mountain trolls

Ages of Midgaard
The Before Time
The Dawn Age: First Age
The Age of Myth and Legend: Second Age
The Age of Heroes: Third Age
The Age of Enlightenment: Fourth Age

Combat Maneuvers, Techniques, and Styles
Dyvers' thrusting maneuvers; Dwarvish overhand strikes; Cernian technique; Sarnack maneuvers; Lengian cut and thrust style; Valusian thrust

Military Units of Lomion

Squad: a unit of soldiers typically composed of 3 to 8 soldiers, but it can be as few as 2 or as many as 15 soldiers.

Squadron: a unit of soldiers typically composed of two to four squads, totaling about 30 soldiers, including officers.

Cavalry Squadron or Troop: same as "squadron" but often has additional support troops to tend to the horses and supplies.

Company: a military unit composed of 4 squadrons, totaling about 120 - 150 soldiers. Mercenary Companies can be of any size, the word "company" in their title, notwithstanding.

Brigade: a military unit composed of 8 companies, totaling about 1,000 soldiers

Regiment: a military unit composed of 4 brigades, totaling about 4,000 — 5,000 soldiers

Corps or Army: a military unit composed of 4 regiments and support troops, totaling about 20,000 — 25,000 soldiers

Military Ranks of Lomion

(from junior to senior)

Trooper; Corporal; Sergeant; Lieutenant (a knight is considered equivalent in rank to a Lieutenant); Captain; Knight Captain (for units with Knights); Commander; Knight Commander (for units with Knights); Lord Commander (if a noble); General (for Regiment sized units or larger)

ABOUT GLENN G. THATER

For more than twenty-five years, Glenn G. Thater has written works of fiction and historical fiction that focus on the genres of epic fantasy and sword and sorcery. His published works of fiction include the first ten volumes of the *Harbinger of Doom* saga: *Gateway to Nifleheim*; *The Fallen Angle*; *Knight Eternal*; *Dwellers of the Deep*; *Blood, Fire, and Thorn*; *Gods of the Sword*; *The Shambling Dead*; *Master of the Dead*; *Shadow of Doom*; *Wizard's Toll*; the novella, *The Gateway*; and the novelette, *The Hero and the Fiend*.

Mr. Thater holds a Bachelor of Science degree in Physics with concentrations in Astronomy and Religious Studies, and a Master of Science degree in Civil Engineering, specializing in Structural Engineering. He has undertaken advanced graduate study in Classical Physics, Quantum Mechanics, Statistical Mechanics, and Astrophysics, and is a practicing licensed professional engineer specializing in the multidisciplinary alteration and remediation of buildings, and the forensic investigation of building failures and other disasters.

Mr. Thater has investigated failures and collapses of numerous structures around the United States and internationally. Since 1998, he has been a member of the American Society of Civil Engineers' Forensic Engineering Division (FED), is a Past Chairman of that Division's Executive Committee and FED's Committee on Practices to

Reduce Failures. Mr. Thater is a LEED (Leadership in Energy and Environmental Design) Accredited Professional and has testified as an expert witness in the field of structural engineering before the Supreme Court of the State of New York.

Mr. Thater is an author of numerous scientific papers, magazine articles, engineering textbook chapters, and countless engineering reports. He has lectured across the United States and internationally on such topics as the World Trade Center collapses, bridge collapses, and on the construction and analysis of the dome of the United States Capitol in Washington D.C.

CONNECT WITH GLENN G. THATER ONLINE

Glenn G. Thater's Website:
http://www.glenngthater.com

To be notified about new book releases and any special offers or discounts regarding Glenn's books, please join his mailing list here: http://eepurl.com/vwubH

BOOKS BY GLENN G. THATER

THE HARBINGER OF DOOM SAGA
GATEWAY TO NIFLEHEIM
THE FALLEN ANGLE
KNIGHT ETERNAL
DWELLERS OF THE DEEP
BLOOD, FIRE, AND THORN
GODS OF THE SWORD

THE SHAMBLING DEAD
MASTER OF THE DEAD
SHADOW OF DOOM
WIZARD'S TOLL
VOLUME 11+ *forthcoming*

THE HERO AND THE FIEND
(A novelette set in the Harbinger of Doom universe)

THE GATEWAY
(A novella length version of *Gateway to Nifleheim*)

HARBINGER OF DOOM
(Combines *Gateway to Nifleheim* and *The Fallen Angle* into a single volume)

THE DEMON KING OF BERGHER
(A short story set in the Harbinger of Doom universe)

Visit Glenn G. Thater's website at http://www.glenngthater.com for the most current list of my published books.